AND THE RESTLESS

QUEERS OF LA VISTA

KRIS RIPPER

Riptide Publishing
PO Box 1537
Burnsville, NC 28714
www.riptidepublishing.com

This is a work of fiction. Names, characters, places, and incidents are either the product of the author's imagination or are used fictitiously. Any resemblance to actual persons living or dead, business establishments, events, or locales is entirely coincidental. All person(s) depicted on the cover are model(s) used for illustrative purposes only.

The Queer and the Restless
Copyright © 2016 by Kris Ripper

Cover art: L.C. Chase, lcchase.com/design.htm
Editor: May Peterson
Layout: L.C. Chase, lcchase.com/design.htm

All rights reserved. No part of this book may be reproduced or transmitted in any form or by any means, electronic or mechanical, including photocopying, recording, or by any information storage and retrieval system without the written permission of the publisher, and where permitted by law. Reviewers may quote brief passages in a review. To request permission and all other inquiries, contact Riptide Publishing at the mailing address above, at Riptidepublishing.com, or at marketing@riptidepublishing.com.

ISBN: 978-1-62649-438-1

First edition
October, 2016

Also available in ebook:
ISBN: 978-1-62649-437-4

THE QUEER AND THE RESTLESS

KRIS RIPPER

TABLE OF
CONTENTS

Chapter 1 1
Chapter 2 9
Chapter 3 13
Chapter 4 23
Chapter 5 29
Chapter 6 41
Chapter 7 49
Chapter 8 55
Chapter 9 63
Chapter 10 77
Chapter 11 85
Chapter 12 89
Chapter 13 99
Chapter 14 111
Chapter 15 119
Chapter 16 125
Chapter 17 131
Chapter 18 141
Chapter 19 149
Chapter 20 155
Chapter 21 161
Chapter 22 173
Chapter 23 181
Chapter 24 187
Chapter 25 193
Chapter 26 203
Chapter 27 207
Chapter 28 213

CHAPTER 1

I sat in my chair on the day after the Fourth of July holiday, drinking coffee and staring at the wall. Since I didn't have the energy to actually start writing, I switched the calendar over my desk to July: a picture of a massive cruise ship on a spectacularly blue sea with the words *Find the destination of your heart* in script below it.

It was one of those times when I really wished I had darts. One in the hull of the ship. One in the benevolently shining sun. The rest in that perfect ocean, taunting me with its blue depths.

Caspar, my desk-mate (and by "desk" I mean "table with delusions of grandeur"), snorted. "The fuck does that even mean?"

"No idea. My heart's just fine where it is."

"Ha. Funny, Masiello."

It wasn't meant to be funny. But oh well. Caspar was forty-five and didn't give a fuck about anything. I knew this because he found a way to put DGAF in every email he sent me. *Potter's on the warpath. Too bad I DGAF. Alder is lurking, saw him in the coffee room. DGAF myself, but you might try to look enterprising.* Which was stupid, because I actually worked. I didn't have to look like I was working. You'd think he might know that after a year and a half sitting next to me, but no. Mostly because he didn't give a fuck.

"Ed! How's the blind cat story coming?"

Speaking of Potter. I rolled my chair out until I had a line of sight to my editor's office doorway. "You mean, the blind cat that can sense when people are dying? Actually, it's weirdly interesting. You'd think the cat wouldn't be so popular, since it's basically a death omen, but the residents all seem to relish the idea they might be next."

Potter—who was tall and probably had been good-looking at some point in the past, before the long hours in a desk chair and weekends steeped in beer got the better of him—shook his head. "I want a nice story, Ed. Can you do that for me? No death, no dying, no clever euphemisms for death and dying. Give me twelve inches on the nice blind cat and the little old lady who brings it to visit the seniors. Okay?"

Sure. Take everything interesting out of this story completely.

"Got it." Arguing wouldn't get me anywhere. Plus, I could write twelve feel-good inches about the nice blind cat if I had to. I rolled back to my half of the table.

Caspar snickered. "'Just write a *nice story*, Ed.' What a fucking stooge."

I packed up my notebooks. "I'm gonna go see what the blind cat's up to."

"Oh, I bet. Hey, if this gig doesn't work out for you, maybe you can get a job ferrying handicapped pets around making old people happy."

"No one uses 'handicapped' anymore," I muttered, aggressively zipping my bag shut.

"I just did." He laughed, this kind of guffaw he does when he's bored and poking people for fun.

"That's a great idea, Caspar. I'll definitely take it into consideration."

He was still laughing when I slipped out the back of the conference room, which had a fire door that wasn't wired into the security system. I'd go see the blind cat. Maybe it would make me feel better about having landed the reporter job I'd always wanted only to discover that "general assignment" mostly meant "a bunch of crap that reporters who've been here longer don't want to waste their time on."

This was not the destination of my heart.

I texted Cameron on my way out of the assisted-living center, wiping wet hands on my pants. The blind cat was nice enough, but it shed like crazy, and even washing didn't make me feel clean. Obviously the thing I ought to do now was go back to work and write my twelve inches. But I thought I'd take a chance that Cameron had a lunch movie on and could hang out for a few minutes.

The Rhein dominated the north side of Mooney Boulevard in downtown La Vista. Big florid arches and molding, scrollwork around the more modern theater signs, and a red carpet Cameron replaced every five years, just like his parents and grandparents and great-grandmother before him. The Rheingolds had opened the theater in 1936, and it'd been La Vista's favorite movie theater since then, though it'd been steadily losing business since the Cinema 18 opened in the big shopping center out in the suburbs.

Today's lunch movie was *Jurassic Park*, and I settled into the ticket booth with Cameron right around the time the T-Rex escaped its pen. I angled for a view of the tiny monitor that always ran the current movie as it played. "Not your usual lunch movie."

"I have a soft spot for it. It was the first PG-13 movie I ever saw." He stretched his legs in one direction and leaned over to reach for the minifridge in the other. "I was six."

"Did it scare the hell out of you? I don't think I saw it until I was older."

"Yeah. I had dinosaur nightmares for months. But after that I wanted to be a paleontologist for a few years, so I guess it ends up being a good memory. I have carrots and hummus?"

"You don't have to feed me, Cam."

He pulled out the carrots and hummus, spreading an honest-to-god handkerchief on the counter between us. "Of course I do. You're my guest."

He was three years older than me, and he'd gone to the Catholic school instead of La Vista High, so we hadn't met until I covered the premier he'd hosted for a local indie filmmaker. I'd liked him immediately. Cam was one of those guys that I had conflicted feelings about, one of the guys who'd confused the hell out of me when I was younger, and a lesbian: did I have a crush on him? But it hadn't been a crush. I didn't want to kiss Cameron; I wanted to *be* him.

Case in point: brown wool trousers, crisp white shirt with a club collar (that *didn't* make him look like an English boarding school boy), embroidered vest in deep blue and burnt umber, and oxfords that looked both worn-in and cared-for.

Okay. I've been on testosterone for a little over a year, I actually feel all right in my clothes on most days, but I still kind of want to be Cameron.

He picked up a carrot. "Eat. Tell me what story you're dodging today. Any time you're not working in the middle of the day, I know it's a good one."

So I told him about the blind cat and its psychic powers. And how I wasn't allowed to report on anything interesting about it.

"You're saying the residents aren't afraid of the cat?" He propped his long legs on the counter behind me.

"It's more like they look forward to their turn. Cam, I watched it happen last week. The cat sort of . . . *flirted* with everyone, winding between their legs, scratching its head on their wheelchairs. And they all held their breath waiting to see what would happen next."

"What happened next?"

"It—*he*—finally jumped up into the lap of this little old man, curled up, and fell asleep purring as the man petted him. The guy . . . looked so peaceful. Petting the cat, talking to it. There was this audible sigh among the other residents, but no one was disturbed. It was the strangest thing."

"And the old man died?"

"I didn't follow up. I guess I didn't think about it. It seemed like a foregone conclusion." I hadn't seen the old man earlier today, but he could have just been in his room or something. That was bad reporting. If the old man lived—well, it didn't erase the cat's history of having selected out the people who were going to die, but it made it a little less compelling. "You're right. Maybe he didn't."

"I'm not sure it matters." Cameron crunched a carrot thoughtfully. "If the residents all believe the blind cat tells them when they're going to die, the effect is still the same. That's really interesting, Ed."

"I know. But for the paper I'm writing a human-interest story about a nice little old lady and her blind cat, which she takes to the nursing home every day."

"Wouldn't a human-interest story about people reclaiming a fear of death and making it into something peaceful be a much more powerful story?"

"Exactly."

He pushed the hummus toward me. "How's everything else? Your parents still being difficult?"

I ate a carrot, thinking about that one. Cameron, being Cameron, didn't fill the silence with words. He ate a carrot too, without fiddling with his phone or shuffling papers.

"They're okay. As long as I avoid my dad, things are all right. I try to go see Abuela before he gets home."

"And your mom? Tell me she's at least getting your name right."

I shrugged. "She tries to avoid calling me anything. Kind of the bitch about Spanish, you know? All those gendered nouns. So now she just doesn't address me at all." I didn't tell him that sometimes, in the middle of the night, I tried to manufacture my mother's voice calling me mijo, that I'd done it so many times I could almost make it real: *my boy, my son*.

"I guess it'll take time." His voice was low and even.

If I were attracted to men, I think there could be something between us. I think Cameron wouldn't balk at the fact that my dick doesn't look like other guys' dicks, or that once I take my binder off I have breasts again. He's gay, but he's seen me as a man since the first time I introduced myself, and when I went on T he was one of the only people I told. We weren't that close at the time, but I'd just needed to tell someone, and I'd been at the theater interviewing him about a fund-raiser he was doing for the high school's Gay-Straight Alliance. (An assignment dropped on me because who else would bother covering the story? Potter had as good as said, "Go interface with your people and give me ten inches about local business owners supporting the youth.")

Cam was still looking at me. "If you need anything, let me know."

"Sure." I grabbed another carrot. "I should go back to work."

He checked the monitor showing *Jurassic Park*. "Did I tell you about my Cary Grant series?"

"No. What're you doing?"

"Well. You know about my love for Cary Grant."

"You have a love for Cary Grant?"

"Ed. Mr. Grant and I go back a long time." He flashed a playful smile.

"I had no idea, though it makes sense. You are very Cary Grant."

"Why thank you. In any case, I'm holding a Cary Grant film series in the fall. Starting in October, running through December. Spend Saturday night with Cary Grant! Then snacks and fruit juice after, something like that."

"Really? That sounds great. I'll totally come."

"I'm hoping to generate some, ah, habit-forming behavior. Follow up with movies of the same era, at the same time. We always play *It's a Wonderful Life* near Christmas, which is right after the end of the series. Really, I'm trying to . . . engage, I guess."

I raised my eyebrows. "That's . . . good."

"It sounds awful. Part of me is dreading it. But I think if I want the Rhein to stay important to people, I have to do more than hide here in the booth. I'm the only Rheingold who hides in the booth, Ed."

He was the only Rheingold still breathing, but I took his point; both of his parents had known me on sight when I was a kid because I'd scraped money together to go to the movies whenever I could. "It was always good, walking up to the window when your folks were selling tickets. It meant something that they knew my name and the kinds of movies I liked."

He nodded. "That's exactly it. And it's the thing we have that the big theaters don't have. I don't know why it took me so long to see it, though I guess I was . . . hoping it wouldn't come to that."

"Is the Rhein in financial trouble?"

"Nothing I can't think of at least a dozen ways to turn around. Just gotta make myself do it. So I'm starting with Cary Grant, but I'm trying to seed the audience with people I know, so when I'm attempting to make small talk I won't feel quite so ridiculous."

"You can make small talk, Cameron."

"It is not my strength, like it was Mom and Dad's. But I'll try." He reached for the lid to the hummus and packed it and the carrots away.

That was probably my cue. I waited until he stood, tugging his vest down as he did so—two sharp tugs on both sides, effortless masculinity and grace.

"Thanks for letting me crash your lunch," I said.

"Anytime. Good luck with your blind cat story."

"Thanks."

I drove back to work thinking about the ways I was different than my parents expected, thinking about the ways Cameron was probably different than his parents expected. I looked at him and saw my quirky friend, who wore clothes eclectically, who never seemed to lack for confidence. How much of that was something he did intentionally, the way Cary Grant had changed his mannerisms and his accent to be who he wanted to be? How much of any of us was real, versus what we projected for the benefit of other people?

The blind cat would probably know the answers to all these questions. If it weren't a cat.

CHAPTER 2

After work, I went by to see my abuela. Not just because I was avoiding my roommates, though avoiding my roommates was always a good idea. There was nothing really wrong with them. And I *thought* I passed enough so they hadn't twigged to me being trans yet, but my policy of avoidance had worked pretty well so far, so I went with it.

And I love Abuela. She's the only person I miss. She's definitely the only reason I ever visit the house.

Abuela is my mother's mother. My dad is completely estranged from his huge Italian-American family because of some fight he had with his parents when he was in college. They've tried to reconcile over the years, but he's too much of a pigheaded jerk. Once, when my mother told him she thought it would be more healthy if he maintained a connection to them, he told her that he'd sworn he would never speak to them again and he never will.

The last time he spoke to me he said I could be his daughter or I could be dead to him. I couldn't be his daughter, so that didn't leave a lot of other options. He never got home before six, though, so I had a little time to visit before I had to get out.

Abuela is always glad to see me. Even if she misgenders me like crazy.

"Here's my flaca, come to see me!" She kissed me on my cheeks. "Why don't you ever eat? I looked up that thing you do, eating only plants, and it's not healthy!"

"Beans and rice are plants, Abuelita."

She made a kind of growling sound. "I looked it up on your mother's computer. Being *vegan*." The way my abuela pronounced *vegan* made it sound a lot closer to *bacon* than *vegan*.

"It's a plant-based diet, and there's a lot of evidence to support it. And anyway, it makes me feel better, so it doesn't really matter." I sat down on the coffee table in front of her chair. "How's your day been?"

"Es bueno. You know. But you tell me about *your* exciting day, mija."

It's hard to describe how it feels when someone you love more than life calls you "my girl" when you aren't. When I was a kid, Abuela used to come in at night and brush her hands through my hair over and over again until I fell asleep. This is like she's brushing her hands through my hair but there are needles on her fingertips; I want it to feel so good, but it hurts, too. The kind of pain that never lets me forget how much it hurts.

I told her about the blind cat who could tell when someone was about to die.

"And you met this gato?"

"I saw it sleep on someone's lap, this old man. But he might not have died."

"Animals can sense things. They know things."

"I know, Abuelita."

She patted my hand. "Do you want to hear about the ladies?"

"Definitely."

Abuela has a group of "ladies," this mixture of white and black and Latina women she plays bridge with down at La Vista Rec. They're basically a running telenovela that I tune in to every time I visit Abuela.

I never stopped looking at the clock.

My mother got home before I was able to escape, greeting me with a kiss on the head and a slightly wary expression. If I stayed too long, it would cause problems between my parents, but I thought she liked seeing me. The way I liked seeing her, probably, some tentative combination of love and distrust.

"I gotta go, Abuelita," I said as Mom unpacked groceries in the kitchen.

"All right, flaca."

Being misgendered in front of my mother felt a little extra ugly to me, a little humiliating. When it was Abuela and I alone, I could still pretend to be her granddaughter. But in front of Mom it felt more like giving in, or maybe like me being who I am was the phase they said it was.

But I don't correct Abuela, so I bit down on my cheek and excused myself.

I went home, successfully got into my room without being seen, and ate a cold dinner of cashews, salsa, and black beans rolled in cabbage leaves. It was actually pretty good, so I wrote it down on my list of meals to make again. Trying to quit meat and cheese after growing up in a Mexican-Italian home was almost impossible, but the absence of all those heavy foods made me feel better about myself, as if that weight in my guts was particularly female and leaving it behind meant more than just dietary change. None of which actually made sense, but it worked for me, so I let the weird associations slide.

Today had a blind cat. I wondered what tomorrow would bring me.

CHAPTER 3

I hadn't paid much attention to the story, the way you don't when a story is awful, but not *too* awful. A twenty-one-year-old boy died on his birthday. Beaten to death and left at the waterfront down beyond where people usually went. A woman taking a jog on a Monday morning with her dog had found the body. She'd thought it was a pile of garbage at first, until she'd noticed the shoes, still on feet.

Not garbage. A man. Steven Costello. Just home from his third year at UC Santa Barbara. His parents said he'd gone out for his birthday, but not with friends, or at least, none that they knew of. They had no idea where he'd planned to go, but he liked movies, so they assumed he'd gone to a movie.

If he'd been younger, I probably would have paid more attention. If he'd been tortured or sexually assaulted. If he'd been a more obscure race, maybe, and not a nondescript brown-haired white boy. If he'd been found anywhere other than the waterfront, a mostly foul stretch of the Bay that hits La Vista on the far side of the freeway in a tangle of weeds and trash and stinking debris from nearby cities. But I'd skimmed the story, felt a momentary pang at the prevalence of such crimes, and forgotten it. The *Times-Record* ran the story on Thursday, June 23. I started paying attention on Friday, July 8.

I was in the kitchen at work, getting my third cup of coffee. Someone had been doing the *Chronicle* crossword at the counter, so I added to it, only getting one clue while the coffee finished brewing. (One good thing about my job: free coffee all day long, as much as you want to make.) I did all right through Wednesday's and Thursday's crosswords, but the weekend puzzles were more challenging, so as I stood there trying to find any clue to the answer, I also did a lot of random glancing around, like inspiration would just show up on the bulletin board, or the refrigerator.

The bulletin board. Someone—probably Amie Arry, who wrote a lot of our "big" stories—had started pinning murder articles to the bulletin board. Even though Steven Costello wasn't interesting enough for an Amie Arry byline, he still had been murdered, so he was on the top of the stack.

Steven Costello, whose face from his UCSB ID card smiled at me from just below the headline. I'd seen him before. I would have sworn it. I'd seen that smile. I had no idea where, and he was way too young to be someone I'd gone to school with, but damn it, I knew his face.

I read the article while I stood there. And when the coffee was done, I unpinned the article and took it with me back to my desk.

Died on his birthday. No suspects. No leads. I could read between the lines. Kid didn't have a lot of local contacts, and had recently come home from college. His parents were the last people known to have seen him, but they didn't know where he'd gone to celebrate his birthday, and they had no idea who he'd gone there with.

I picked up the office phone that sat in the middle of the table between me and Caspar and dialed the extension of Joe Rodriguez, who'd written the article. Since I didn't really want Caspar to hear my probably stupid questions, I asked Joe if he had a minute to talk.

Joe, being one of the older guys, had an actual office he shared with a constantly rotating cast of staff. Right now the other desk was taken by a woman named Star, who spent the day with her headphones on, "editing" the *Times-Record*'s social media accounts. She seemed nice enough, as much as I could tell from someone who only communicated via 140-character email requests for 140-character articles.

"Eddie! What's going *on*, man?" Joe shoved a stack of notebooks off a chair and gestured me to sit.

"Not much. Yesterday I reported on a blind cat who can sense when people are dying."

He laughed. "I heard about that. Tim Potter was all up your ass. All he wants is a story that makes people *feel good*, damn it, but you always have to make it *dark*."

"I wasn't! The whole point of it— Never mind. I'm not here about the damn blind cat."

"What're you here about? How can I counsel you, young Padawan?"

I put the Costello article on his desk, carefully moving a picture of a kid in a karategi. "What's the story with Steven Costello?"

He picked it up, but I could tell by his eyes that he wasn't really reading it. "Yeah, that was a bummer. Lady's out for a jog, finds the body, calls the cops. At first they thought someone put him there figuring he'd be pulled out to the water, though he was a little above the high-tide mark. But the more they looked around, you know, he was killed right there. Beaten all to shit, Ed. Kid's face looked nothing like this."

"You saw the body?"

"I saw the photos. He was a fuckin' piece of meat." Joe put the article back down and smoothed over Costello's face. "If he was a girl, maybe it was some kind of hookup that went wrong. If he'd been raped, you know, maybe it was that. But this was just a kid out at the waterfront, killed in the middle of the damn night."

"Drugs?"

He shrugged. "That's what the cops are going with, unofficially. He wanted to celebrate his twenty-first with some refreshments of the illegal chemical variety, so he tracked down someone he knew could get it for him, arranged to meet. Maybe he didn't have the money. Maybe he had too much money. Bad things go down, he gets beat. But he had twenty-five bucks sitting in his wallet. No fingerprints to make it look like anyone even went through it. What the fuck drug dealer kills a grown man and doesn't take his cash?"

"None," I said. "That makes no sense."

"Yeah, and I'll tell you something else." He smoothed over the kid's face again. "I talked to the mother, asked her if there was anything else she could tell me about her son, you know? 'Straight-A student gets beat to death,' that kind of thing. And she just . . ." Joe paused. "I don't know, man. She didn't say anything, really, but it felt like there was stuff she wasn't saying specifically—stuff she could be telling me but didn't want to. So maybe it *was* drugs. Maybe our clean-cut college boy had a problem. But he grew up here and his parents couldn't name a single friend they thought he might be out with. That's a little weird, right?"

"Well, I grew up here, and my parents probably couldn't, either. But yeah, that's strange. He's pretty young for them to know nothing about his life."

"Yeah, look, everyone grieves differently, but if you talked to my mama a week after I was killed, when I was missing for two whole days, she'd be accusing every kid who ever spit on me or tripped me in line for hot lunch, you know? And Mrs. Costello was just . . . quiet." He shook his head and handed me the article back. "Dead ends. Cops had nothing to go on. Sorry, kid. Why're you asking about all that, anyway?"

"I don't know." I hesitated, not sure if I should mention how familiar Costello's face was. "I have it in my head that I've seen him somewhere before, but I might be making that up."

"You should think about it. And call up— Fuck, I forget his name. Green, I think. Detective Green was the guy on that case. Call Green if you think of anything."

"Sure. Thanks, Joe."

"No problem. You got any more blind cats to write about?"

I withheld my sigh. "I have a church bingo game that's donating money to the homeless, and a sweater drive down at the rec center. You want to trade for whatever you're working on?"

He laughed. "Fuck no. I did my time writing shit like that. You'll live."

"Thanks again, Joe."

"Don't mention it."

I went back to my desk, but I didn't put the Costello article back on the bulletin board. I stared at it a little longer, then started to google.

Before I got this job, I'd thought every story I covered would be a labor of love, at least in some sense. Sure, some might be boring, but I loved digging out details, and writing facts in a way that made them not only readable, but inspiring.

If you'd told me I could force myself through inches of words that I didn't care about, that I could write entire articles without hardly learning the facts of them, I wouldn't have believed you. I didn't think I could be that jaded about reporting. By the time I finished the bingo article (both the online version, which was little more than bullet points, and the print version), I wanted to write my younger, more dewy-eyed self a letter. *Dear self, on some days you will be so bored at work you'll become obsessed with the murder of a poor kid just to keep yourself awake. I'm sorry. Love, your future self.*

It had been a surprisingly tough week, though part of that was having Monday off. Even working four days felt long when you had three days off before them. (I hadn't done any big Fourth of July things, either. I'd spent that time reading the newish Sarah Vowell book and trying new vegan recipes, most of which had been terrible.) But whatever the reason, by Friday night I was in need of some light entertainment, so I headed out to Club Fred's.

Fred's is *the* queer club in La Vista. It's basically the anchor of queer nightlife, and rules one corner of Steerage, which is an L-shaped alley that runs between Mooney and Water Street. The other side of Steerage plays host to a dive bar called Bayside Saloon that might have been straight twenty years ago, but was now, at the least, "lifestyle optional" if not outright queer.

I don't go to the Bayside much. Not really my crowd. Club Fred's is all about music, and camp, and seeing everyone you've ever had sex with all in one place. Which sounds more gruesome than it actually is; if you really want a place where everyone knows your name, in La Vista, that place is Club Fred's.

I got myself a beer and started wandering around, chatting with different people, different groups. I passed a poster proclaiming next Friday "F*ck G*nd*r Night," which would be entertaining. When I was done with my beer I hit the dance floor, and immediately found Zane Jaffe (whose dancing was . . . unique).

"Baby!" she shouted over the music. "It's been too long, tell me everything that's happened since I saw you last!"

"It's only been a couple weeks!"

"Yeah, like I said, too long!" She tugged me closer, putting her hands on my shoulders and leaning in to speak in my ear. "How's it, Ed?"

"It's good." Now that she wasn't throwing her limbs everywhere, we could settle into a fun little grind. I liked Zane a lot, at least in part because we'd never dated, so she was one of the only lesbians I knew who didn't make me feel like I had to explain my transition to her.

I wanted to ask her about the Costello kid, but that hardly seemed like dance-floor conversation. "How're you?"

"I'm not fucking pregnant. Christ, Ed, it's beginning to fucking wear on me. Doesn't matter. Maybe this cycle it'll work, right?"

"Right! That's a good attitude to take." I'd gone to her two "conception parties," but she'd stopped throwing them. "Sorry I can't help you out, Zane!" I leaned back enough so I could adjust my crotch.

She laughed. "Oh baby, if only you could! I would totally mate with your genes!"

No joke, that was a really cool compliment. "Aw, thanks."

"Hey, you gotta talk to Jaq tonight, okay? She's got a student she wants to pick your brain about."

"Okay. Is she here?"

"Not yet, she's off with her girlfriend! Have you met Hannah?"

I shook my head.

"Oh, just wait until you do. I'm gonna go eat something disgusting, babe. See you later!"

She did some kind of wild shuffle in the direction of the bar, grinning when I turned back. Zane was hilarious. She'd also added a streak of pink to her purple hair since the last time I saw her, and while pink and purple might look little girlish on a lot of people, on Zane it just looked fierce.

After ten years of coming to Club Fred's, I felt pretty comfortable dancing by myself, or with whoever was around me. In the early days—when I was poor Steven Costello's age—I'd only gone to Fred's if I had a date or very close friends with me, so I would never have that moment of feeling by myself in a crowd.

Then again, these days I know so many people the difference is a little moot.

I registered the hand grabbing mine even before I registered the words.

"Hey, you."

"Hey, Alisha." It was easy to smile at Alisha. Alisha was full of smiles.

She moved in close against me, and I had a momentary flash of feeling revealed. Could she tell I had a binder on? But she'd known me for years—obviously I didn't have to hide that I wasn't born with a Y chromosome.

And anyway, Alisha didn't look the least deterred, whether she could feel the binder or not. "Looking good, Ed. Dance with me?"

"Sure."

Hell yes, I'd dance with her. I put my hands on her waist, and this wasn't quite the playful dancing I'd done with Zane; Alisha kept looking into my eyes and I kept looking back, far too long to be casual.

Her eyes were blue. Dark in the club, but I bet if we were outside they'd be bright, like the sky.

Dating had been the hardest part of transitioning for me. I dreamed sometimes about moving somewhere totally new, where I didn't know anyone, where no one knew me. Where no one remembered me awkwardly attempting to embrace being a "tomboy" as a kid (I always hated that word), or butch as a teenager, or transmasculine in my twenties before I let myself admit that I couldn't keep pretending the voice in my head that knew I was a man would go away. It was scary. Really scary.

And that was before I started telling people.

I still dated, but it was tricky. My old group of friends were gay in a binary sense, and a lot of them still had trouble understanding the difference between me now and me then, that even if I look pretty much the same on the outside, I'm not. And I'm probably more paranoid than makes sense; I always think the second I meet someone new, they'll talk to someone else and that maybe after that they won't want to date me because I'm trans, or they won't want to date me because I'm not trans enough, because I only started T a year ago, because my dick's not that big or my breasts are *too* big.

Alisha and I had been acquaintances a long time, but we'd never run in the same circles that much. She certainly knew I was trans, and whatever she was seeing, it was working for her.

"I'm glad you're here tonight," she said into my ear. I could barely hear her over the almost-intolerably loud beat pounding through the speakers.

"Me too. I mean, I'm glad you're here."

She grinned, little dimples in her cheeks making me flush. "I had to come out. Got this feeling something was gonna happen tonight that I needed to be here for."

I got up closer, my lips almost brushing her ear. "That sounds mysterious. Has it happened yet, or are you still waiting?"

"I'm not waiting anymore." She stepped back, dancing for a moment by herself, long hair down her back, arms upraised, her entire body undulating to the beat. Still looking at me. Still smiling.

I flushed hotter. I couldn't help it.

Alisha laughed and returned to my arms, running her hands down my sides. "I like the way you look at me. Makes me feel beautiful."

"You are. You are beautiful." I kissed her, because she was pressed against me and it seemed like the thing to do.

"This is why I came out here tonight," she murmured.

"You came out here to kiss me?"

"To be kissed by you. There's a difference."

Her hands guided me loosely until both of us were moving together. I touched her hair, her shoulders, her arms, sheathed in sheer black sleeves that were loose at her wrists.

It was still fun, with a thin vein of something serious running through it. We danced, laughing at each other, kissing a little more, but never too much. Her hands on my body didn't make me feel exposed. I may have made her feel beautiful, but she made me feel something else, something precious. Dancing with Alisha made me feel handsome, like a boy out with a beautiful girl.

My chest went tight, so I forced myself to stop thinking and just enjoy this moment, this dance.

I wanted it to go on forever, but eventually, sweaty and disheveled, we kissed again and she leaned in.

"I have to go. I hate my job, but I kind of have to be at it in like six hours."

"Sorry." I wasn't sure if I was apologizing for her job, or how late it was, or what.

"Are you kidding? This is the best night I've had in months! I knew coming here was a good idea." She grinned. "See you around, Ed. Are you coming to F*ck G*nd*r next week?"

"Definitely. Are you?"

"For sure. This is my favorite so far, I think. Mostly because Fredi used those little asterisks in it."

Of course that would be her favorite part. The asterisks. "I'll be interested to see how everyone fucks gender. You should go home and get some sleep, Alisha. I'll see you next week."

"You better believe it. Good night, handsome." She kissed me on the cheek and turned, melting into the crowd while I stood there, staring after her, thinking about the word "handsome" and how fucking powerful it was. It was my goal, my desire, an almost tangible mountain I'd set myself to climb.

Five foot seven inches tall, hair long enough on top to gel, seriously restrictive binders to hold my D-cup breasts in so they didn't screw up all of my shirts. When I looked in the mirror I saw all the ways I'd never measure up. My facial hair was still practically nonexistent, even after a year on testosterone. I'd never be taller. I was lifting weights a little, but I was far from strong, and nowhere near buff.

I had no idea what Alisha saw when she looked at me. Except that tonight she'd seen someone who was handsome.

I hung out for a while longer, opting for a soda instead of another beer, which the bartender, Tom, comped me. Sometimes I could find Cameron at Club Fred's reading a book, but not tonight. I laughed and talked and drank my soda, all of it with this thin sheen of detachment, trying to understand how people saw me, how they saw each other, how much of it was performance. Some people, like Fredi, Club Fred's ferocious owner, seemed to be entirely honest, as if she'd be as gruff and loud in her own home as she was at the bar. Some people, like Zane, definitely had a "public" persona.

If Steven Costello were here, what would I see? A secretive, overwhelmed straight boy? A depressed twenty-one-year-old hiding in drugs? Something else?

I finally went home, grateful for the quiet, grateful that no one in my house was having a party. Most of them were probably still out, though the kettle was warm when I heated it for tea, so clearly someone was up. I made my tea in peace and took it back to my room.

Alisha. Dimples. Her hands, unhesitating on my sides.

I drank my tea, took a shower, and crawled into bed. Where I may or may not have jerked off to the memory of Alisha's hands and her eyes never leaving mine.

CHAPTER 4

I live in one of the older detached houses downtown, three levels, with a little wrought iron fence out front. I'm the only one with a bedroom on the first floor, which is convenient sometimes, less so when my roommates are having parties. To be fair, they're all guys, and they're mostly grad students in their late twenties, and they've been pretty cool to me, even if the notion of having a full-time job is a little foreign to them.

I had a full-time job in undergrad. But I think they all come from enough money to not worry about their bills, so I guess they probably didn't work in undergrad. Or didn't work much. Or I might be assuming that they're all entitled white boys when maybe they aren't.

There're four of them. The guy in the attic is José, who definitely isn't white, and might not be all that entitled. I've only seen him like four times in the last six months. He has a girlfriend who lives somewhere else. Troy and JP are two tall, blond, white hipsters who look so similar it took me a long time to tell them apart. JP wears bowler hats a lot. The fourth guy is David, who's kind of a hipster, but the decaf version. Despite the fact that he spends the most time in the kitchen, I don't know him that well. I think he hangs out with Troy and JP, though it's a little hard to say, what with the avoiding and all. He cooks a lot of Indian food, but I don't think he's Indian.

Saturday morning was blissfully quiet in the house, so I made a tofu scramble and ate it standing over the stove after propping my generic e-reader against the salt, with the pepper making sure it didn't slide away.

I'm not a fan of tofu. Reading makes it less likely I'll taste it. I keep meaning to go to the new vegan restaurant in town to see if maybe they can make tofu interesting, but it's expensive, and for some reason my brain has it classified as more of a date-night thing than a "get lunch before heading back to the office to write more feel-good drivel" thing.

I was just cleaning up when David came downstairs and zombie-ambled his way to the coffeepot.

"Hey," he said.

"Hey."

Tofu was easier to clean off pans, but I still had to scrub it for a minute, which was apparently long enough for David to find his words.

"Uh, hey, can I—can I ask you something?"

"Sure." I looked over. He was standing at the coffeepot like it was an altar and he was preparing for worship.

"Uh, so, are you gay? Like, not that it matters, just, we were thinking, you never bring guys back here, and if you want to, you could. Unless that's offensive or something. I mean, it wouldn't be a problem. For us. If you were worried about that. Unless you aren't gay. Uh."

Quite a speech to deliver to the coffee machine.

I almost said, *Yeah, I'm gay*, before I remembered that if I said that, it'd give him entirely the wrong impression of the guests I'd be bringing home. If I ever brought guests home. I definitely couldn't say, *I'm straight*. That felt crazy-wrong.

"I date women." There. That sounded right.

David looked over, eyes wide. "Seriously? Uh, I mean, cool. But like . . . really? Like all the time? Shit, never mind, forget I said that. Not that—not that I thought a lot about it. We just kind of figured, uh . . ."

At least this answered the question about whether or not I passed. I apparently passed as a gay guy.

"But thanks." I finished my cleaning as fast as I could. "That's good to know. I don't currently have a girlfriend."

"Hey, me neither. Though really—" He waved a hand at the house. "This isn't usually the place they want to be, when I do. You know girls. They have all these expectations, like toilet paper. And clean dishes."

I set the pan aside to dry. "I'm pretty good on both those fronts, so maybe I'll have more luck. See you later, David."

"Yeah, see you."

I made it all the way into my bed before I started laughing, muffling it with my pillow. My roommates had been stressing over possibly making me feel too uncomfortable to bring a date home. I was such a jerk. Even if they were entitled white boys (except for José), they were apparently socially aware enough to try really hard not to be homophobic dicks. It was almost sweet.

And, god, was I really straight now? I'd never felt any romantic attraction to men. But that couldn't possibly make me straight. I didn't *feel* straight.

I muffled another bout of slightly hysterical laughter.

I could pass as a man, just not a straight man. I decided I was definitely okay with that.

Time to fire up my computer and get some work done.

I hit Togg's site first.

Togg was a mystery. His site was called thetruthisinvisible.com, and his About page only said, "The Original Gay Guy reports the truth you won't find in your mainstream publications." Which could be the description of any site from *Daily Kos* to one of those Fox News fan sites that regurgitates whatever Bret Baier says.

Except.

Togg was good. Really good. He was faster than the *Times-Record* at getting news up. When a drag king was murdered back in March, Togg had been the only person who reported it until the paper came out the following Thursday; it hadn't been considered big enough news to make the website, despite the fact that we frequently published irrelevant junk about bingo. No one had any idea who Togg really was, if he was one person or a collective of people. He was clearly local; only someone who knew La Vista well could talk about it with such a mix of contempt and disappointment. And I was relatively sure he was within five years of my age on either side. He referenced things that he would have only been likely to pay attention to if he'd been a teenager during a certain time period.

I'd read his entire archives. Twice.

I wasn't really closer to figuring out who he was than when I first started reading him. People at the newspaper treated him like a joke, but the only thing that kept me from thinking that he might be one of them was that none of them were gay and out. It was hard to imagine someone calling himself "the original gay guy" being in the closet and having a boring day job where he pretended to be straight. Then again, maybe that would actually explain why he seemed to put so much time and energy into the website. Maybe it was projection or something.

But I didn't think he had a day job with set hours. The speed at which he reported things, no matter when they happened, made me think he definitely had a lot of flexibility where his time was concerned. And I hadn't ruled out the idea that he might have a mole on the paper, in the police station, or both. On two separate cases that I'd heard of, Togg's post hit his site while our editors were still scrambling to assign the story.

I was pretty sure someone at the *Times-Record* was paying attention to him. Maybe my potential mole. Maybe someone else, who derided Togg even though they quietly recognized that he was doing a lot more serious work than we were, most of the time.

The posts were a mix of classic news-type reporting and more ornate editorials, as if he was his own entire news team. I was jealous of the way he wrote his editorials, never going too far into the kind of manic prose it's easy to tune out, always coming back around to his points until he'd built his entire argument cleanly. His style was way too consistent for him to really be more than one person, though the amount of work he put up daily was sometimes considered proof that he *must* be at least two or three people.

I scanned back through the archives to read more about the drag king, Mistah Olmes, who'd been found in an alley in the Harbor District on a Saturday morning, head bashed in, face disfigured. Togg had stayed on the story for a solid week, posting updates. He'd talked to the cops, but he was cagey about which ones, and when, and how. (He had a mole. I could feel it.) Then I went further back.

La Vista's pretty small, one of the mini cities that makes up the East Bay. We have our share of gangs and drugs and violence—lower than some places, higher than others. We have our share of hate crimes, and sexual assaults, and carjackings. A few years ago there was a nasty string of home invasions that eventually led back to a group of high school kids who "didn't mean to scare people" as they waved incredibly realistic guns around and duct-taped men and women and children so they couldn't scream.

Togg did a weekly round-up of local crime, but he saved his actual reports for things that had to do with queer people. I read back about a year without knowing what I was looking for. Then another year. By the time I'd gone almost all the way back to 2012, I was finished. After an article about a brutal gay bashing that left a boy in a coma, I shut down all my tabs.

I kept looking at Steven Costello's picture and trying to place him. Hard to do with a generic ID photo. Obviously wherever I'd seen him, he hadn't had a monotone background and a bland smile on his face. Still. He looked so familiar. I tried to find him on social media, but he didn't seem to have any accounts, at least not under his real name. I found a few other local Costello families, but the only ones who had kids in range to be siblings were black, and I doubted that matched this Steven Costello (and Joe's description of his parents). Joe hadn't mentioned siblings, anyway, but it would have accounted for how familiar/not familiar he looked.

I couldn't make Costello into a real story, but after I'd taken a break for trail mix, I decided that wasn't actually my issue.

I wanted more. More than blind cats. I'd only been at the paper for a year and a half, but I'd interned there when I was at the community college. That had to mean something. Maybe. And it didn't hurt to at least *try* to get a better position. Or expand my current one.

For the next two hours I crafted, revised, deleted, and rewrote an email to Potter. The first version was a full-on persuasive essay, high school style, with five perfect paragraphs citing my past credits, how I'd helped out senior reporters, and my value to the paper. The final version was one main paragraph and a sentence thanking him for his time. I kept it short. *I just want my work to mean something.* The most he could do was laugh at me, right?

Then, stupidly, I hit Send. It took about five minutes for the regret to hit, and another hour before I was actively brainstorming ideas on how I could break into the office and delete the email before he saw it, except most of the editors had their email shoot straight to their phones.

He might have already seen it. If so, he hadn't—I hit Refresh again—replied.

I paced my room, coming up with elaborate excuses about why I'd been so foolhardy as to write that email, and a long apology that was embarrassingly abject, which I'd never actually say to anyone.

I made myself stop and steal half a cup of David's coffee, which now needed to be reheated. There was no microwave in the house, so I stood there swirling a tiny amount of coffee in a sauce pot over low heat, bemoaning my stupidity.

Research fatigue. That was what it was. Too many hours lost in research could make a man do strange things, and that was clearly what had happened here. There was no other explanation. I'd let myself get all wrapped up in this crazy conspiracy where there probably wasn't one, and it'd taken over my brain.

I dumped the coffee in a mug and took a walk. And prayed that Potter didn't fire me.

CHAPTER 5

After a Sunday spent under a self-enforced internet ban, I was eager to get in to work on Monday morning, timing it so I managed to be at my desk and working before Potter arrived. My nerves were tightly strung, but he hadn't replied to my crazy email, and a quick check of the *Times-Record* site and Togg didn't reveal anything all that interesting having occurred during my self-restriction.

Togg had an interview up with a couple of guys who were starting a drop-in center for queer kids down at the Harbor District. I took a few notes on their names and checked out their website. I might pitch that as an article. Sometimes we ran token articles like that, and if I had to write feel-good junk, I might as well find some that actually made me feel good.

My pacing and internal rants came to nothing; aside from the usual good-morning grunt (about which Caspar assured me he didn't give a fuck), Potter didn't say a damn thing to me all day. I got the usual emailed assignments, but that was it.

The week passed mostly the same. I got permission to write fifteen inches about the drop-in center and set up an interview for next week. I stayed on task and generated easy posts for the website, took my turn coughing up links for Star to put out on Twitter and Facebook, and sent in all of my articles on time. Another boring week in the life, which I told myself to stop complaining about since I had the job I'd always wanted, lived in a house where people were generally cool to each other, and made slightly more than enough money to live. Things were good.

I made myself stop thinking about Steven Costello and put the article back on the bulletin board in the break room.

Abuela had gone out of town with her ladies, so I didn't have any reason to stop by the house, which was kind of a relief. I kept thinking that I had no excuse to feel so restless when in fact I had a pretty good life, but I couldn't shake the feeling that I was missing things—maybe big things, or small things, but *something*, I was missing *something*, and it ate at me a little every day.

By the time Friday rolled around, I was so ready to F*ck G*nd*r it wasn't even funny.

If your entire life is gender-fucked, coming up with an appropriate outfit to fuck gender is a challenge. I could have gone in a suit or a dress and been pretty much fucking gender either way, but I opted for a white button-down, a bow tie, and a long flowing skirt I'd never gotten rid of.

It felt weird to wear a skirt.

I'd been raised on skirts and dresses, and had balanced the scales by wearing jeans underneath them. When I was old enough to have a job and shop for clothes with my own money, I'd bought men's T-shirts and jackets, trying to cover up any hint that I didn't have a man's body. I'd stopped wearing skirts completely, for years, but when I checked myself in the bathroom mirror, I didn't look like my old self, like someone whom everyone saw as an awkward girl. I looked like who I was: a boy in a skirt.

I looked like I was fucking gender, and I was.

Club Fred's was packed by the time I made it there, more busy than it had been since Drag Night back in March. People had grumbled about Fred's starting up theme nights, but I thought it was kind of fun. A lot of people came in funny costumes, and even those who didn't seemed to be in on the party. Drag Night had included actual drag performances, but it looked like F*ck G*nd*r was going to be everyone doing the usual thing, but more of us and more deliberately fucking gender.

Also, the Men's and Women's signs on the bathrooms (which to be honest had never been more than suggestions at Club Fred's) had been papered over with *F*ck G*nd*r* on yellow construction paper.

My kind of night.

I saw Honey before I saw anyone else, wearing a white wedding dress and holding court at a corner table in the front, telling stories. She paused long enough to kiss my cheek and compliment my skirt before going on about some kind of horrific gender reassignment surgery a doctor had tried to talk her into back in the eighties. That turned into a huge argument with her ex-and-current-boyfriend about trans authenticity, so I slipped away.

Funny thing about dramatic fights: there are the people who see them and take that as a cue to back away slowly, and the other people who see them and are pulled in as if they're magnetic. I almost passed Alisha without recognizing her as she was getting caught up in the fight excitement.

"Hey," I said. Like a dolt.

Apparently seeing me was enough to cure her of wanting to go watch the fight. She immediately detoured into my orbit.

"Ed, I am so glad you're here. You look fabulous."

"You too. I like the tie."

"Isn't it great? I bought it from Obie a few weeks ago, but this is the first time I've had an excuse to wear it. Have you met Obie?"

I shook my head, barely tracking what she was talking about. The tie, the crisp black shirt, the quilted jacket that went down to her boots over skinny leather pants. Alisha looked damn good. I wished I hadn't wasted my compliment on a mundane *You too*.

"Buy us a drink, Ed, come on."

We found a spot to stand at the bar and I bought her mojito and my beer. It would have been an awkward silence while we waited for our drinks, except that the club was throbbing and pounding around us.

She nudged me. "Thought about you all week, you know. Hey, I was wondering, do you know how to drive a motorcycle?"

Did those two thoughts relate to each other? Had she been thinking about me driving a motorcycle all week?

I shook my head and took a sip of my beer. "Nope. Always wanted to learn, but I never did."

"*Ed.*" She grabbed my hands. "Let's learn together! There are classes you can take at the DMV and get your license!"

"Well, I don't actually have a motorcycle, so—"

"That doesn't matter! I mean, what if you're in a foreign country sometime and you're trying to get around and the only vehicle you have to rent is a motorcycle or something? You'd need to *know*."

"No, you're right. You're so right." She was right? What, that I'd be in a foreign country where the only way to get myself from place to place was a motorcycle? That made no sense.

"Will you do it with me? Please? It's like $250, okay?"

Whoa. "What's $250?"

"The *class*, silly. But I so want someone to do it with. It'd be fun!"

I found myself agreeing, though I had no plans to be in a foreign country without transportation (surely I'd be able to walk or take a bus . . .). It seemed to make her deliriously happy to tipsy-plan an imaginary motorcycle class, so we did. After that we tipsy-planned a trip to China, where we'd motorbike all over the country (though I was pretty sure most people there used regular bikes).

Alisha's eyes were bright. "Don't you just want to go *everywhere*? I feel like I'm standing in place here, you know? Like the entire universe is out there"—she gestured widely, almost cracking the kid behind her—"and I'm in La Vista, getting stagnant."

"You are not stagnant," I assured her.

She grinned, deepening those dimples. "Thanks. Neither are you. But you know what I mean. Do you ever feel like one of those shots in a movie where the entire background is a blur of energy and excitement, and the main character's standing right in the middle of all of it, perfectly still?"

"Yeah. Yeah, I know what that feels like."

"See? So we should travel. We should ride motorcycles together."

"Even though we don't have motorcycles?"

"We'll borrow them! I bet we know people who have motorcycles!" She grabbed my hand again. "I want to *do* things, things that aren't going in to work every day and just sitting there."

"Where do you work?" Somewhere boring, probably. An office job filing paperwork and sorting mail.

"Oh, at the Adventure Connection."

"The what?"

She rolled her eyes, executing some kind of alluring head-tilt thing that shook her hair free of its bun. "The Adventure Connection? We coordinate these trips for people—white-water rafting, skydiving, that kind of thing. It's like a travel agency for extreme sports, you know?"

I didn't know. But any questions I might have had were a little wrapped up in watching her pale fingers working through her hair, then braiding it, then twisting the braid back into a bun.

"So, like, I'll answer the phone and it'll be Pasty Beer Gut Accountant. And that's not shitting on accountants or anything, it's just the first thing that came to mind. Anyway, Pasty Beer Gut wants to go skydiving because he just had his, like, twenty-year frat reunion, and he feels like he's never done anything cool in his entire life, and he got a divorce and whatever, so he calls me up and says, 'Hi, can you hook me up with an airplane so I can jump out of it?'"

"Seriously?"

She laughed. "Seriously. This is my life. So I give him the whole rigmarole and get him signed up for our services and I take down all the information—"

"Wait, what information? Like, what more can he say after 'I want to jump out of a plane'?"

"Oh, tons of stuff. Does he want to do it here in California? A day trip? Does he want a weekend in Napa with wine tasting as well as skydiving? Maybe he wants to go to New Zealand and work in some backpacking, you know? People have these very specific dreams about their perfect adventures, and it's my job to give them exactly what they want."

"That seems—" I shuffled a little closer to her. "That seems actually really cool."

She sighed. "I know. That's why I got the job. It sounded cool, and my interview made it seem all, like, romantic and fascinating, connecting people to the adventure they've been waiting for all their life! But, I don't know, now it all seems so . . . made-up. Pasty Beer Gut wants to go to New Zealand for two weeks of adventure. He wants to stay in hostels and experience the outdoors and eat cheap food. But three days into his big adventure he calls me to bitch about how his three roommates at the hostel all snore and his feet hurt and they don't even have Foot Locker in New Zealand, so what is he going to *do*? Because he had this whole thing in his head about how it would be, and it wasn't. So I get him a room at a hotel, and he spends his days at the pool, eating room service, and if I'm lucky, he doesn't blame me for his failed adventure, but he's still not satisfied."

"Does that happen a lot?" I couldn't imagine being in another country and crapping out because my feet hurt, but then again, the only other country I'd ever been to was Mexico when I was four, and my dad hated it so much we never went back.

"Oh yeah. Not all the time, but a lot. We do these follow-up calls to check in with people after they get home. It helps us keep up on where the best service is at our contracted sites, and it makes it more likely that people will come back to us the next time they want to go on an adventure. Sometimes people had, like, the greatest time of their lives, but probably the majority just sound sort of... dejected about it. They can't pinpoint anything that was really wrong, but it wasn't what they'd hoped it would be. And it's just so *sad*, that all these people invest so much in their dreams and then miss the adventure they're actually having."

"Yeah. That sounds— Wow. Yeah." I studied her, trying to imagine her traveling the world. It was easy, picturing Alisha with a backpack and a boarding pass. "So then what's your idea of an adventure, if it's not skydiving?"

"Oh, I'd skydive. But I wouldn't want to plan it weeks in advance, or anything. I'd just want it to *happen*. And if it didn't happen, then maybe I'd go hiking somewhere really cool. Or find a street vendor selling a food I didn't even know how to pronounce." She pushed a bowl of nuts across the counter, maybe to illustrate mundane food choices. "I want something different. I want to sit somewhere that isn't here, look up at the sky, breathe in the air. Not rely on some kind of dream of what a 'real' adventure looks like, but make my own."

"That sounds incredible. Seriously, Alisha. That sounds absolutely amazing. You should do that."

"It'd be a lot more fun if I had someone to do it with." She didn't exactly bat her eyelashes at me, but her voice sounded like eyelashes batting all the same.

"I've kind of got work," I mumbled.

"I'm quitting my job. I've decided. I have to. I hate it."

"Yeah, but don't you have, you know, rent and stuff?"

"*That's* why I haven't quit my job—yet. But I have to, Ed. It's sucking my very soul out through my ears. Every time the phone rings and it's another middle-aged, middle-class white guy who's bored, I want to scream."

I raised my beer. "To not screaming at work."

Her glass clinked against mine. "I'm sorry I'm complaining. It's just getting to me more and more. Like there are some days when it's fine, it's even okay, and I don't want to kill anyone. But then there are these *weeks* where everything is so mind-numbing that I feel like I might literally die. Like just sitting there, at my desk, no cause of death, no foul play, one hand on the phone, the other on the keyboard, eyes wide open, totally dead."

"Okay, no. Don't do that."

She grinned. "Okay. I won't. But tell me about your job, now that I've bitched and moaned about mine. Let me guess: it fulfills you, right? It's what you always wanted to do, you worked your ass off to get there, and now all the hard work was worthwhile?"

"Not exactly. I mean yes, in some ways. Kind of. I work at the *Times-Record*."

"Ohhh. That must be really interesting."

"I . . . thought it would be. It turns out it's not that interesting. At least at my level. I mean, obviously it'll take years before I get to work the really interesting stories, but I'm in a rut right now. Or maybe I'm just super impatient."

"So what does that mean? You work boring stories?"

I took her hand, gravely, and patted it. "Do you want me to tell you about the blind cat that can predict when people are about to die?"

"You're *lying*."

"Nope. I've seen it do the prediction, though I don't know if that particular one came true."

"But, like, seriously?"

"Seriously."

She shook her head slowly, eyes never leaving mine. "I really want to meet this cat, Ed. Like a lot."

"You do? Why, you still planning to die at your desk?"

"No, like, I don't know. I want to pet the cat that knows when people are dying. That is so freakin' *intriguing* to me."

"Me too. I mean, the lady who owns it takes it over to the assisted-living place on the north side pretty much every day, so I can probably actually introduce you if you ever want to go."

"Wait, are you for real? Because I *totally* want to go."

"Sure."

"That's awesome. I can't wait. I can't wait to meet the cat." She tipped her drink back and pushed away from the bar. "I gotta get home. I'm required to answer some very important adventure questions in the morning."

"You really work Saturdays?"

"Yeah, and I'm off Mondays. I guess more people realize they absolutely *need* to go parasailing in Hawaii on a Saturday. We get more couples on the weekend too." She leaned in to kiss me, and I could have pretended that everything until that moment was casual, but Alisha's lips were anything but. She lingered, looking right at me.

I didn't gasp when she broke contact. I think.

"You could come home with me for a little bit, you know. If you wanted."

The offer took me so by surprise I couldn't process it for a minute. Then, when I did, I had no idea what it meant. Was this a one-night stand? Did she want to talk more about adventures? Hell, was she even attracted to trans guys?

"Um," I said. Like a genius.

"Maybe next time." She kissed me again and slid her index finger under the knot of my tie. "Really like the look tonight, Ed. See you around."

She didn't wait long enough to hear my weak "You too." Which was probably for the best.

What just happened? What did I do?

"There, there, boy." The guy on the next stool patted me on the back. He was Carlos, which I knew because Club Fred's only had one regular who was a little person, so even though we hadn't actually met, I knew who he was.

"What did I just do?" I blinked at my empty glass. "Oh my god."

He laughed. "Either dodged a bullet or missed the chance of a lifetime. Tom, would you get this man another pint and put it on my tab?"

The incredibly tall blond bartender put a beer down in front of me. "She's a good kid. Mostly."

Carlos laughed again. "Sure, she is. Dancing with that girl is like dancing with fire: it's gonna be hot, and you'll definitely get burned."

"I don't know what she was asking! I have no idea what I just said no to. I didn't mean to say no!" I sucked on my beer, and he patted my back again.

"Don't be too hard on yourself, kid. She'll be back. I saw that look she gave you. Alisha never takes three steps when she could leap off a cliff instead."

I almost said, *What if I want to leap off the cliff with her?* Except that would have been pathetic, so I didn't. I stewed in misery instead. Much less pathetic.

Beside me, Carlos hooted laughter. "Now, look what the cat dragged in. Sweet, sweet Jaqueline! Here with her lady love."

"Quit mispronouncing my name, you buffoon. Oh good, Ed, I've been meaning to call you."

I managed to drag my face up, though I didn't bother trying to look less miserable. "Hey, Jaq." Then I did a double take. "Whoa."

She twirled to whatever extent she could twirl with people pressed pretty close against her on all sides. The satiny hot-pink dress she was wearing attempted to twirl too. "You like?"

"You're, uh, definitely fucking gender." I'd never seen Jaq in a single article of women's clothing. Let alone a pink dress.

"Bet your ass I am. Hannah, you gotta meet Ed. Ed, Hannah."

Hannah was wearing a suit, which was also pretty awesome.

"Good to meet you," I said.

"Oh, you too. Tom? Be a love and get me a glass of wine and Jaq a soda?"

"Sure thing. You two look great."

Both of them preened.

"What's up your butt?" Jaq asked me, backing all the way into the woman on the stool behind her (who muttered "Hey" so low that Jaq ignored it).

"Nothing."

"He turned down Alisha," Carlos said helpfully.

"I didn't! I didn't turn her down. I just didn't know what she wanted."

"She said, 'Come back to my place' and you said 'Uh.'"

Oh god.

Jaq laughed. "If Alisha's anything, she's forgiving. I'm sure the next time you see her she won't even remember that happened. Now, are you in a sulking mood, or can I ask you a few questions?"

"Questions?" I took a sip of my beer. "What kind of questions?"

"I have this student who I think might be trans. What's the protocol on that? I mean, I assume I don't say anything to her, but I'd like to find some way of being less than a fucking dumbass about it."

"Why do you think they're trans?"

She pointed at me. "Like that. I keep saying 'she' even though it feels off to me, but you said 'they.' Why didn't I think of that?"

Hannah nudged her. "Tell him about Merin, sugar. I'm going to bring my knitting woes to Honey."

"Because Club Fred's is the perfect extension of knitting group. Go on. I can survive without you for a couple of minutes."

"That's all you have." Hannah held up her glass of wine. "When I'm done with this, I'll require dancing."

"I'll be right here, ready to do your bidding," Jaq shot back. She focused on me again once Hannah was lost in the crowd. "Listen, even if Merin was the kind of kid I could walk up to and be overt with, I wouldn't, because it'd be inappropriate. But there's got to be something I can do so if—or when—she needs anything, I'm available. Damn it, *they*. I'm waiting for QYP to open, which would I think at least help, but right now it's a great big warehouse with practically nothing in it."

"QYP? I saw that somewhere recently. Wait, is that the drop-in center? I just scheduled an interview with them."

"Yes! So you know about it? That's good. I was starting to think no one had ever heard of it but us. Listen, are you going down there to talk to them? The place is at the far end of the Harbor District where the waterfront kind of takes over for a few miles of old cars and dead washing machines before it becomes Albany, and Merin's been working to clean it out, so she might be there. Will you— Fuck, Ed,

I don't know. If you see Merin, will you at least tell me if I should be worried?"

"Because I'm the only trans person you know well enough to ask? It's not like there's a secret language, Jaq. How would I know if you should be worried?"

"Shit. Sorry. You're right. Fuck, you're right, I'm sorry. And I know that. But her girlfriend's leaving for college soon and I'm worried that she's going to be totally isolated after that." She shook her head. "I don't know if I can switch pronouns outside of class, and I know for sure Merin would kill me if I tried to do it in class. Damn, this is complicated."

"Well, I'll keep my eyes open when I go down for this interview," I said. "And whatever you're already doing is good, Jaq. I'm sure this kid knows they can talk to you if they need to." I wasn't sure I'd have the balls to be out if I taught high school, but Jaq was not only out, she ran the Gay-Straight Alliance.

"I hope so, but I doubt it. Hell, I really am sorry for treating you like some kind of trans whisperer, Ed."

I waved it off. "It's fine. I'm not offended or anything. I just don't have any big wisdom to share. Sorry."

She leaned in to kiss my cheek. "Gotta go. I can see Hannah meaningfully up-ending her wineglass from here."

"Have fun."

"You too, kid. And don't worry about Alisha. She will totally be back. Trust me."

"Thanks." God, now half the damn bar thought I was mooning over a woman I totally wasn't mooning over.

I settled back in to drink my beer and pointedly not-moon.

CHAPTER 6

Dark. Dark and humming. Hummm. Hummm. Wait, no, that was vibrating. What the hell?

I groped for my phone, which I always turned facedown at night so the notifications light wouldn't keep me up. I blinked and aimed a finger at the green Answer slider.

"Hello?"

"Masiello. What're you, sleeping?"

"Who is this?"

But when he laughed, I knew.

"Joe Rodriguez. Sorry, kid, did I interrupt a pleasant dream?"

"I think I was in a way deeper sleep stage than that. Uh. Joe, what's up?"

"Potter said you want to do things that matter and I can feel free to use you, so I'm using you. Get your ass out of bed. There's a body at the waterfront."

There's a body at the waterfront.

I scrambled out of bed, nearly dropped the phone, and managed to turn the lamp on. "A body?"

"Yep. And since you volunteered to do unpaid overtime in the interests of reporting the news, buddy, you get to be my assistant. Two creams, one sugar, and I'll meet you in the parking lot. Be quick about it. I'm not waiting longer than five minutes."

Click.

"What the hell just happened?" I asked my empty room. Last night's beer weighed heavily in my limbs, but a quick impromptu drunk test assured me I was safe to drive (thank god). Still: what the hell just happened?

Also, if this was going to be happening more often, I'd need to have a work outfit and go bag ready at all times. The thought thrilled me a little, and I couldn't tamp down the excitement, even when I realized it basically hinged on people dying. What else would get Joe Rodriguez out of bed at— Seriously? It was just before 5 a.m.? No wonder it was still dark out.

I tugged on jeans, shoved myself into a binder, and pulled a dark shirt over it. Black? Dark blue? I had no idea. I covered that with a sweatshirt (he'd said the waterfront, right?) and grabbed my keys.

One creamer, two sugars? Two creamers, one sugar? I couldn't remember, so I stopped by the gas station and picked up one of each, then promptly forgot which was which. Fuck it. Joe could bring his own damn coffee if he wanted perfection.

For a second I thought I'd beaten him there, but when I pulled in to a space right outside the cop cars I saw him talking to an officer I didn't know. Not that I knew a lot of La Vista cops or anything, but the handful of them who work the high school have nicknames like "Butt Pads" and "Carrot Top." This was just some nondescript white guy, younger than Joe but older than me.

I walked up with the coffees in my hands, only at that second realizing I'd forgotten to bring my active notebook. Or a pen. *Fuck, fuck, fuck.*

"Hey, Ed. Officer Smith, this is Ed Masiello, one of our new guys."

A year and a half and I was still a "new" guy. I withheld a sigh, handed one of the coffees to Joe, and shook hands with the cop. "Good to meet you."

"Yeah, you too, kid. Stick with Joe, okay? And don't look too closely at the body if you're gonna puke."

"That bad, Jay?" Joe asked.

"She's pretty busted up, yeah. Nothing you haven't seen before."

"We'll see you out there."

The cop nodded and started walking toward the pier. I watched long enough to see him split off to the left, but Joe snapped in my face to get my attention. I was ready to be irritated, but he wasn't smiling.

"He's right. That's a dead human being out there, and we'll probably make indecent jokes about it later, because that's what you do, but this is your first and he's right, Ed. You don't have to look. You got nothing to fuckin' prove, not to me, not to anyone. Got it?"

I swallowed. "Got it."

"Good. Thanks for the coffee, though I was joking."

"I don't mind stopping."

"Can't help but see you got no paper with you to write on."

Shit. "I'm trying to keep more notes on my phone so I can use the computer to search for them later," I lied. I hated digital notes. Everything made more sense when I could see it written down in my own handwriting.

"Whippersnapper." He cuffed the back of my head. "Let's go. Take a walk if you need to."

"I'll be fine."

"Sure, kid. That is what literally all of us say. Come on."

I didn't quite follow him. We walked side by side and I tried not to look like I was copying Joe's moves exactly. He'd set his face in a deliberate, stiff expression, whether because we were walking out to see a dead body or because of the biting wind off the Bay, I didn't know. I tugged my sweatshirt in tighter and tried to remember where I put the app on my phone that was supposed to be good for taking notes.

The Bay lapped at the rocks below us, inky dark still, and San Francisco was mostly an eerie glow of fog across the water.

Easy to tell where the body was. Cops were grouped around it and caution tape was already up, strung from the low wooden fence at the edge of the path all the way around some bushes, ending at the rocks. La Vista's waterfront is far from a thing of beauty; they managed to maintain the jogging path pretty well, but years of litter and pollution showed on the rocks and sparse vegetation that separated it from the water. As we approached, a white plastic grocery bag snagged on a spindly branch, waving in the wind like a flag of surrender.

Then my eye was caught by something else, also white, also highlighted in the low lights of the parking lot, still visible in the distance, still casting a mute glow in the gloom.

A couple of the cops greeted Joe with "Rodriguez" or "Hey, Joe." One of them said, "I didn't know old men like you got up this early in the morning for work."

"Well, I was pretty sick of boning your sister, anyway, so the timing was good, Johnson."

"Ohhh hell no. You did not just say that about my *sister*."

I tuned out the banter. We weren't the only ones standing at the caution tape. A few people who looked like joggers, one or two other people dressed like I was, in dark clothes and hoodies.

I forced my eyes back to the white bundle on the sand, forced my brain to sort it into a person: those were legs, one foot missing a shoe, and that was an arm, and that—that must be a head, though it was hard to tell if the person was face-up or -down.

A free-standing light came on, and I saw her, not as pieces, but as a whole.

Honey. I knew that dress. I'd seen her a few hours ago, wearing a white wedding dress. I bit down hard on my tongue as a cop knelt beside her body.

"Think we have a bride here? Maybe too old, though."

"Old people get married too, Bolshov!"

"Christ, really? Murdered on her wedding night? I'm taking odds it's the husband."

"No fucking pockets, though."

They rifled through her dress searching for identification, and I almost shouted at them to stop. They had to stop. *Stop touching her!* But I didn't say anything, just watched their hands and the way she didn't respond, the way she didn't slap their hands away, the way a breeze picked up her veil and blew it back at a cop, making him scramble away.

A hand clamped down on my shoulder and I almost screamed.

"Look away."

"No, I—"

"Damn it, Masiello, this isn't a fucking competition. Don't look if you don't want to see it."

"Her." Could I be wrong? "I think I know her."

"Jesus, Ed, you know a lady who got married last night and ended up dead this morning? Come on, man, I'm beginning to think this was a bad idea—"

"If it's her, she has a heart tattoo on her ring finger." I turned to look at him, keeping my voice as steady as I could. "Can I ask them?"

"Shit. Hey, Baker."

One of the cops glanced over, an older black guy with broad shoulders. "Busy, Rodriguez."

"My colleague wants to know if she's got a tattoo on her ring finger."

That got his attention. He stalked over to us, and I didn't let myself feel intimidated by his looming since he was doing it so deliberately.

"Who's this?"

"Ed Masiello, Tony Baker."

I shook his hand, barely feeling the sensation. My fingers were numb. "That looks like Honey Jansen."

"This Honey have some reason to be in a wedding dress?" he shot back, and all the cop shows I'd ever watched hadn't quite prepared me to face a real cop, with a real question.

"It was— There was— There's a club, on Steerage. Club Fred's. It ran a theme night last night and Honey came in a wedding dress. As a . . . costume. Kind of."

"The gay club," he said, staring me down.

Fuck. Not that I was in the closet, exactly, but that my queerness no longer lined up with people's expectations. "Yeah."

"So this Honey's a lesbian?"

"No. No, she's trans." I held his gaze, wishing like hell I didn't have to explain. Wondering what the hell Joe was thinking right now.

"Trans. As in, she used to be a man and now she's a woman."

Probably this wasn't the time to get into an argument about the permanence and retroactive nature of trans identity. "She transitioned like twenty-five years ago."

"When was the last time you saw her?"

"Last night."

"What *time*, Masiello?"

You see people on those real-life police shows stumble over their words and you think maybe they're on drugs, or maybe it's a sign they're hiding something. But I wasn't hiding anything and I was completely sober, and I still had trouble getting my brain to count back in hours to figure out when I'd left Fred's, and when I'd last seen Honey.

"Right after midnight. That's when I went home, and I said good-bye to her before I left." Oh god. I'd said good-bye to her. She'd kissed my cheek and told me she just bought a few skeins of yarn that would look fantastic on me and I should look forward to getting a scarf from her before winter.

I took a step back, forgetting about Joe, and Detective Baker, and my job. Honey was lying there, tangled on the rocks. Her heavy dress rippled in the wind, but her veil blew up into the air in a way that was so undignified it was almost offensive. She'd kissed my cheek. I could still feel the warm imprint of her lips, and smell the Elizabeth Taylor perfume she always wore.

"If it's her, she has a tattoo on her ring finger of a heart," Joe said.

Baker grunted and moved toward the body. I watched him crouch on the rocks, watched him lift her left hand toward the light. She was stiff but still movable, so rigor mortis hadn't made her into a grim statue yet. Which meant she'd only been dead a few hours.

I knew by the way he looked up at me that the hand he was holding had a heart tattoo on its ring finger. A heart that Honey had once confided belonged to her first love, a man who'd died in the AIDS wards in the eighties, holding her hand.

This time I did turn away, abruptly sad. Sad for the man whose heart that was, sad for Honey, who'd died without anyone holding her hand.

"All right, drink your goddamn coffee. It helps, Ed, drink."

I raised the cup mechanically to my lips and sipped. No longer scalding, but too sweet. I sipped again and wondered if I was going to cry, or if I even could.

Honey, with two skeins of yarn at home that would never become a scarf.

"Good friend of yours?" Joe asked, and this time when he slammed his hand roughly on my shoulder he left it there.

"No. Not exactly. It's hard to explain." Friend? Maybe. Mentor, more like. Honey, who'd been trans back when it meant you could be institutionalized for it, who'd said doing drag was the worst thing she'd ever done because it was like being pressed up against the window of womanhood without ever getting to go inside. "I didn't know her that well, but she . . . took me under her wing, I guess." Why was I saying this to Joe? I'd presented as male the entire time I'd been at the *Times-Record*, and I was pretty sure no one remembered me from when I interned there in college, or at least they hadn't put the pieces together.

"Sorry," I muttered.

"Sorry I called you for this."

"No, it's okay." I made myself turn toward her again. Not Honey, but her body. "Maybe it'll help them figure out who did this if they know her name right away. I don't know."

"Yeah, kid. Listen, I gotta stay here, but you should head home. Take a shower, throw a little whiskey in your coffee, take it easy, all right? Hey, Baker! Ask Ed your questions so he can leave."

I wanted to argue with him, but it was easier not to. Baker sent Smith over, and word was getting around, because Smith didn't meet my eyes as he asked me about Honey. Did he know she was trans? Did he suspect I was? Probably that was paranoid. Maybe I shouldn't have said how long ago she'd transitioned. That was random. Cis people don't keep track of stuff like that.

I gave him her phone number, told him I thought she'd lived in the nicer part of the east side, but I wasn't sure where. I gave him Zane's and Jaq's numbers too, so they could start narrowing down the timeline of when Honey left the club. I listened to my voice and paged through my phone contacts and I must have been functioning, processing his questions, but I couldn't remember them seconds later.

When Joe Rodriguez shoved me in the direction of the parking lot with one final pat on the shoulder, I went without a backward glance.

I shouldn't have been able to sleep with all that coffee in my system, and the lingering afterimage of Honey's body in my brain, but maybe unconsciousness was the way my mind tried to protect me from feeling it too much. I climbed into bed after taking off shoes and pants, leaving my hood tightly pulled over my head, and crashed hard.

Hours later I woke up. The room was bright. I was sweating in my clothes. It took an entire minute and a half to remember about Honey.

I stayed in bed the rest of the weekend.

CHAPTER 7

Monday morning Togg posted a long, in-depth exposé-flavored article about how La Vista PD was hiding a killer who chose trans and gender-bending targets. He covered Honey, and the drag king Mistah Olmes, and went on to cite a history of local cops dismissing, mocking, or allegedly assaulting trans victims of violent crimes. When he was done nailing the police, he broadened his scope to include the media, news outlets, and queer community itself, which he accused of "ignoring at best and smothering at worst the complaints of our most vulnerable members, especially when they aren't photogenic or unthreatening."

It was a brutal piece, and I read it with a sick lump in my gut. Not because I disagreed with it, but because so much of it was true. The cops *did* regularly harass trans people who couldn't—or didn't want to—pass as cis. The community that arguably should have protected and nurtured its trans members was often scornful or pitying, with some of it going so far as to start a petition to drop the "T" in "LGBT," as if they could divorce themselves from us by a slight change in branding. As if straight people would like them more if we weren't lingering on the fringes, complicating matters.

Togg's words were aggressive, his tone imperious, his disdain riding the surface of something that felt a lot more like rage. I didn't think he was trans. It took my breath away that he'd even noticed all of this shit going on around him if he didn't have to. I couldn't escape it; a stranger who called himself "the original gay guy" probably could have gone his whole life without sparing a thought for people like Honey. Or me.

The comments section was, as expected, a clusterfuck. I didn't know why I was reading it except that I wasn't done with my coffee yet, and Caspar was late to work, so I didn't have to worry about being jeered for reading trash.

Togg's comments sections are often the kind that keep good people from opening their mouths, but this article had already gathered, in the six and a half hours since he'd published it, some real doozies.

SoHomo argued that "the trans minority should just shut the fuck up and be happy anyone's paying attention to them at all." He further theorized that Togg himself must be trans "or why the fuck do you care?" Which I would have found offensive, if I hadn't had basically the same exact thought.

SoHomo annoyed me for about fifteen seconds, until I hit a few way more horrifying comments along the lines of "she probably looked like a hooker and deserved it" about Honey, and "Olmes was a dick and had a beating coming to her" about Melissa Loren.

Jesus Christ. People were sick.

I should have quit there, but I didn't.

On the other side of the coin, a few people claiming to be trans wanted to make it clear that "transgender" and "drag" were not the same things, and criticized Togg for his apparent misunderstanding. Even though he'd gone out of his way to point out that the nuances of gender, while at least acknowledged by people inside the community, would be less clear to someone targeting it from outside.

It wasn't all hate. The usual Togg fans piped up to laud his "investigation" and pledge their support. A few others, who'd known the folks mentioned in the article, shared their grief and hopelessness. One or two had me tearing up, so I skimmed down. Togg himself rarely commented on his own site, leaving the impression that the skirmishes waged at the bottom of the page were far beneath his interest. He never turned the comments off, though, and they never collected spam, so he was clearly monitoring them. Or he had the best spam filter on earth.

I refreshed when I got to the end, just for the hell of it. Sixteen more comments had hit while I read, probably from people staring at the screen with their coffee like I was. The same, mostly, except for one lodged seven minutes ago, by someone calling themselves

WarriorTruth: *An artist's work is never truly appreciated until he is dead, unfortunately.*

That was it.

What the actual fuck did that mean? I stared at it, read it a few more times, refreshed again, but no, it was still there, a few comments deep now, slowly but surely about to be buried by Togg's traffic the rest of the day.

On a whim I took a screen shot of it and messaged Togg. I'd talked to him once before about an article he'd written that I'd tentatively requested additional sources for, because I'd wanted to pitch it to Potter as something we could cover. I'd spent a day and a half on that email, trying to make it perfect so he'd understand that I wasn't interested in plagiarizing his copy, or stealing his work. He'd messaged me back almost immediately with a list of books and articles, and after we talked for a few minutes he'd offered to give my name and information to two of the people he'd interviewed.

He'd been generous and direct, but I still didn't know exactly how to say what I found so disturbing about that particular comment. I sent it with a postscript: *Am I being paranoid, or is that creepy?*

Fifteen minutes later, after I'd closed the tab and gotten to parsing my assignments, Togg messaged back: *Don't think I'm not keeping records and digging into IP addresses.*

That was it. I sent *Good call* and got on with my day.

Who would read an article about the systemic mistreatment of a group of people, leading in some cases to murder, and write a comment about art? It wasn't any form of spam that I recognized. Which made it, what, a joke?

I had to stop thinking about it in order to proceed with the important work of covering La Vista Repertory Theater's announcement of its fall schedule. I thought about asking Joe how the article about Honey was going (he'd already posted the web-optimized version to the *Times-Record* website), but I didn't need to know and maybe it was better if I tried not to dwell on it any more than I already had. Or something.

Abuela would know the minute she saw me that something was wrong, and I couldn't deal with her *mija*-ing me today. I decided to hit the gym instead. Maybe I could sweat the fear and gnawing anxiety out.

Free weights still made me feel a little inadequate, so I opted for the mindless drone of an elliptical machine and plugged my earbuds into my phone, pulling up a radio station I liked. Quick-paced punk rock with lyrics I couldn't always make out, sung mostly by young angsty white men agonizing over their privilege. I didn't care what the music was. I needed to get out of my head, so I pushed myself harder, chasing exhaustion and its pleasant white-noise buzz.

Half an hour into my workout someone tapped my machine, almost scaring me into tumbling off. Zane waved apologetically and climbed up on the next elliptical over. Jaq waved from the treadmill on her other side.

I waved back, my bubble of physical absorption popped. Now I felt the heaviness in my calves and the strain in my thighs. My back ached, and my shoulders protested. I kept it up for a while longer, losing all hope of recapturing that sensation.

When I finally gave up and tugged my earbuds out, Zane said, "Sorry I scared you, Ed."

"'S okay." I started to slow my pace. I could do a cooldown, get chitchat out of the way, and—what? Go home? Sit in my room? Refresh Togg's site and rake myself over a new batch of heartless comments?

Or not.

I tried not to rush my cooldown. "Are you guys going to Club Fred's after this?"

"Please yes," Jaq said. "I cannot deal with that smoothie bar, Zane. Fred's is better."

"I'm trying to lose weight!"

"Have you even looked at the nutritional info for that smoothie you love? I think it's got an entire day's worth of sugar in it."

Zane pouted. "Fine. So wait, are you saying I might as well get fried mozzarella? Because that's what I'm hearing."

"I'll buy the first round of mozzarella sticks," I said. "I need to be out in the world."

"Sure thing, buddy," Zane said, and I had the impression that "buddy" was a last-second revision of "babe" or "hon." Jaq hadn't seemed to struggle that much with me transitioning. She'd slipped up sometimes early on, but she'd apologized and it wasn't a big deal. Zane had slipped *once*, telling someone I'd graduated a few years after them, calling me "she" accidentally, and she'd been totally horrified by it for weeks.

I wouldn't have minded "babe" or "hon," which were terms she used for everyone. Not that it mattered.

"I think I'm done. I'll see you guys over there." I left as they were debating whether or not they should cut their workout short in the name of mozzarella sticks.

Jaq's voice lectured as I walked away. "So you're trying to lose weight and this is how you're doing it? Shorter workouts and more fattening food? Good luck with that."

The men's locker room still felt a little like no-man's-land to me. It wasn't the alienating experience that being in the women's locker room was—where I'd always felt splintered, divided into two people, the one who could "pass" as female, and the one who couldn't help being male despite appearances—but it didn't quite feel like a place I belonged. I hoped that would change the longer I was on T. Right now my body hair was thicker than it used to be, which helped, and my voice had evened out lower than it was before. Testosterone was cumulative, though, so while I could kind of pass now, in time I'd probably feel more confident.

Cameron told me once that he suspected "passing" wasn't really about hormones or appearance. That at least part of the battle was in my head, and a lot of it had more to do with making eye contact and keeping my head high, and not looking like a guy who was trying to avoid being noticed. I thought of that every time I entered an all-male space, like a bathroom or locker room. A space where I'd be among strangers, not people who'd already slotted me into however they considered me in their head.

I kept my chin up and didn't seek out or avoid eye contact. Then I grabbed my stuff and locked myself in a shower stall, relieved to be alone.

It was still warm outside when I got in my car to drive downtown. Club Fred's was quiet on a Monday night, and I nursed a beer and hung out with Zane, keeping one eye open to see if Alisha would arrive. She didn't, so once I finished my beer, I went home.

CHAPTER 8

Togg kept posting updates about Honey to his site while the *Times-Record* hadn't even published her name yet. When it came out Thursday morning, I read the final copy of the story and found it basically identical to the version of the facts Togg was telling. Nothing new, nothing novel, nothing that gave me any hope the case would ever get solved. I gave in and knocked on Rodriguez's door late in the afternoon.

"They don't have a fucking clue." He swiveled all the way around and leaned back in his chair. "And to be honest with you, Ed, they're not exactly tripping all over themselves to figure it the fuck out, either."

He sounded more angry than I would have expected. Since it wasn't a brush-off, I sat down. "They connect it to the drag king murder back in March?"

He made a face. "You've been reading *that site*, haven't you?"

"Um. I plead the Fifth."

"The kid's sharp, I'll give him that, but not everything's a fucking conspiracy." He shook his head. "I tell you my boy is gay? My son. A little younger than you are. I really hate that the read I'm getting from this shit is that they'd look into it harder if anyone who actually mattered had bit it."

"Now who sounds like a conspiracy theorist?"

"Oh, that ain't conspiracy. That's just plain fact. You want your murder to count, you better be white, straight, and have enough money to make you sympathetic. Baker's doing his best, but no one else gives a flying fuck why a lady with a dick let herself be lured to the waterfront in the middle of the night to be beat to death."

I wanted to argue with his phrasing, but it seemed like there probably wasn't much of a point. "She wasn't stupid. I don't know why she'd've done that."

"People who aren't stupid do a lot of stupid things. They hauled the boyfriend in, but Baker said he alibied out pretty fucking fast. You know the guy?"

"Max? Not well. They were always fighting, though. It was part of the charm in their relationship, I guess. If one of them was going to get violent, I'd bet on her, not him."

"Yeah, well, if he didn't do it, they have no leads at all. And her friends weren't necessarily forthcoming, some of them."

I didn't know if he expected an apology on behalf of the community, or commiseration that we're a bunch of distrustful fools who don't know how to help ourselves. "I don't think anyone actually expects the cops to solve it. Melissa Loren died months ago and no one's bothered."

"Loren had a lot of people in her life who didn't particularly like her. Not like this Honey. No one says a damn word sideways about her except her parents." He grimaced. "They pissed me off. Acting like she had it coming. The parents always piss me off, Ed. Because I know what it feels like to have your kid upend everything you thought you wanted for them. You gotta be the fucking grown-up with that shit, you know?"

Not really. I raised an eyebrow. "I'll take your word for it."

"Yours too? Jesus. What the fuck is wrong with people?"

It was the closest we'd ever come to acknowledging that I was queer. Maybe he thought I was gay, like his son. Or maybe he'd figured out I was trans. I could tell him, but it didn't really seem important at the moment.

"I don't know what's wrong with people. I wish they'd at least find whoever killed Honey. She was good people, you know? She helped me when I didn't even know how much help I needed."

"Sounds like that might have gotten her killed, if she wasn't out there looking for tail." He shook his head. "I'll keep you posted, kid. But focus on your shit. And I'm sorry, again, that I called you out for that."

"You couldn't have known. Thanks, Joe."

He grunted and I left.

I wasn't really sorry that he'd called me out for it. At least one person standing there that morning had known her, mourned her. Had looked at her fingers and remembered knitting needles, and drinks, and the way she used to stand out in the alley at Fred's with the smokers, lighting match after match and watching them burn down to her fingers.

I'd asked her once why she did that. She'd said, "I like to be reminded of impermanence, honey. 'Nothing gold can stay,' you know." I'd teased her about quoting Robert Frost at me in a stinking alley off Steerage Street, but she'd just smiled and burned her matches.

My assignments were done early, and I slipped away with enough time to visit Abuela before Mom got home. When Zane texted me to meet up with her at Club Fred's later, I jumped at the chance. Anything was better than being at home with my notebooks, getting no closer than the cops to figuring out why Honey had died.

Fred's was tame and quiet, a Thursday evening crowd more interested in talking than dancing. It took me a few minutes to realize that Honey was the main topic of conversation, and the reason everything was so subdued. It had probably been the same on Monday, but I hadn't noticed, too lost in my own thoughts.

No Tom tonight, so Fredi served me, placing a pint on a coaster and lingering for a minute. "Heard they called you out of bed to go down to the waterfront Saturday morning."

I didn't bother trying to figure out where she'd heard that from. I already knew Togg had been there; it wasn't all that unlikely that another one of those random people had been queer, chatty, or both.

"Yeah."

"You saw her?"

"Yeah."

She flattened one hand on the bar in front of me. "You're on the house tonight, Ed. I'm sorry you had to see that."

"Me too. And thanks, I guess."

"It ain't much, but I don't suppose there is much that'd make up for seeing what you saw."

"No." *She was beaten so much her face was black. Her dress kept rippling in the wind. I proved it was her by her tattoo. Do you remember her tattoo? A little heart, right there, where a wedding ring would be if she'd ever wanted to get married.*

"The cops came around, wanting to know exactly where everyone was on Friday night, who she talked to, who she left with."

"Did she leave with someone?" I asked, interested in spite of my grief.

"I didn't see it. A few people thought she was escorted out by a boy half her age, but I don't take that altogether seriously. Half her age wasn't really Honey's style."

I shook my head. "Not really."

"Unless she was helping someone, anyway."

"I know they took Max down for questioning." I kept my voice low and watched her face, but clearly this wasn't the first she'd heard about it.

She waved a hand in dismissal. "They had that fight, and everyone saw it. Nearly everyone who talked to the cops mentioned it."

I wondered how many people had refused to talk to the cops at all. "They let him go, so I guess his alibi checked out." It hadn't even occurred to me that Honey's death might be a straightforward domestic dispute, something easily explained by the unstable cocktail of rage, love, and alcohol.

"Sure it did. He was still here until I closed up, then went down the street for last call at the Bayside. He's real broken up about it." Someone called to her from the other end of the bar, and she tapped the counter one more time with her palm. "Take care, Ed."

"Thanks, Fredi."

Max must be devastated. He and Honey had been going back and forth for years as far as I knew; by the time I was regularly showing up at Club Fred's, they were *that* couple, the one most likely to get into a screaming match and leave with other people, then most likely to come around hand in hand a week later.

Now she was dead, and she'd died after one of their blowouts, but before the reconciliation. I had a feeling Max was going to regret that for the rest of his life.

I nursed my beer and greeted Zane and Jaq when they arrived, taking stools on either side of me, grateful for the distraction.

They were mid-bicker.

"Why would I do it if I'm not interested?" Zane dropped her purse on the ground at her feet. "Why would I bother? What would I gain?"

"You still haven't actually addressed the question of *why* you aren't interested. If it's because you just don't care in general and you're happy being alone, then fine, but—"

"I'm dying of thirst over here, Fredi!"

"Keep your shorts on, Jaffe!"

Zane sighed. "She so hates me. What were you yammering on about?"

"Answer the damn question!"

Flicking a lock of purple hair out of her eyes, Zane leaned toward me confidingly. "I don't even remember what the question was, to be honest. Don't tell Jaq."

"You are so fucking infuriating, Suzanne Amanda Jaffe! Ed, have you ever used one of those online-dating things?"

"Um."

"Tell Zane it's a totally normal thing that totally normal people do."

Fredi showed up at that moment and took their drink orders. I tacked on an order of mozzarella sticks for them as well, hoping the diversion had permanently derailed Jaq's conversational choice.

No such luck.

"There's nothing wrong with using an app or something to meet people, or just to talk to people."

"I talk to people all day long," Zane countered. "What am I doing right now? Fucking talking to people."

"You're talking to me and Ed. It doesn't count. Neither does work. It's about *companionship*, babe. Where in your life are you leaving room for something new?"

"This is that thing where you hooked up with someone and now you want to wave fairy dust over the rest of us as if it's some kind of prescription?"

"No, Zane, this is the thing where for the first time in our entire friendship you didn't say you're happy being single. *That's* what this is."

"I'm fine."

Jaq sat back with finality. "Exactly."

I tried to focus on my beer, but it was no use. "Can you guys... not fight around me? I mean, literally, in space, if you're going to fight with each other can you at least sit on neighboring stools? I don't mind listening to you bicker, but it's harder when I'm in the middle of it."

"Sorry, Ed. I just have one more thing." Jaq leaned over to address Zane. "All I'm saying is that if someone was interested in companionship of the affectionate variety, that person might benefit from branching out. That's it."

Zane reached around me to shove Jaq's arm. "All I'm saying, Jaq, is cram it."

Jaq sighed.

We split the order of mozzarella sticks (there was only so long I could smell mozzarella sticks without tasting them; I'd be a better vegan tomorrow), they went to hit the dance floor with Jaq's girlfriend, and I was contemplating another beer when Alisha appeared.

Obviously she must have gotten there like anyone else. She'd driven or taken the bus, said hi to the bouncer. She must have walked from the door to the bar, but to me it was like one second there was a void in space and time, and the next she was filling it.

Her hair was pulled back in a few dozen tiny braids.

"Hey." I wished we knew each other well enough for me to tuck a loose braid behind her ear.

"Hey yourself. You got room for me here, or do you want to dance?"

Just like that, as if it was a foregone conclusion that whatever happened next, we'd do it together.

"Neither, really," I admitted. "I was thinking about another beer, but I might go home. I guess I'm not much in the mood for dancing."

She grinned. "Come back to my apartment and have a beer there. Cheaper and the company is assured."

I searched her eyes (blue, but liquid blue, like topaz), but I still had no idea if she was propositioning me or not. Tonight I didn't care. "Sounds good. Do you have a car? Should we take mine?"

"You can follow me." She grabbed my beer and sucked down what was left. "Wouldn't want you to pay for a drink and not finish it."

"Actually, Fredi comped that, so it was okay."

"Fredi *comped* a drink? How'd you manage that?"

I stood up and patted down my coat to make sure I had everything. "It was a 'I'm sorry you had to see Honey dead' drink, I guess. I'm ready to go."

She clearly wasn't. She stared at me long enough for me to note that she had three holes in each earlobe and none of her earrings matched.

"Honey died?"

Oh hell. "I'm so sorry. Yeah, didn't you hear?" It was on our site, on Togg's, and Club Fred's didn't have a corner where at least one table wasn't discussing what had happened. How did anyone miss that kind of information?

"No. No, I—I had no idea. I mean, not that I knew her well, like I don't want to be one of those people who capitalizes on grief and like steals it for myself, but obviously I—I definitely *knew* her, like everyone did." She took a seat on my abandoned stool. "Oh my god. How?"

"She died sometime early Saturday morning. They found her down at the waterfront."

"God. Ed. That's awful."

"Yeah."

She reached for my hands, gripping them tightly. "You saw her? Why?"

"I, uh, you know how I'd said I was sick of my job, of the kinds of assignments I keep getting?" She nodded. "So I asked my editor if I could do more challenging work. That was the first case they called me out on, to basically train with another reporter. But he ended up sending me home, because I was so— I wasn't much help."

"That's terrible. I'm so sorry."

"Me too."

She stood up, pulling my hands a little. "Come on. We're going to my apartment and I'll make us tea or something."

"Okay." At that point I would have agreed to anything that meant leaving Fred's. "And I'm sorry I told you so badly. I guess I figured everyone had heard already."

"I never hear anything. I kind of like it that way. Especially when stuff like this happens. I drive a bright-yellow VW bug, okay? You can't lose me. Come on."

I followed Alisha out the door.

CHAPTER

Alisha's studio was one rectangular room with an Ikea kitchen built against the exterior wall and a bathroom. Scarves were thrown up over the two lamps I could see from the front door and a longer piece of fabric had been tacked up around the fluorescent light in the kitchen, giving the whole place a kind of mystical feel, muted spheres of color meeting at the edges. The living area was blocked off from the bedroom with a bookcase on one side and a curtain on the other. Somewhat to my surprise, everything was neat and tidy. I'd imagined Alisha to be more bohemian with her domestic chores.

She really did make us tea. I was a little worried that she'd want to have some kind of deep conversation now, but that wasn't Alisha's style. Pressing a steaming mug into my hand, she led me to the sofa, which—along with the bookcase and a small television—made up the living area.

The books I could see from where I was sitting were almost entirely travel books. The spines proclaimed wild locations: Mali, Beirut, Cape Town. "Have you gone to a lot of places?"

"I don't even have my passport. How terrible is that? I filled out the form and never brought it in."

"I'm not actually sure where you go for that."

She grinned. "The *post office*. Isn't that weird? Like, I'm not sure what the post office has to do with anything, but that's the best place to submit your passport. Actually, I have no idea where I put that form now. Huh." She swiveled her upper body to stare at her bookshelves. "It must be here somewhere. Oh well. Or I'll just fill out a new one."

"So you have all those travel books and you've never been to any of those places? Do you . . . read them for fun?"

"Oh, I do more than read them." The twist became a stretch as she pulled out a book. "There's this, like, *structure* off the coast of Copenhagen, built right into the ocean, and it's like a kind of deck in a circle with the sea in the middle, so people swim and stuff, and there are bathrooms, and places to sit." As she paged through the book I could see sticky notes poking out in a dozen places and a little stub of pencil dropped into her lap. "Oops. I wondered where I put that. Here."

I took the book and tilted it toward the nearest lamp. "The Kastrup Sea Bath."

"I want to go there. I want to jump off the highest part of it."

"Looks kind of shallow there."

Alisha laughed. "That's very practical of you, Ed. But people jump off it all the time and live. That's what I want to do. I want to take it on faith that it'll be okay and then just do it."

It took hardly any effort to imagine her as one of the people in the photographs: braids flying out behind her as she fell through the air, maybe crying out, maybe laughing even as she hit the water.

I cleared my throat. "What would you wear? I'm assuming not a bikini, for the sake of propriety. I'm, uh, asking so I can better picture you there. You know. So when I'm sitting at my desk and you're in Copenhagen, I'll be able to see it in my mind's eye."

"Oh, I only wear bikinis." She leaned in close to take the book back. Very close. Close enough so I could see little starburst imperfections on her skin. "You know, you could come with me."

"I don't think my boss would pay me to go diving in the ocean off the Copenhagen coast with a beautiful woman. Unfortunately."

"No, you'd have to save up for it. I save every penny I can, outside what I spend going out for drinks. Which you know, if I stopped doing that, I could afford to travel way sooner. But then I'd hate being here more, so I have to kind of balance it out."

"I get that. I guess I do save money, I just never had a goal with it." Except maybe top surgery someday. And even more than that, to not be poor. Abuela had come from people with a little bit of money in Mexico and being poor was her greatest fear. But it was one of Mom's rare Spanish phrases that came to mind sitting in Alisha's living room. "De dinero y bondad, siempre la mitad."

"Something about money? Two years of Spanish with Señora Trujillo and that's all I've got."

"Money and goodness, yeah. Well there are a few ways of looking at it, but the one Mom always liked was about seeking balance—never too much money, or too little."

"There's such a thing as too much goodness?"

"I think it means don't let yourself be taken advantage of." I shrugged. "Like, the other way of looking at it is that you shouldn't believe anyone's claims of money or goodness because they're probably full of shit. I mean, I'm not sure which way's 'right.' My mom used to say it, but she kind of shuts down if you ask her questions about anything Mexican. But I think it's about balance, about finding a middle ground with money and goodness. And everything else."

"Wow. Yeah. That's *exactly* it. Exactly." She brushed her lips against my cheek. Not a kiss. "You so get me, Ed. It's hot."

I turned my face. "You're pretty hot yourself."

"For a while I was worried you weren't interested. Which, obviously, is hard to believe, since I'm, like, *so* sexy. And available."

"Why did you think that?"

She sat back, setting the book on her little coffee table. "I don't know. You seem a little . . . restrained. When we were dancing you were into it, but I almost feel like you aren't quite sure you want me. It's weird. People don't usually say 'no, thank you' when I invite them home."

"I didn't tonight."

"I know."

"The first time— I don't know. I wasn't sure if you wanted to have sex with me or watch a movie like besties. There've been a couple of times lately when I sort of misjudged someone."

"Like you thought they were into you and they weren't?"

"Or I thought we were hanging out and then they wanted more."

"And you didn't?"

"Kind of. At least, I don't want to be a novelty. Not that *you're* thinking that. But sometimes I get the feeling that maybe a person is interested more in seeing what it's like to be with me than they are actually *being* with me. I probably sound foolish." I definitely felt foolish.

"You mean because you're trans." Her voice was totally steady, maybe even warm.

"And everyone who already knows isn't interested, which leaves the people I have to tell. Who either aren't interested once I've told them, or get this... look. In their eyes. That makes me feel like a freak show attraction."

I hadn't meant to say all that. To anyone, really. It made me sound ungrateful. Or maybe like I was ridiculously picky. I studied the books on her shelves and waited for her to laugh at me.

"I don't think you're a freak. And I know what you mean, about people. Like sometimes what they want from you is this experience, and you're mostly just an actor playing out some script they have in their head."

"That's— Yeah. How'd you know that?"

"You think it only happens to you? I got breasts when I was like *eleven*, Ed. I was all kinds of curvy woman by the time I started high school. I got hit on by teachers and bus drivers and the guy who used to own the liquor store on Twelfth. Remember him?"

"Balding and always wore sunglasses?"

"Yeah. Well, the day he asked me if I wanted to see something special he had in his storeroom, he tilted his glasses down, like he was real cool." She shook her head. "I was fourteen. I *did not* want to see his storeroom."

"Shit." I felt a rush of pointless anger. "What douche bags."

"They weren't all men. It doesn't matter. No one ever did anything to me, but sometimes I played it coy to get away from them, like when they had something to hold over my head. So I kind of played the game and it made me feel powerful, but it also made me feel sick, all at the same time."

I nodded. "I think I can understand that."

"You were wrong before."

"Um. Okay. About what?"

"You said everyone who already knows isn't interested in you, but I'm sitting right here. And I am."

Which was obvious, or should have been, since the first night we'd kissed on the dance floor. "Was I really stupid about this? I'm feeling really stupid about this."

"You aren't stupid. Drink your tea and I'll tell you more about all the places I'm gonna go someday."

"That sounds wonderful."

I liked watching her. The way she moved her hands when she spoke, as if they were hummingbirds, quick and flashing, illustrating her stories with wrist-flicks. For years we'd lingered at the periphery of each other's small worlds, and during that time we'd probably never been alone together long enough to exchange pleasantries. Now we sat on her sofa and she described faraway places, painted pictures in the air with nimble fingers, and I could see every one of them.

The written word has always been more comfortable to me than speaking, but the way Alisha spun a story required me to see it the way she saw it, which was the kind of skill I thought only related to especially good writers.

When we finished our tea she put aside the four—no, five—books she'd pulled off her shelves. She stood up, drawing me up beside her. "I'm not gonna lie, you totally turn me on. But I don't think it's because you're trans. I always liked you, Ed."

A chill hit my spine, making my breath catch. That I've always been Ed, even when I was called something else, was something not a lot of people understood. I wanted to believe that Alisha did.

"I've always liked you too."

"Cool. Want to see my bedroom? If you look through the shelves, you can see it right now." She bent down, peering into the space above some books.

I laughed a little and did the same. "I wouldn't mind a closer look at your bedroom. If you're offering."

"I'm pretty much insisting."

"That would be good."

But before she pushed back the curtain she grabbed my wrist.

"You actually like me, right? I'm not just the person you're doing because you're bored and you haven't been laid in a while."

"Hey, who's been talking? How do you know the last time I got laid?"

Her fingers tightened.

"Alisha." I brushed that damn braid back. "I definitely like you. The night you asked me here and I said no—Carlos bought me a drink to drown my sorrows because I was so depressed after."

"Then why did you say no?"

I shrugged. "Some nights it's worth going home with someone, even if they end up not getting me. Some nights it's not."

"Do I get you?"

I really hope so. "Let's find out."

She kissed me. "Yeah."

We went through the curtain and into her bedroom.

Someday I probably won't feel like this every time I have sex with a new person, this roiling, impossible sensation that I'm standing at the edge of a cliff and the only way down is a flying leap. I want to be confident and cool, but until I get top surgery, until I've been taking T longer, when I take off my clothes I still feel like a guy wearing a woman suit.

I sat on her bed and pulled her toward me, skimming my hands up her sides. "We're having sex, right? I don't want to misinterpret."

Alisha laughed, touching my jaw, tilting it higher. "Hell yes."

"Good." And it was. I ran my hands under her shirt now, and kissed the swell of her belly. She sucked it in, and I brushed my knuckles over her skin. "Are you self-conscious?"

"You know, I try not to be, but, like, everywhere you look there are these pictures of gorgeous women." She slid her fingertips between mine, pressing deeper. "I'm soft where I wish I was hard. But I'm not going to spend every hour in the gym, and I'm not going to stop eating, either."

"De dinero y bondad, siempre la mitad. Only with food and exercise and self-image." I pressed my lips to her. "You're gorgeous. Not that it matters what I think, but you are."

"Thanks." She pulled her shirt off, which I took as an invitation, sliding my hands higher. Her breasts were plump and round with nipples I desperately wanted to tease with my teeth, but I settled for running my thumbs over them until she shivered.

My heart was pounding. "Thank you," I whispered, looking up at her.

"For what?"

"For this."

Her fingers grazed my collar. "Are you okay with taking off your shirt?"

My binder suddenly felt impossibly tight, a life jacket protecting me. "I haven't had top surgery yet."

Alisha leaned down, kissing me sweetly. "Your chest isn't what makes you a man, right?"

"No."

"Trust me to know that, okay?"

I did. I trusted her. She unbuttoned me slowly while my heart pounded like it was about to explode. Even after she slipped the shirt from my shoulders, she didn't touch the binder. I was glad, suddenly, that I'd worn one of my two relatively decent binders. If I decided to take it off, I would look more like a contortionist, but older, looser binders just looked kind of silly.

We stared at each other for a long moment, her face in dark shadows staring down at me.

I swallowed. "Do you have a light in here?"

"Kind of. Watch." She leaned all the way over and fumbled with something at the wall, lighting up a double string of white Christmas lights strung along the wall in an L-shape above her bed. "Come on."

Alisha sat back and held out her hand.

Once both of us were on the bed, her room—part curtain, part bookshelf—became a little bubble of white light.

"This is really cool." I made myself comfortable beside her, glancing around. "You have different books on this side."

"Yeah. That side's all stuff I can make conversation about."

"And this side?"

"More for me. Silly stuff. Mystical stuff that, you know, has a lot of meaning to me, but probably other people would find ridiculous. Do you have books like that? Like, they changed your life completely even though you'd probably be embarrassed to tell people that?"

My eyes skimmed over her shelves, thinking about my own. "I guess a few. I mean, I loved the Harry Potter books. I used to read them and reread them for days. And, uh, I kind of didn't hate *Fifty Shades of Grey*, either."

She gasped. "You. Did. Not."

"Well like, okay, the writing, and yeah, wow, over-reliance on bad tropes, but they kind of held my interest—"

Her face was arranged in comic shock.

"Never mind. Shut up. Jerk."

"Oh man." She swung a leg over mine. "You want me to pin you down, boy?"

"Maybe I want to pin *you* down." I ran my hands up to her breasts again, rolling her nipples.

She threw her head back, thrusting them harder against my palms. "Hey, read some better kinky literature and then we'll talk."

"You got anything here? I'll start right now."

"I could find you some more appropriate reading material. Oh god, Ed, keep doing that." Both hands slammed down on the wall over my head. "That feels so good."

This position was better. I arched up and took one of her breasts into my mouth, playing my tongue against the hard nub of her nipple.

She groaned. "Ohhh yes."

I slid my hand inside the back of her pants, squeezing her ass.

"You better make good, you brat. Damn."

I'd make good. But I needed a little more freedom of movement. "Can I take these off? Not that I'm complaining about how tight they are, but right now—"

"Take 'em off."

I was already moving, thumbing the button, tugging the zip. I needed to be inside Alisha, and *now*. Right now, before I lost my nerve, before whatever spell made me feel this confident departed. I pushed her pants down, and she laughed, tumbling to the side, trying to shimmy out.

"This isn't how I normally get undressed." Her braids shook loose, spilling all around her head as she tried to wriggle out of her pants, and she just kept giggling, like this was the most hilarious thing she'd done in months. "I must look ridiculous, oh god, Ed, help."

"Do you usually have assistance to get undressed? I'm, uh, willing to volunteer for that job, if you're hiring."

"What, you'd come over every night and assist me in taking off my pants? Like what would that even pay?"

"I can think of a few worthy trades." I shifted down to corral her pants at her feet. "Seriously, how did you get them on in the first place?"

"I must have been more coordinated then."

Between us we managed to finally get the damn things off, and then it was just Alisha, black underwear, no bra, braids every which way, lying back against the head of her bed with white lights making her look slightly wild.

I crawled up over her legs, kissing a trail that wound slowly toward the inside. When I reached the elastic of the panties I pulled them out enough so I could press my tongue beneath them.

"You— Ohhh, fuck yeah—"

More of a tease than anything else because I didn't really want to go down on her with her panties in my way, but I did want to tease her, surprise her, delight her, and I definitely wanted her to keep making the little moans she was making as she tried to thrust up into my mouth.

I shifted a little and pulled the fabric tight over her skin, rubbing my cheek against it. She smelled spicy and almost sharp. I wanted to turn her on as much as possible without actually touching her.

She tried to hump my face, but I withdrew before she could.

"You're such a bastard. Get up here."

"Are you sure? I'm not exactly done—" Before I could even finish my sentence she was dragging me up until she could kiss me and, fuck, that was good, that was fantastic, that was marvelous, Alisha's tongue battling mine, her hand hard at the back of my neck, both of us tangling into each other.

"You're messed up, you know, teasing me like that," she panted in my ear.

"I do my best."

"I want you on top of me. But I need you to talk, Ed. I need you to tell me what works for you and what doesn't."

I went stiff, but she kept kissing me, nibbling at my earlobe, letting me hide in her hair.

"Yeah, I get you want to be the strong silent type right now and please me without demanding anything for yourself, but that's not how I roll. It'll be so much better for me if you tell me what you want."

"I shouldn't have to do My Body 101 just because I'm trans," I argued. Weakly.

"If *everyone* did My Body 101, people would have way better sex." She rolled until we were on our sides and I could no longer hide. "What do you usually do? Get your partner off and hope for the best?"

"Sometimes. Most of the time. I mean, that works for me, so it's okay—"

"Who the hell have you been sleeping with who don't care if you're actually having a good time?"

I narrowed my eyes. "Lesbians." Which wasn't fair, but at the moment I was seriously considering getting the hell out of here. This was too intense, and I didn't know if I could deal with someone looking at me the way Alisha looked at me, as if she wanted to see into me.

She laughed a little and shoved me lightly into the pillow. "Don't be a dick. Lesbians who treat your body like a woman's body?"

"They knew I wasn't. But when I take my clothes off . . . I guess I can't really blame them."

"Well, you can't blame them because you didn't talk to them, but I think anyone who approaches sex with someone new like it's a language they already speak is totally missing the point."

"Oh yeah, wise one? And what's the point?"

She grinned, tracing my lips with one fingertip. "The point is that this is an adventure, Ed. The point is that every time you open your world to someone, it's an adventure both of you are taking, without even leaving home. You've had sex with women, but you've never had sex with *me*, so that makes this new. Right?"

"Speaking of sex."

"I want you on top of me. When I've fantasized, that's what it's been, you fucking me like that. If you don't want me to touch you, it's okay. It's so totally okay. But can we give that a shot? I mean, unless you don't want to."

"I definitely want to."

"Oh good." Eyebrows raised. "So. Your pants?"

"Yeah. Right."

It was harder taking off my pants now that we'd made this "talk about sex" rule. With other people, sparse though they'd been, it had been less about talking and more about pleasing, which suited me. I was good at pleasing. But trying to explain how my body worked, what it wanted, what it liked, made me feel horribly exposed. And I suspected that the questions would intensify from here.

My disrobing was a lot more dignified than Alisha's. I hesitated over the binder.

"Leave it on. I swear to god, baby, it's fine." She tugged me down over her again and sighed. "Oh fuck yes. I love this feeling. I love having someone on top of me."

I could definitely get used to being on top of her, pressing between her legs. I ground down against her, and she latched on to me, trying to tug me in tighter.

"Oh fuck, I can *feel* you. Jesus, Ed—"

She was hot and wet, and I played with the sensations, rubbing side to side, up and down, making her cry out.

"Yes, damn it, keep doing that—"

"What?" I smiled against her lips.

"All of it!"

I pulled back, both of us panting now. My cock was lit up like a fucking Christmas tree, ready to blow, but I didn't want to come yet. An orgasm that fast wouldn't be any good, and I wanted this to be good. Quickie orgasms were more my brain's way of testing the works, always slightly dissatisfying. Especially because now it seemed inevitable that I'd get off, so I could relax instead of trying to steamroll pleasure.

"You are a fucking tease." She forced my head down to hers, kissing me hard. "I want to feel your dick more."

The words sent shivers all the way to my toes, and this time when her legs tensed, I let her draw me down again. Alisha took over, spreading herself wider against me, grinding us together, using me—using my cock—as a way to tease herself. She angled up, taking me into her folds, and I shut my eyes against how fucking good that felt.

"Yes," I whispered. "Oh god, yes, that's so good—"

"There he is. Keep talking, boy. Keep telling me how it feels."

Somehow she shifted her weight, and it sparked my imagination; my cock, which would by anyone's standards be considered barely visible, extended in my mind until it was just like any other guy's cock. I thrust into her and she groaned, hands scrabbling over my back.

Now I wished I'd taken off the binder. I wanted to feel her nails on my skin. I wanted to feel her nipples. I wanted us to be pressed against one another with nothing in between us.

She hauled me against her. "Oh yeah, come on, baby, more—"

I gave her more, trying to get a bit of leverage on the bed so I could go deeper. I wanted desperately to give in to the illusion that I was actually fucking her, that my cock was deep inside and that's what she felt, but at the same time, as real as it was, it also seemed ridiculous.

"Ed, *more*. I can fucking *feel you*, give me *more*—"

Screw realism anyway.

I braced one arm on the wall and wrapped the other around her, holding her in place. Alisha gasped in my ear, and somehow she opened just a little more for me, and that was it. I couldn't hold back.

"I'm coming—" *I'm coming inside you, I'm coming inside you, oh god, I'm inside you right now—*

"Me too!" She moaned louder as I thrust and the sound of her orgasm pushed mine higher until I was shuddering, clutching her against me, grinding into her body until I couldn't control myself.

I felt myself come, felt myself come in the imaginary extension of cock, with its thousand-fold imaginary nerve endings. In that moment I was seven inches long, and hard, and ejaculating into a beautiful woman.

Who panted in my ear, almost weeping.

"Oh fuck, Ed, tell me that wasn't the best fucking sex you've had in years. Oh my god."

"It was," I heard myself say. "It really was."

It was the best sex I'd had since I started transitioning. The best sex I'd had for years before that. I collapsed, regaining my breath, a little afraid that if I looked her in the eye the illusion would break and I'd remember that my cock wasn't slowly going soft inside her right now.

"That was amazing. You were amazing." Her fingers traced lazy lines on my lower back, on my ass. "Damn, boy. I'm so glad I went to Fred's tonight."

"Me too."

The moment passed. I had to move. Carefully, trying to hold on to the splintered sensation of my imaginary body, I shifted slightly, and her legs relaxed to let me go.

This would be awkward. No way around it. I started to get up, but she was reaching for a blanket and I hesitated.

"I know you'll want to go home, but stay with me for a few minutes at least. Please."

I'd've felt better with my boxers on, but she was naked and beautiful, and she'd been open with me despite her self-consciousness, so I lay back down, pressing against her side.

The blanket settled over us, and I tucked it around her shoulders.

"Thank you." I looked at her lips, her ears, the line of her jaw. Anything but her eyes.

"Thank you. We did good, Ed."

"We really did. I, uh, like your hair this way."

"Do you? It's my favorite style ever. I'm gonna start playing with the colors this week, I think. One good thing about my job: they totally don't care about piercings and tats and wild hair. I mean, it's a fucking adventure company, right? They probably like me more for all that." She sighed. "Tonight's gonna improve my whole week, by the way."

"Mine too." I was a parrot, only able to imitate her words, even though they accurately reflected how I felt. I wanted to say something more, something heartfelt (and original), but I slipped and accidentally met her eyes, and then I couldn't speak at all.

"You're not going to avoid me now, right? I mean, I could do friends with benefits if you wanted, but making this into a one-night stand would kill me."

"It's not a one-night stand. What's the alternative to friends with benefits?"

Her eyes crinkled with her smile. "You silly. The alternative to friends with benefits is, you know, we get together."

"Oh." *Get together.* "I'm not . . . opposed to that. I mean, if you're not."

"You want to be my boyfriend, Ed?"

I couldn't help it. I hid my face in her neck. "Oh god. When you say that..."

"What?"

"I've, uh, never really—I mean, there have been a couple of people I was with for a while—but I never—"

"So I'd be your first?" She giggled. "You are totally my boyfriend now. I'm telling everyone. I'm going into Club Fred's, standing on the bar, and announcing it to the world. 'Ed Masiello is my boyfriend, bitches!'"

I laughed and it was only a little forced. "Oh my god, shut up."

"What? It's true! You're my boyfriend now. And I'm your girlfriend. Hot. I had no idea I was going to end tonight with a boyfriend. I've never had a boyfriend before. Whee, adventure!"

Her amusement was irresistible. I kissed her, brushing braids out over her pillow. "You're completely crazy, you know that?"

"I know! Isn't it great?"

We kissed for a while longer. When she got up to use the bathroom, I pulled my clothes back on. This had been amazing, but I didn't want to press my luck. Better to go home, wake up alone, just in case none of this seemed like a good idea tomorrow. At least she wouldn't have to see me with indecision all over my face.

"Good night, boyfriend," she murmured at the door. "Please come again soon."

I rolled my eyes at the pun. "I'll call you tomorrow. Is that okay?"

"You fucking better. Except you don't have my phone number."

Oops. I fumbled out my phone and made my fingers punch in the appropriate numbers. "*Now* I'll call you tomorrow."

She leaned in for a final kiss. "Good night."

"Good night."

I may have strutted on my way to my car. I may have whistled.

CHAPTER 10

We saw each other a little bit over the weekend. I took her to dinner after work on Saturday, and we caught a cup of coffee and a walk along the pier on Sunday. I told her about my roommates thinking I was gay and being overly sensitive about it.

She laughed. "Holy shit, that's hilarious. Huh. No, I don't think I could say 'I'm straight' out loud without making it a joke. No offense to straight people."

"Exactly. I don't have a problem with straight people, and I guess that's... kind of what I am now? But I don't even know how it must feel to be straight. There's no way I could seriously claim that as my, like, identity."

"Right? And I was always a lesbian, forever, except now I have a boyfriend. So maybe I'm pansexual? That's so weird. Because 'I'm a lesbian' still feels right. Is that messed up? I mean, does that feel super weird to you? Like I'm attacking your masculinity? Because I promise, to me you're all man."

I considered it for a minute, wondering how Honey had thought about it. She was a woman dating a man, but I'd sure as hell never heard her say she was straight.

And damn it, now I couldn't ask her. The thought hurt my heart, but I refocused on Alisha. "No. I mean, I think of you as a lesbian. Uh. Maybe it *is* weird that it doesn't throw me."

"I could start saying 'pansexual'..."

We looked at each other.

"Whoa." She shook her head. "This is so weird. Like, I've been a lesbian since I knew what the word meant. And now I totally have a boyfriend." Alisha laughed, then clamped her hand over her mouth.

"Wait, is this funny or totally fucked up? Sorry, it's not funny if it makes you feel shitty."

"It doesn't. You can be a lesbian. As long as I'm an exception. To your gold-star lesbianism."

"Or how about this: I only date queer people. Not all ladies, obviously, but only queer people. What's that make me?"

"Queer?"

"Okay. Sold. I'm queer."

"Me too."

"Good. Glad that's settled." She linked arms with me and we walked that way. And the whole time I was trying to focus on the moment, but mostly I was thinking *I'm somebody's boyfriend, I'm Alisha's boyfriend, Alisha is my girlfriend and I am her boyfriend* over and over again.

It was just a word, and it shouldn't have mattered—I didn't want it to matter. I didn't want what other people called me, how other people saw me, to matter as much as it did. But walking down the pier with her, knowing that people saw us together and thought of me as her boyfriend, *did* matter. It meant something to me that for once I wasn't scraping at the edges of passing. Being with her made me feel somehow more real than I'd felt before, which made me uncomfortable, but I couldn't deny it.

We parted late Sunday, after going back to her apartment again and having more incredible sex, and she made me promise that next time we could go to my place so my roommates could see that, in fact, I did have a girlfriend.

I told her I couldn't wait.

I'd forgotten the meeting with the Queer Youth Project folks until I was mid-interview with someone else, so I'd rescheduled it for the following week. For once the irritating notifications my phone sent up for every calendar event were actually useful, as opposed to the ones that kept informing me about knitting group, which I kept dismissing. I couldn't face knitting. Not without Honey there.

Jaq wasn't kidding about how far out QYP was. They'd found a location practically on the edge of the water. "Location" was a polite word for the warehouse with the hand-painted *QYP* sign in a front window. I guess the only helpful thing about having a boarded-up window was that it was much easier to make into a sign.

I tried knocking on the door and got nowhere, so I tentatively let myself inside.

Inside was a whole different story.

The walls were half-painted, literally; each wall had stretches of bold color on it, but none of them had been finished. The floors, though, had been gone over in black until they were clean and shining. The far left corner of the place was in mid-renovation toward becoming a kitchen, with a sink cabinet in place and a refrigerator still wrapped in plastic, but most of the rest of the space was empty save for ladders and drop cloths and discarded cleaning junk.

"Hi there! Are you Ed?"

I turned to the voice, a young white guy, coming out of an office I hadn't noticed in my first spin in the center of the room. "Ed Masiello, with the *Times-Record*."

"Good to meet you. I'm Keith Whelan. Welcome to the Queer Youth Project."

He looked even younger up close, but he shook my hand firmly and gestured me back toward the office.

"Let me introduce you to Josh, then I'll start the tour and he can join us when he's done fighting with spreadsheets."

"Fighting with spreadsheets never ends well."

"I've already done battle with this one, but he keeps thinking if he looks at it just right maybe it will tell him something new."

A call came from the back room. "I heard that!"

Keith grinned and my brain immediately jumped on the idea that they were closer than business partners. "This way, but watch out. This is where all the everything ends up."

It wasn't really an office. It was a large room in which they'd stolen a corner and shoved a couple of desks. The unoccupied one was neat and tidy. A black guy a few years older than Keith was sitting at the other one.

"Josh, this is Ed from the paper. Ed, Josh."

"We spoke on the phone." I shook his hand.

"Really good to meet you, Ed." He turned to Keith. "I can't make it better."

"I know. I told you that already, remember?"

"Yeah, but we were so careful." He shook his head. "Damn it. Sorry, Ed. Let's show you around a bit."

"I told him we'd start and you could join us later."

Josh snapped shut the laptop he'd been working on. "I need to stretch my legs anyway."

"Spreadsheets giving you trouble?" I asked.

"Man, spreadsheets are always giving me trouble. Which is why I try to leave them to Keith, but I really thought this one was holding out on us. No dice. So I figured we'd show you around and describe to you how the place will look when we open, then we can sit down and show you the programming stuff. Sound good?"

"Sure." I'd work in my questions or, if I couldn't, ask them later.

They led me into the main room again, pointing out different areas they planned to section off through the use of furnishings.

Josh gestured widely. "We're trying to make things comfortable without making ourselves a target. No big-screen TVs, and we have a guy coming in over the weekend to install a cage for all the computers. I definitely want kids to be able to come here and search for jobs, or do schoolwork, but the laptops will all go into the cage at the end of the night. We also have an alarm company charging us a small fortune, so I think we're managing potential theft concerns pretty well, but ask me again after someone comes in and busts the place up, right?"

His cavalier tone surprised me a little. "You expect to be robbed?"

"Opening a place in this neighborhood, catering to teenagers and young adults, and not expecting some amount of loss would be like having a kid and not expecting the occasional glass breaking, you know? I don't have any illusions about our target demographic. Some of them will be desperate or angry enough to steal from us, and that's fine. We're willing to accept the risk. I'm a lot more worried about people from the outside who just want to make us disappear."

I nodded. "Are you getting pushback?"

"On the record? La Vista has been nothing but welcoming."

"Ha." I raised both hands. "Off the record, out of curiosity. Things aren't all smooth going?"

"We didn't expect them to be. Funding has been easier in some ways, mostly because Keith can write a business plan that makes people want to fall in love, but the actual nitty-gritty of getting off the ground has been a little more... subtly contentious than we knew to expect."

I tried to work out what that meant. "In terms of what? Again, off the record."

"Oh, nothing overt. Nothing I could describe to you. More a feeling we get, talking to people sometimes." He gestured me through a door and into a hallway. "This corner has been chopped up into smaller rooms. Initially we weren't thrilled about it, but now we're beginning to have an appreciation for the idea. The electronics cage will get a room to itself, which adds a layer of security, and we're hoping to have a room with donated clothes and shoes. We'll also be able to hold meetings here. We'd planned to do that in the room where our office is, keep everything out in the open, but that's not always what people want." He offered a rueful smile. "We have a few consultants who have been very convincing about the need for a certain level of deniability when it comes to QYP. It's the opposite of what I'm going for, but you can't have everything at once."

"I understand that. What kind of meetings?"

"Twelve-step meetings, the high school GSA, maybe. A local youth minister wants to know if we'd be open to a Bible study group."

My face must have done a thing. His smile widened.

"That's about Keith's response. But I believe you can be a queer person of faith, so I'm open to it. Though we'd want them to meet in the big room, at least to start. I liked this lady when she came to pitch her Bible study idea, but I'm wary too. And the whole idea here is that we have to be careful. We're inviting kids who are incredibly vulnerable—economically, physically, legally—into a space that we're responsible for keeping safe. If we get robbed, we open up the next day and repair everything. We will be consistent, and we will not be easily silenced."

"Damn." I followed him back out into the main room. "Also off the record, but I wish this had existed when I was growing up."

"You and me both. That's why we're here. Let's find a place to sit and then Keith can do the real sell job. I'm only here to soften people up so he can seduce them." He flashed a playfully flirtatious smile. "If you're ever interested in coming down here to volunteer, we have a form on our website."

"Good to know."

I scribbled notes and asked questions for the next hour. They took me on another, more in-depth tour, and this time I began to see the place as they saw it. Toward the end of the interview (which had stretched much longer than I allotted for it), a kid walked in the front door, black parka on and hood tugged down over their face despite the heat outside.

Josh immediately walked over, but since he didn't look alarmed I assumed kids randomly showing up wasn't that unusual.

"That's our number one assistant," Keith said. "Hi, Merin."

"Hey, Keith." The kid didn't look over.

Merin. I knew that name. This was Jaq's kid. The one she thought was trans.

Josh said something. The kid replied. For a second they faced off, but whatever it was, Josh won. He nodded his head toward us and the kid followed him back over.

"Ed Masiello, Merin Beighley. We're trying to get Ed to come volunteer down here when we're open."

"I like how you say that like this place is ever gonna be done." Merin reluctantly extended a hand. So, a white kid. I hadn't been able to tell under that parka, with the hood pulled low.

"Good to meet you." I couldn't very well ask if they knew Jaq without it being obvious Jaq and I had talked. "You don't think QYP will be ready in time to open?"

Josh nudged Merin and smiled at me. "Be careful what you say to Ed. He's a reporter."

That got the kid's attention. "Are you?"

"I work for the *Times-Record.*"

"My girlfriend wants to be a reporter. She's gonna be pissed she didn't come in today."

"This probably won't be the last time I stop by. Hey, is there anything you guys need? I could end the article with a call for donations, if that would help."

Josh and Keith looked at each other.

"Not yet," Josh said after a minute. "We're trying not to overwhelm ourselves."

Merin snorted. "That's a fancy-ass way of saying we've already got way too much shit and nowhere for anyone to sit."

Josh nudged Merin. "Truth. The back room is filling up with stuff we haven't yet found a home for when this part of the building isn't even close to ready for the open house, which is in less than a month."

Keith staggered, clamping down on Merin's shoulder. "Did he just say that out loud?"

Merin shook him off, but didn't look all that disturbed. "Yeah, he did. Ha. You jerks need to buy me more paint. And like . . . scaffolding or something."

"We really didn't consider scaffolding. Hell, that's another thing for the damn spreadsheet." Josh ran a hand over his shaved head. "Let's do the paint run right now and pick up lunch or something." He tugged Merin's hood. "You're with me. How many days do you think it will take to do the whole room if all three of us are working? We need to figure out how long we need scaffolding for."

"Shouldn't we paint the bottom parts of the walls first and work it out from there?"

"I'll call the rental place and see. I don't want to leave it to the last minute, or we're screwed if they don't have any available."

"We hired Merin on a whim." Keith kept his voice low. "It's the smartest thing we've done so far. Anyway, if you have any more questions, give one of us a call. The website should be changing over the next few weeks to have a lot more information on it, hopefully, which might be helpful to you."

"I'll write this up and see where my editor wants to put it. It'll definitely go on the *Times-Record* site, but I can't guarantee it will be in the print edition."

He shrugged. "Really, you could scrap the article and come volunteer with us instead, and we'd still consider this a good use of our time." He stuck out his hand, and I took it. "Good meeting you, Ed. We're here from dawn till dusk most days—or at least one of us is—so feel free to come by again."

"Thanks." I probably wouldn't, but then again, I liked the idea of the place, and I liked the idea of volunteering more genuinely than I expected to. "Good to meet you too."

I left the future site of the Queer Youth Project feeling slightly more hopeful about the world.

CHAPTER 11

The first few weeks Alisha and I were together passed in a blur. We saw each other almost every day, and on the days we didn't, we texted constantly. We talked about everything—movies, books, gender, politics. I'd never had to charge my phone so frequently. I took shorter showers so that they wouldn't interrupt our conversations, and kept skipping out on knitting group, which I might have done anyway, because it reminded me of Honey and made me sad.

I didn't want to be sad. I wanted to be happy. With Alisha.

I went back to her place a handful of times, sometimes to make food, sometimes to have sex, sometimes to snuggle on the sofa and watch television with my arm around her shoulders, or her head in my lap.

Part of me felt like I was an imposter, living someone else's happy life with someone else's happy girlfriend, but every time she looked at me I felt so *seen*, as if she was the first person who'd ever looked at me and seen who I really was.

I ignored Abuela, who kept leaving me messages. She'd upgraded me from "mija" and "flaca" to "mocosa," which meant I should probably go see her soon before she got really annoyed. I'd gotten a text from Cameron asking me if I wanted to come for a showing of *All About Eve*, which I'd almost missed completely because I'd been so intent on looking at only Alisha's texts. On a whim I asked if I could bring a friend, then called her and invited her along.

They knew each other, kind of, the way everyone knew each other in La Vista.

"Your mom let me in once when I didn't have any money," she told him, as he was locking up the ticket booth. "I came in with this big group, but they'd all gone in ahead of me and I only had, like, three bucks in my wallet. Super sweet of her."

Cam smiled. "Did she keep the three dollars?"

"No. She told me to use it for popcorn if I wanted."

"Mom loved getting kids in here to see movies. If they could have afforded to let everyone under eighteen in free, they would have."

"Yeah, it's weird I never come here anymore. Not that I go to the Cinema 18, either. I guess I don't spend money on movies."

"Alisha's saving up to go on adventures," I added. "International adventures."

"Oh really? There's a joint here in town that coordinates that type of thing, I believe."

She crinkled her nose. "I know. I work there, actually, but I'm talking about real adventures, the kind that aren't coordinated by anyone, you know? You fly somewhere, get off a plane, and there you are."

"That sounds so exciting." He offered her his arm. "Confidentially, Alisha, you should try to coax Ed into coming with you."

"Don't think I'm not already."

"I'm standing right here," I said, pretending to be affronted.

Cameron laughed and led her away. "Adventure is good for the soul, don't you think?"

"I so do, Cameron, I so do."

I followed them into the theater and we took seats on the top row, left side. The old wooden seats weren't as cushioned as seats in new theaters, and as we walked, the threadbare carpet didn't completely muffle our steps on the floorboards below.

"God," Alisha whispered. "I love the way it smells in here."

"Me too," I said.

Cam gestured us in first, and there weren't more than a dozen other people in the entire theater. I wondered if he was playing it casual when he said the Rhein wasn't in trouble.

The second we sat down, Alisha grabbed my hand.

I love *All About Eve*: the delicious mind-fuckery of it, the twistiness of who you're rooting for when everyone's shallow and selfish, the end, which is so perfect it makes me ache a little and wish I wrote screenplays. I've never loved it more than sitting there holding Alisha's hand, occasionally stealing popcorn.

An hour after I got home, after leaving her at her apartment, I got another text from Cameron: *Now I understand why you haven't dropped by in a few weeks. You two should come to movies more often.*

I wrote back, feeling a little bashful, and promised that we would.

Work was reliably dull through the beginning of August. More feel-good stories. Somewhat to my surprise, Potter advocated for the story about the drop-in center to go into the print edition. I clipped it and sent it to the QYP address, not even sure if they received mail there. I got, in return, an invitation to the open house, which was later in the month.

I thought about going down again to see if they needed help with stuff, but quickly got sidetracked doing other things. Steven Costello's face still looked out at me from the bulletin board when I was getting coffee, and I still couldn't remember where the hell he was from.

Honey's case was cold. Joe didn't think it was all that likely the cops would ever solve it unless someone confessed or new information showed up. Togg, continuing his kick about a killer targeting people who didn't conform to gender norms, went so far as to say that the next murder was inevitable, and when it happened, La Vista would have a serial killer on its hands. Like most of Togg's more extreme stances, even his more defensive commenters couldn't find anything to support in those posts.

I read his site, and my paper, and courted Alisha, and tried to ignore everything that didn't jive with the bubble of "actually okay for once" that I was floating in. I tried to embrace the Caspar ethos of not giving a fuck, and while I wasn't actually successful, it was nice to feel drawn through my days by something happy and hopeful, instead of the thing I'd been doing for months of just getting through each day, bracing for the next.

Being a boyfriend suited me. Not being obsessed with murder, or the dead-endedness of my job, or sneaking over to see Abuela without being seen by my father, also suited me.

But you know what happens to bubbles: they always pop.

CHAPTER 12

Fredi's next theme night was Back to School in the second week of August. Alisha and I went in matching "school uniforms." She made a hell of a school girl, and I wore a tie that matched her skirt and fell only halfway to my belt, which looked somewhat nerdy and worked with the look.

Theme nights at Club Fred's were becoming a thing. Back to School was more crowded than F*ck G*nd*r had been, and I was glad we arrived together, because otherwise it would have been hell trying to find one another.

"This is crazy!" she shouted. "I've never seen this place so packed!"

"Me neither!"

Cam was nestled into a corner at the bar, reading a book, so we said hello and managed to grab beers before wandering around. Josh and Keith were there, at a table, so I introduced them to Alisha. They extracted promises of future volunteering from both of us and assured me that they were on target for the open house.

"Our trusty assistant keeps us in line." Josh tugged Keith closer. "Right, babe?"

"Merin would sacrifice sleep from now until we open if that's what it took." Keith turned and raised his eyebrows at Josh, who laughed.

"Do you two want the table? We're about to go dancing."

"Definitely," Alisha said. "Good meeting you guys!"

"You too!"

They walked away, Josh winding a proprietary arm around his date.

Alisha leaned in to speak directly into my ear. "No shit, if those two made porn, I'd watch it. They had definite sparks."

"What about us? Do we have sparks?"

She pinched my side. "You gotta ask?"

As tight as the crowd was, our table ended up being a nucleus of all kinds of conversations. Zane hung out for a while with a book about quilting, trying to get people to help her choose a pattern. (I didn't even know quilts had patterns.) When she went off to do her bizarre flailing dance, she stole Alisha, and every now and then I could see flashes of Zane's bright pink-and-purple streaks, or Alisha's braids, maybe half of which she'd dyed blue. Cam sat in Alisha's chair sometime later, getting his fill of "practice small talk."

"You know you already make small talk with people, right?" I asked.

"But not intentionally. Accidental small talk doesn't count."

He'd never officially met Jaq's girlfriend, so I introduced him to Hannah, who charmed him, as she seemed to charm everyone. But when Jaq walked up later—she'd been "wrangling grooms, even though that's Zane's job," she said—Hannah's demeanor changed. She focused all of her energy on Jaq, pulling one hand up to kiss her knuckles.

Jaq visibly swooned. "Damn, woman. Get your ass over here. We're dancing." She led an unprotesting Hannah away.

"That seems to be going well," Cam said.

"Guess so."

He nudged me. "It's nice to see you and Alisha, you know. It's nice to see you being real with someone."

"I'm real with people!"

He patted my arm. "We all wear armor, Ed. Finding people we can let our guard down around is a boon."

Did Cam ever let his guard down? Looking at him, sitting ramrod straight in his seat, phone still out on the table in front of him as if he might urgently need to return to his book in the middle of a conversation, I doubted it.

I wanted to say something profound, to express that he could be himself around me, if he wanted, but instead the thing that came out of my mouth was, "If we were attracted to each other, would you go out with me?"

He blinked, forehead creasing. "I'd go out with anyone I was attracted to. What on earth are you asking?"

"Just—" I gestured to myself, feeling ridiculous. "You go out with guys. Would I—I mean—"

The frown smoothed out. "Oh. Of course, Ed. I mean, I assume you're not asking, but theoretically, of course. Do you worry about that?"

"I kind of have to. And no, sorry, I'm not asking— I mean, not that I wouldn't but—"

"We aren't compatible in other ways. I should be asking you that question," he teased.

"Yeah, I'm sort of irrevocably attracted to women, I guess."

"I'm irrevocably attracted to men, which is a group you belong to." He patted my arm again. "See, like this. This is fine. This is not small talk, it's . . . real talk. It's talk about real things that matter. My issue with small talk is that it's talk about superficial things that don't matter."

"I guess small talk matters because you can't always discuss deep stuff, you know? Because of the people you're with, or because it would be too exhausting."

"And people don't appreciate silence as much as I do."

"Ha. Probably. Let's find small talk you don't hate. Tell me more about Cary Grant."

"Bite your tongue! Cary Grant is *anything* but *small*."

I laughed, and he told me stories about Grant and his leading ladies, and Grant and his leading men. When Alisha came back, having lost Zane to a group of roller derby women, Cameron surrendered his chair to her with a bow.

"Treat him well, my lady." He grinned.

"Thank you, kind sir," Alisha replied. We waved as he walked off.

I touched her hand. "You want to get out of here soon?"

"Definitely. Take me back to your place? I mean, if it's okay. I've wanted to see where you lived for ages."

"It's okay. It's great. I want you to see where I live too."

She kissed me. "I really hope I meet your roommates so they know you're banging a super hot chick."

"Jerk," I muttered, but I secretly hoped she met my roommates too.

Having Alisha in my space was an entirely new experience. David had been right: I'd never brought anyone home with me. I'd gone home with a couple of one-night stands, but I'd always made sure I could leave when I was done, when I needed to regroup on my own.

Letting her into the house, showing her the living room and kitchen and bathroom, then taking her into my room, felt right. Felt good.

Kissing her in my bed felt even better.

We made out for a while, slowly shedding our clothes. I'd gotten pretty comfortable with her, in or out of my binder, and she never treated my breasts like they were anything special, but she didn't ignore them like they were off-limits, either, which was apparently the perfect amount of attention.

I'd made my way down her body and she'd pulled my legs over so she could kiss my thighs, the beginning of what promised to be a hell of a sixty-nine, when a commotion at the front door alerted us that my roommates were home.

The house was old; despite the door being closed, we could hear every word they said.

"—could have totally hit that, if you hadn't—"

"That girl was so far out of your league, you aren't even the same species, Troy!"

I smothered giggles into Alisha's belly and kept listening like they were a radio play.

"Okay, okay, be cool."

"She wasn't out of my league! She liked me!"

"You guys, shut up."

"But—"

"We aren't the only ones home, asshole, shut up."

They lowered their voices, and JP continued to make peace while David teased Troy about the girl who was out of his league as they stomped up the stairs.

"Oh my god, you live with frat boys," she said when we could no longer hear them. "Ed. *You live with frat boys.*"

"Grad students, but yeah, feels like about the same thing, only with less alcohol poisoning." I rolled off her. "Bastards totally screwed up the mood."

"Right?" She giggled. "She's not even the same species! Ha!"

"Seriously, they're like caricatures." I reached out to run a finger along her shin. Alisha didn't shave her legs, which was kind of cool. I liked it most when she wore skirts. Something about the inherent *fuck you* of it made me happy. "Oh my god. I so can't have sex right now. Sorry."

"I know. Okay, so let's make snacks. Do you have snacks?"

"I have hummus in here, but I don't feel like carrots right now, so we'd have to brave the kitchen for dipping devices."

"Dipping devices it is!" She smirked at me down the length of her body. "I guess we have to put clothes on?"

"Naughty brat. Yes, you have to put clothes on." I tugged my jeans on before contorting myself back into my binder and T-shirt.

"What is *this*? Ed, I have to wear this."

I turned. She'd been poking through the rack over my door and unearthed an old black satiny cover-up I'd forgotten I owned. "You can have that if you want it. An old girlfriend gave it to me, but it was too nice to throw away when we broke up."

"Giving me your ex's gifts, huh?"

"Shit. You're right. That sounded bad." I took it from her. It had probably cost a fortune and the ex had liked seeing me in it, but it always made me feel ugly and wrong. After a second I held it open for Alisha, sliding the dark fabric over her incredibly pale skin. "Looks better on you than it did on me."

"I can't imagine buying you something like this unless it was for Halloween. Damn, but it's nice." She twirled a little and the fabric flowed out from her. "You like?"

"If it's not creepy, you should definitely keep it. Or at least wear it when you're here. What do you want to eat?"

"Don't know. I'm more into the idea of wearing this in front of your roommates. What do you think the likelihood is they'll come downstairs again?"

It was only midnight. "They'll definitely come downstairs if they hear that I have a guest."

She twirled again. "Any objection to me wearing this and nothing else?"

"Uh, what possible objection could I have to that? As long as you let me take it off you after."

"Sure thing, big boy." She batted her eyelashes and I laughed. "Let's go see what you've got in your kitchen." Alisha swept from the room, still tying the belt around her.

God. She was sex in black satin, bending over to look deeper into the refrigerator than anyone could possibly need to look.

"You spelunking in there?" I asked.

She wiggled her ass at me. "What's wrong, baby? You don't like the view?"

"Far from it." I rubbed against her, getting off on the clash of textiles, my denim and her satin. I wanted to fuck her like that, bent over, at my mercy. My cock was trying to get purchase inside my jeans at the thought of it.

"You're a fucking tease, Masiello." She pushed back at me. "Damn. What the fuck am I doing right now? I forgot."

I kept hold of her hips, sorely tempted to reach inside the flimsy robe.

"*Ed—*"

A clatter on the stairs.

I sprung back, blushing so hot I could feel sweat at my temples. "Oh shit."

Alisha's laugh sounded strange inside the fridge, and she was still laughing when all three second-floor roommates galloped into the kitchen.

Their "we're so surprised, we had no idea you had company" act needed some refining.

"Oh jeez, Ed, so sorry to interrupt!" Troy said, staring between me and Alisha's ass.

JP hit him. "Hey, you making food? We, uh, thought we'd make some food."

Alisha straightened and turned, surveying each of them one at a time.

"Alisha, these are my roommates. Troy, JP, David. Guys, this is Alisha." I hesitated, then added, "My girlfriend."

Her face lit up. "So these are the famous roommates, huh? Good meeting you." She shook their hands, and they all chorused "good meeting you, too" back, but were clearly having trouble reconciling the beautiful woman with the butt-length blue braids and "Ed's girlfriend."

"We're just getting a snack," I said.

"A light snack," she purred. "I never eat anything heavy this late at night. Heavy food gets in the way of other activities, don't you think?"

I bit my lip to keep from busting up, and the boys goggled.

"Oh, uh, yeah, definitely," David said. "Sure. We should—we should eat a light snack too."

"Really?" She raised her eyebrows, looking between all three of them. "I would not have guessed." Then she turned back around. "Babe, I don't see anything dippable in here."

"Toast?" I asked, covertly watching JP try to explain sotto voce that David had just implied the three of them were having sex.

"Wait, *what*?" David mumbled.

"We're not together," JP said to Alisha's back. "I mean, not that it matters, but in the interests of, uh, clarity. We're only roommates."

"And friends," Troy said.

JP elbowed him.

"What? We are, aren't we? I think of you guys as my friends. Most of the time."

"Stop talking. Everything you say is embarrassing."

God, if they kept up, my lips would be in ribbons from me biting them so hard. I put two slices of bread into the toaster.

"To be honest, you were more interesting when I thought you were banging." Alisha finally withdrew from the fridge. "So, boys, big night out on the town?"

Troy honest to god pouted. "I *would have* had a big night, if these two clowns hadn't totally cockblocked me."

"We did not. You're dreaming." David shook his head at Alisha. "He's dreaming. Some guys don't know how to stay inside their zone, and not get in over their heads. Like the girl Troy wanted was in the hot-girl zone, so she was out of his league."

Holy shit.

"The hot-girl zone," she repeated over Troy's protest. "Tell me more about this."

David, obviously thinking he was imparting Great Wisdom, warmed to his subject. "You gotta know your limits when it comes to girls. Not every guy is gonna land a hot girl, right? There aren't enough hot girls in the world for every guy."

Alisha's mouth hung open. I would have been more offended if I wasn't so entertained by her reaction.

"David," JP mumbled.

"What? It's so true. Right? I mean, come on, Ed, you know what I'm talking about. You don't walk into a bar and hit on the hottest girl there."

"I'm pretty sure I did, actually." I sketched my best imitation of Cameron's earlier bow at Alisha across the kitchen, and she nodded regally in return.

"Well okay, there are exceptions, but that's all they are."

"I don't know, David, I think that's kind of dumb." Troy sagged back against the counter. "I mean, maybe hot girls don't always want to go out with only super hot guys, right?" He glanced up at me as if tempted to use me as an example of a not-super-hot guy who'd magically landed such a woman, then deciding against it.

JP shook his head. "This whole conversation is brain-dead. Seriously, I know you read some stupid book that made you think this is how dating works, but it's ridiculous. People aren't attracted to other people based solely on how they look, David. Or you'd *never* get a date."

"Hey!"

Troy laughed. "Ha, right? Who wants to go out with that face?"

"Assholes! And that's not what I'm saying, anyway, it's more about having realistic expectations."

"Oh, I agree with you there," Alisha said. "A man who treats women as if their appearance slots them into a predetermined role in the world should definitely have realistic expectations of his appeal as a dating prospect."

As if we'd timed it, the toast popped, like it was punctuating her sentence.

"She *told* you," Troy said. "Man. I'm having a B of C. Anyone?"

"Stop *saying that*. It's not an abbreviation if it takes the same amount of time to say," David muttered.

JP was already poking into the cabinets. "I'll have one. Lucky Charms?"

"Cocoa Puffs."

I gathered our toast and herded Alisha out of the room before she could say more (probably about their cereal choices).

"That was the most fun I've had in forever," she whispered. "I can't believe that just happened."

"I can't believe I've never asked them about the hot-girl zone before. I feel like we learned so much about straight cis dudes tonight."

"Not all straight cis dudes. But definitely that one."

I spread a blanket on the floor and got the hummus out of my minifridge. "Do you want almond milk?"

"Sure." She grabbed me for a kiss. "I'm so glad I met your roommates."

"Yeah, that was hilarious. And unbelievable."

"It really was."

After a picnic of hummus and toast, we got back to what we'd been doing before, and regardless of our various "zones," the sex definitely qualified as super hot.

CHAPTER 13

Alisha went to work early on Saturday, and I screwed around at my house, trying not to count the hours until she was off again. We'd decided to make dinner at her apartment, so I was half-heartedly trolling the internet for recipes. I'd found a few, but nothing I was super excited by, so I hit Togg's page.

And almost immediately wished I hadn't.

Third Body Found. Is La Vista's Queer Population a Target?

I scanned the article, then read it again, then a third time. A woman named Stephanie Hawkins, who I didn't think I'd ever met before, had been found beaten to death at the Waterfront.

Three times reading it, and I still wasn't sure what I was looking at. Hawkins was a reproductive rights advocate who'd just married her wife in March. Togg called her an "activist outspoken about bi-erasure, who sometimes offended people by refusing to be invisible."

I pulled up a message window and typed, *If it's not about gender, why do you think this is the same killer? Bodies by the waterfront could be anyone.*

The response, less than five minutes later, was: *Check a calendar.*

I couldn't decide if it was a douchey response or a busy one, but I decided to give Togg the benefit of the doubt. He was smart. If he was telling me to check a calendar, it couldn't hurt.

I flipped to a new page in my notebook and made a list.

MELISSA LOREN - discovered 3/5

HONEY JANSEN - d. 7/16

STEPHANIE HAWKINS - d. 8/13

All Saturdays. Since I was using my personal calendar, the one in my phone that told me when I needed to be where, I could see something else about all those dates.

Each of them fell following a Club Fred's theme night. I added them to my list.

MELISSA LOREN - discovered 3/5 - after Drag Night
HONEY JANSEN - d. 7/16 - after F*ck G*nd*r
STEPHANIE HAWKINS - d. 8/13 - after Back to School

I studied my list for another long moment, trying to think. Work backward. It could still be a coincidence. Queer people went out to places other than Fred's. Though I knew for a fact both Melissa Loren and Honey had been at those particular theme nights.

Maybe Togg knew more.

Was Hawkins at Back to School @ Club Fred's? I sent.

She was tagged in pictures on Facebook, so yeah.

*I was there on Drag Night and F*ck G*nd*r.* I paused and added, *I saw Melissa Loren perform, and I spoke to Honey that night.*

Me too. It's how I made the connection.

Damn. Togg went to Club Fred's? Had I seen him? Had we interacted? Had he known Honey well enough so she was more than just a name on a screen? I couldn't remember now if there had been other events between March and July. I paged back through my calendar again.

Only one. Come As You Are. June 17. But no bodies following it.

It was too early to go to Club Fred's, but I really wanted to talk to Fredi. And Alisha was working for hours, so there was no chance I'd be able to ramble about all of it to her. Still, I needed to get the hell out of my house, so I packed up my knitting, my notebooks, and got on my bike.

I'd planned to ride down to the pier, but ended up at Sobrantes instead.

A hot cup of Triple Bridge Blend and a comfortable chair made it easier to feel like myself—a little less cold and overwhelmed—but I couldn't focus on anything for longer than a minute or two. My mind careened from one thing to the next without any rhyme or reason that I could discern. Was I crazy to think someone was actually using Club Fred's theme nights to kill people? Togg was widely thought to be a bit of a conspiracy theorist, so how mad was it that everything he was saying right now made perfect sense to me?

When you jumped out of a plane, were you thinking about the state of having jumped out of a plane? Or were you just thinking *Please don't let me die, please don't let me die*? Did Honey beg whoever had attacked her to let her live? Had she screamed and no one heard her?

I pressed the coffee to my lips again.

My brain ran ceaseless circles. Was I losing it? If I pitched this to Potter, he'd roll his eyes and send me to a church luncheon for a feel-good story.

Damn it. I had to stop thinking. I tried to get some knitting done, but before I'd finished a row I was teary. Honey had taught me how to cast on. How to knit and purl. She'd put her hands over mine and showed me what to do.

When I first met her, before I started on T, when I was still trying to be vaguely transmasculine, she'd told me that there was no "right" way to be trans. That whatever I was, I could be that. Without worrying I wasn't trans enough. Or that if I transitioned I wouldn't be trans until I passed, completely, a hundred percent of the time. In a way, I guess she'd taught me how to be myself. And now she was gone.

It would have been one thing if I saw her all the time. But as it was, I still sort of expected to see her soon. My mind hadn't fully caught up with the fact that she was dead.

I shoved my knitting back into my bag and wiped my tears away.

I finally pulled out my phone. I couldn't focus enough to read, but I could look at things. Togg hadn't updated the Stephanie Hawkins post, and I nobly avoided the comments.

Maybe I'd been watching too much *Criminal Minds*, and in the real world people attacked whoever they wanted. Maybe the beatings were unrelated. Maybe they had nothing to do with Club Fred's.

Nothing else on Togg's site. I tried, again, to remember the people who'd been at the waterfront after Honey's death, attempting to cross-check them with the crowd at Club Fred's. Now that I knew Togg had been at both places, surely I could figure out who he (or she, or they) was. Who had been there? A couple of joggers. A dog walker. Random people attracted by police cruisers and the promise of drama. Togg had blended in perfectly, in no way betraying his mysterious identity.

I opened a search tab, but had nothing to search for. Google was good, but I doubted it could answer *Is there really a killer hunting queer people in La Vista, CA?*

Pictures, then. I regularly went through phases of taking more pictures. The current batch was all Alisha. Alisha over dinner, Alisha lying in bed, Alisha's braids in the sun. Alisha over drinks at Fred's, smiling at me like I was the only person on earth. My photo stream had been somewhat desolate before Alisha. I wished I had more of Honey, but there were a few. Honey's fingers demonstrating a stitch I hadn't learned yet, which I'd tried to catch in a series of pictures until I'd given up and taken video instead.

The video would have her voice. I didn't watch it. I couldn't bear to hear her voice right now, soothing, assuring me that it wasn't nearly as complicated as it seemed.

Random shots I'd taken for stories. A lot of pictures of the blind cat. Pictures I'd tried to be artistic with to send to Star for the social media sites: signs around La Vista, a panoramic of the Rhein, capturing the entire marquee.

A series from Come As You Are at Fred's, right after I'd gotten this phone. I'd taken slow motion videos and panoramas of the bar, used every filter Instagram had on offer (just to see if it looked different on this phone than it had on my last). I'd gone by myself and ended up talking to Cameron for most of the night. I had pictures of his nails, which he'd painted an uncharacteristically gaudy rainbow of colors for Pride. Then I'd taken pictures of him looking at me disapprovingly for taking pictures of his nails.

There were only a few more, mostly because Cam didn't like being caught on film. Funny thing for a guy who runs a movie theater.

I skipped back a few photos before my brain told me to return to the ones of Cameron. At first I didn't realize why, since I'd seen them a minute ago. But something needled me and I looked again, a little more carefully, trying to figure out what.

Cam's nails, meticulously painted. The bar counter. Used coasters. A glimpse behind the counter at glasses drying, lemons in a little bin. Close-ups on different bottles, which I'd then cropped, telling myself I had interesting angles. Another few of Cameron—eyebrows raised above the wire frame of his glasses as he tried to give me the kind of look that would make me put my phone away. A blur of people behind him. A bright light causing a flare in the upper left corner.

The next picture was virtually the same shot, but slightly shifted to avoid the flare. Now I could see Tom in the background at the other end of the bar, pouring drinks for someone with purple hair who was probably Zane.

I skipped one more and froze.

The camera had gone out of focus, turning Cameron's crisp lines into a slight smear. Instead it had focused on a beer tap right where the counter curved around. Beside the tap a boy sat talking to Zane's group, grinning, caught in profile, face tilted just enough toward the camera so I could see his features.

Steven Costello. I'd swear it on my mother's life.

I zoomed in, then exported the picture to an app so I could make it lighter and save different versions. If the focus hadn't shifted, I'd never have been able to tell I was looking at the same kid. But I'd stared at his photo in the newspaper article long enough to know it by heart. He had a cowlick in the front of his hair, which made it flop on the side facing the camera. I'd noticed it in the straight-ahead ID card shot, but it was even more obvious when I zoomed in.

Could that be a different kid, a different white boy with floppy hair? Was I making this up? Togg was getting to me. Clearly. I was just inventing this, right?

But no. I was almost certain it was him.

The *Times-Record* website was no help; it had the article, but no photograph. I hit Google again, but Costello's bizarre lack of social media pages meant I didn't have any better luck there.

I wasn't about to go in to work on a Saturday, but there was one other chance. I picked up my coffee and headed home.

The house paid for a subscription to the paper, but I didn't think anyone read it. The subscription predated everyone currently living there, but it was rolled into the rent, so no one seemed to mind. What was a few more bucks a month? I'd seen the paper used for gift wrapping (because nothing says "great boyfriend" like "wraps with newsprint"), and to Windex the windows. The porch roof leaked in April and a bunch of the newspapers sopped up the water.

Hopefully, the one with the Costello story hadn't ended up being domestically recycled yet.

I pulled all the June editions and spread them out on my floor. It only took a few minutes to find the right one.

They'd found his body on a Monday. Monday, June 20. Three days after the picture I'd taken at Club Fred's. Three days after Come As You Are. If I slotted Steven Costello into my list, he'd fit perfectly.

It was him. I folded over the paper until the Costello article was front and center, then put it beside my phone for a comparison. Despite the grayscale and the lack of resolution in the blown-up photo, it was clearly the same kid.

Someone barreled down the stairs and slammed into the kitchen. Not David or José, which left Troy or JP. I tugged the page with the picture out of the rest of the paper and brought it into the kitchen.

JP looked up. "Whoa. Totally didn't know you were up."

"Sorry. Can you help me with something?"

He shrugged. "Sure, man. What's going down?"

Was "What's going down?" some kind of new slang I was too old to understand? I spread out the paper and put my phone next to Costello's ID photo.

"Is this the same guy? I've been staring at them, but I can't tell."

JP leaned all the way down, squinting, bringing his face right up against the table. "Same dude. Right? I mean, there's his hair, and look, he's smiling more in the one on your phone, but it's kind of the same smile, isn't it? Like, it's the natural progression of the smile in the other picture."

I exhaled. "Okay. Thanks."

"Sure. What's this about?" He nudged my phone out of the way and whistled as he scanned the article. "Shit. You have a dead guy's picture on your phone, Ed? Fucked up."

"I don't remember ever meeting him, but I'm pretty sure that's him."

"Who's the blurry dude?"

"Oh." I took back my phone. "That's Cameron. He owns the Rhein downtown? He's a friend of mine."

"Uh-huh."

Cue awkward pause. I refolded the paper carefully.

He shifted on his feet. "Listen, uh, I wanted to apologize. For David last night. Or all of us. We totally meant no disrespect to your lady, you know?"

"She took care of David," I said. "It's no problem."

"Okay. Just wanted to make sure she, like, feels comfortable here."

I had to take back the shitty things I'd assumed about them. Maybe they were, mostly, entitled white boys, but they were trying.

"Really, JP, it's cool. We normally go to her place because she's got a studio, but she feels comfortable pretty much everywhere."

He exhaled. "Oh. Good. Uh, sorry about that dead guy."

"Me too."

Three and a half hours before I could pick Alisha up at work. How early did Club Fred's open on a Saturday? Did they have a lunch menu?

Fred's didn't have a lunch menu, but they did open at two. I slipped inside, not used to the shocking darkness because usually it was matched by the darkness outside. Somehow, during the day, the place looked a little more grim than usual, the silly fake "Club Med" decor not only dated, but shabby. The thick rope twisted around the walls at chair rail height was more frayed and dusty than I'd noticed before, and the fishing nets over the dance floor, which served mostly to cast cool shadows when Fred's was hopping, just looked like someone had failed to clean up after some maintenance job that required netting.

Two cops passed me on their way out the door, and my stomach dropped. Should I call out to them? Should I show them the picture on my phone? But no. It still felt too much like a conspiracy theory.

I made my way to Fredi, who looked pale and angry.

"Have you heard this happy bullshit? Don't tell me you're here for the fuckin' paper, Ed Masiello."

"I'm not. At all." I pulled out the paper and my phone again, setting them up on the bar. "Fredi, do you recognize this kid?"

She looked between them, squinted, then reached for a pair of glasses. "Huh. I don't know. That the same kid?"

"I think so. But I don't remember ever meeting him."

"Hell, it could be any kid. The kids all look the same." She pushed them back toward me. "Don't tell me you're buying into this crap. You know the cops think I have something to do with these deaths."

"I don't think you have anything to do with anything." And probably neither did the cops. "But Fredi, four people have died after being here."

Her eyes narrowed and she thumped her knuckles down on the grainy photo of Steven Costello. "This the fourth? The cops only said three."

"Three for sure. But I took those pictures at Come As You Are. His body was found the following Monday, and he'd been dead a few days. If that's him, then it's four."

She stepped back, lips pressed tightly together, leaning against the back counter. "I can't believe it. I don't want to fucking believe this. Someone's using *my bar* to kill people?"

"It seems like they're finding victims here and luring them away."

"Jesus." Fredi crossed thick arms over her chest. "That's sick."

"Are you sure you don't recognize him? He was clearly at the bar."

"I told you, all the kids look the same."

"It was his birthday," I added, hoping it would jog her memory. "He turned twenty-one that night, and came here to celebrate all by himself as far as anyone can tell. Even his parents didn't know he was here."

"Fuck. I remember him. Damn it. Looking like he was scared out of his mind to be here in the first place, and I remember thinking it was ironic that this frightened child turned twenty-one on Come As You Are night." She took a slow breath and let it out. "Goddamn it. Talk to Cameron Rheingold. And Zane Jaffe. She's the one who ordered his birthday beer, but Cameron bought him one after that. I don't know if they actually talked—you know Cameron—but they definitely sat here for a while."

"I'll talk to him." I was losing her. Fredi's eyes were fading as she stood there, master of her domain, as if she were watching their ghosts walk past. "I'm really sorry, Fredi."

"I can't believe this shit."

"Yeah."

I got out of there.

Detective Green. I'd written his name down back when I asked Rodriguez about Steven Costello. I almost picked up the phone to call, but waited. I'd start with Zane and Cam.

Zane didn't remember Costello. "I definitely remember we had a new recruit that night, but I didn't talk to him, Ed. Sorry."

"If you remember anything about it— I mean—"

"I know. I'll call if I remember anything."

Cameron's phone went straight to voice mail, which meant he was in a movie, but I asked him to call me back later. If Cam remembered the kid, I'd call Green. Between him and Fredi, and the picture on my phone, this was beginning to feel less like a conspiracy I was inventing, and more like a real thing.

I gave up on distractions and played Minecraft until it was time to get Alisha.

She looked more exhausted than usual and sank into the passenger seat of my car with a sigh. "Babe. I had a day."

"Me too. You tell me yours first."

"I'm so glad to see you." We kissed. "Same old stuff. I just— I have to quit. I can't deal with Wing Tips and his bullshit."

Wing Tips was the code name she used for her boss so she could talk shit about him in public without worrying it would get back to him.

"What did he do now?"

"Nothing! He did nothing. He sat on his ass all day and sniped at me, and when I ignored him he pulled on my hair, like a dick."

I grimaced. "What the hell?"

"Yeah, it's his way of getting my attention, since he's basically twelve years old."

It sounded a little more like sexual harassment to me, but I doubted Alisha needed me to point that out. "That's pretty obnoxious."

"It really was. And I had a client call and yell at me for seven straight minutes because the hotel I'd made reservations at for him and his wife didn't allow them to have their dog in the room."

"Um. Is that the kind of thing you check beforehand?"

"I would have, *if they told me they were bringing their dog.* Seriously, what am I, a mind reader? How would I know that? One time—one!—did someone ask me if their dog could come on their adventure with them. I made appropriate arrangements, you know? I even paid to have the hotel leave a doggie goodie bag for the damn thing!"

Which was so totally her that I kissed her hand as I drove, and held it in my lap after. "I'm sorry you had a crummy day. And that people are so unrealistic, what with their expectations of your psychic powers."

"Right? It's ridic. What's up with your day?"

I shook my head. "I think I'm coming around to the conclusion that we have a serial killer targeting people who go to Club Fred's on theme nights."

"Wait. *What*?"

"I know it sounds crazy, but if you look at a calendar, it actually makes an alarming amount of sense, based on the dates and the fact that all four of the victims were at Fred's right before they were killed."

"Ed, oh my god, *what*?" She took back her hand.

"Sorry. Just, I've been trying to figure out where I knew this guy from—the one who died in June—and today I figured it out."

"You knew a guy who died? Ed, you gotta start from the beginning, but not until I eat something. Nothing you're saying right now makes any sense."

"It might not if I start at the beginning, either." I'd planned to stop by the Rhein to see if Cameron was in the booth, but maybe that wasn't the best idea. "So, grocery store?"

"Yes! Please, yes. Do you know what we're making?"

"I looked up like a dozen recipes and gave up. How does tacos sound?"

"Vegan tacos? I can't wait. I didn't know you could make tacos without cheese."

"If I have good avocados, I don't miss the cheese. Much."

"Sounds perfect. And I gotta plan a trip tonight. Even if it's just up the coast or something. I need to get the hell out of La Vista for a few days. *Especially* if there's a serial killer."

I shivered. I hadn't thought about it quite like that. In my brain La Vista had splintered into two planes: the one where I kissed Alisha, and the one where people died. From my plane I could research and obsess, but I wasn't afraid of anything. I'd been quick to buy Togg's theory, but slow to apply it to my own reality.

The grocery store was comfortingly mundane, belying any notion of danger outside its brightly lit aisles.

CHAPTER 14

Tacos were a hit. When we were done with dinner, I cleared everything away and Alisha got out her books and computer. I'd never seen her go full-on adventure planning, but something about it kind of inspired me. And washing dishes while she mumbled to herself about distances and reservations and weather felt charmingly domestic.

I finished up and sat down next to her. "So."

"So basically I need to quit my job and travel full-time forever."

I kissed her. "Sounds good."

"It really does. Back here in the real world, I can maybe do a weekend up the coast. Point Reyes has a hike-in campground I haven't been to yet. And if I want to drive farther north, there are a few good spots." She sat back. "I wish we had the same days off, you know? I don't mind going alone, but it'd be fun to take you along. You know. Bust your cherry, so to speak."

"You trying to say I can't hold my own?"

"Can you?"

"Um. Probably." I waited a beat. "So . . . what's a hike-in campground?"

She hit my arm. "Very cute. Hell, I don't know. That would be a stopgap. I want a *big* adventure, Ed. I want to be gone for two weeks at least. I want to come back changed, like my whole perspective is different."

"I hear that. I feel like that all the time. I mean, I like my life, but sometimes I feel really disconnected from it too. If that makes sense."

"Totally. Like life is going on, and I'm in it, but in another sense I'm barely there." She tucked her braids back and kissed me. "We need to plan a trip, Ed."

"I don't think I can get that much time off work."

"Neither can I, but I'm gonna start planning for it anyway. Where do you want to go? London? Cairo? Amsterdam?"

"Mexico City," I said without thinking.

"Mexico City."

"I mean, you're thinking way more, uh, outlandish, sorry. Mexico probably doesn't seem like much of an adventure to you. I don't even know why I said it." Except that I'd only been there once, and it was where my mom's entire family was from. It was where Abuela was born and raised.

"Ed, taking a walk down the street is an adventure if you look at it the right way. Hold on." She unfolded from her chair and went to kneel beside the bookcase. "Ha. I thought I still had this. I meant to go when I was in high school, but no one would come with me and I chickened out at the last minute. You know, all those stories about vulnerable white girls getting abducted and killed. Though I guess maybe we don't have to leave the country for that, do we?"

The title said only *Mexico*. The cover photo, though, was a sprawling city with the ocean in the background and clear blue skies.

"I'll pick up the Rough Guide for Mexico City," she said. "But we can start with this."

"Oh— But— I mean, I really can't get that kind of time off, so maybe—"

"Planning is part of the adventure, and it's fun even if we never do the rest."

"Okay." My phone buzzed. Cameron, finally.

Just locking up. You want to come over for a minute?

Damn. Alisha was settled in for the night. And I'd planned to be settled in with her, but the rush of chasing down Steven Costello was tempting.

"Ha. Who texted you? You look hungry, babe."

"I'm not. Well maybe. It's Cameron. I asked him if I could put these pictures in front of him, see if he remembers the Costello kid. Fredi said she thought they talked one night."

Alisha gestured me closer and tugged me in for a kiss. "Go, if you want to. I'd rather you talked to Cam about murder and serial killers than to me anyway."

She'd adopted the nickname immediately. I was always so careful about things like that, as if there was an accepted protocol, but Alisha just went for it.

"Are you sure? I mean, part of me definitely wants to stay here with you."

"And part of you wants to investigate more. Why don't you head over there and come back here after? No pressure or anything, but I definitely wouldn't mind waking up with you in the morning."

"That sounds perfect." It did. More perfect still, I didn't feel like she was telling me what I wanted to hear. She was surrounded by books, with a stack of sticky notes, different colored pens, and her computer. Nothing about that picture really required my presence.

I kissed her and lingered for a second. "I'll see you later."

"You better."

"Lock up after me."

"Oh, you know I will."

I waited until she'd shot the dead bolt and texted Cameron to let him know I was on the way.

"Oh no. That poor boy." He studied the picture on my phone, a single line creasing his forehead. "Fredi's right. He sat next to me and I heard Zane teasing him about his birthday, so naturally I bought the sad young man a drink. He thought I was hitting on him." Cam shook his head. "I assured him it was merely tradition to buy twenty-one-year-olds a beer to celebrate. It never occurred to me that this was him, that he was the boy found down at the waterfront."

"I think he must have been in the closet. If he was even gay, though I assume if you go to Club Fred's on your birthday, you must be queer." I let my voice cant up at the end, making it the slightest of questions.

"Oh, we didn't discuss it, but I'd guess he was. He was jumpy, like someone who lives in the closet and doesn't dare come out." He handed me back my phone and picked up the newspaper. "He reminded me of myself. In looks, more than demeanor. He was cute, for a kid, but he probably wanted to be seen as a man. He sat there at the bar studying the reflections as if looking for himself in the masses. I can't believe he's dead. Mentally I'd . . . imagined I'd see him again, later, when he was more comfortable in his skin. Such a loss to all of us that he'll never get there."

That was certainly a positive identification. But I still asked, "Did he introduce himself?"

"I introduced myself, and he said his name was Steven. I remember because I asked him if he preferred Steven or Steve, and he blushed. He probably still thought I was hitting on him."

Most definitely a positive identification.

"I have to talk to the detective who investigated the case." I sat back on Cameron's sofa. I'd never been to the upstairs apartment in the building next door to the theater, but it was very Cam, almost like the theater's apartment alter ego, with plush indigo drapes and this incredibly soft red velvet sofa. "It's okay if I give him your name, right? You might have been one of the last people to talk to him before he left. Did you notice him talking to anyone else?"

"No. I'm sorry. He sat at the bar long enough for me to finish the book I was reading and begin another, but the next time I looked up, he was gone. I assumed he'd slipped away alone." Cam's eyes focused on mine. "He wasn't seeking companionship that I could see. He was too afraid for that. Almost paralyzed with it. I hope they don't try to make this into one of those stories about over-sexed gay men getting what they deserve."

I could picture the critique of *that* on Togg's site, and the hundreds of comments that would follow.

"Well, if he's part of this pattern, I doubt it has anything to do with companionship. Honey had a boyfriend, and Stephanie Hawkins was bi, but she had a wife. Plus, Loren was a lesbian, so even if you could argue that Hawkins was stepping out on her wife with a man, you still wouldn't be able to convince me that all four of them were potentially attracted to the same person."

Cameron picked up his coffee cup and sipped it, watching me maybe too closely. "How is Alisha?"

"I— She's great. We just had dinner. Why?"

"Just wondering. You two should come to another movie soon."

"I'm sure we will." I leaned forward. "Listen, if you remember anything else about Steven Costello, will you call me?"

"Won't the police be handling this?"

"Well, yeah, but they haven't shown a huge amount of motivation to handle any of these cases before, so I'm trying not to let all of them go cold. No one's even looking for this guy, whoever it is, Cam! This guy is fucking *hunting us*, and no one even cares. Including us."

He raised his eyebrows. "That's hardly fair. We can't care if we don't know what's going on, and until now didn't it seem like unrelated beatings?"

"Unrelated murders you mean, and maybe, except how can they be unrelated if they keep showing up beaten to death at the waterfront?"

"Then again, with such different victims, I can see how it was easy to miss the connection. And didn't you say the first one was found in an alley?"

"Yes, but— What's your point?"

"My point is that nothing good can come out of you allowing this to consume you." The intensity of his gaze made me want to look away. He took another sip of coffee. "I understand being frightened by it, wanting to solve it, but surely the police have people to do that job, and more resources with which to do it, don't you think?"

"You think I should drop it? Togg keeps reporting it, so I keep reading about it, and I can't just turn off my brain."

He shook his head. "I've never thought Togg—whoever they are—represented an especially healthy outlook on life. And no, don't turn off your brain, but wouldn't your life be more enriched by Alisha's company right now than it is tracking down people who may have seen a depressed boy on the night he died?"

"Depressed? Wait. Do you think he might have been more than depressed?"

"I don't think he committed suicide by beating himself to death, no. But it wouldn't surprise me, either, to hear he'd taken more risks than were necessary. He was a very lost-seeming young man, Ed."

Which was basically what I'd already figured, and didn't help much. "Fine. But Honey wasn't lost. And Stephanie Hawkins was practically a newlywed. And the next person could be any of us, Cam. All we know is that all four victims went to Club Fred's."

"I want them caught, whoever they are, the same as you do. But I also want you, as my friend, to not lose yourself in the hunt."

It was the same word I'd used to describe the killer, and it gave me chills. "I'm not hunting."

"All right."

A somewhat awkward silence descended between us. Casting for something to say, I complimented his tie, which he was still wearing, even retired for the night. It had seemed like a black tie with odd white dots on it until I realized the white dots were stars in the shapes of constellations.

"I adore it. Thank you." Long fingers smoothed the tie down over his shirt. "Do you know Obie Magovney? If not, you should, Ed, you'd like him. He actually *makes* neckties. I bought this one from his online store, really just to support a local businessperson, but now that I see how high quality it is, I definitely plan to buy more."

"Wait, I think Alisha mentioned him, but I wasn't paying attention. You can *make* ties?"

"Exactly! It seems a little like magic. You can't tell it was handmade by a guy in La Vista, either."

"And you picked constellations." I grinned. "Nerd."

"He introduced himself to me one night when I was wearing it at Club Fred's. When he realized I was a Rhein Rheingold, he promised to find me a fabric suited to being worn at the theater."

"That's so cool."

"You should look him up. Or I'll try to introduce you if we're all out at the same moment. Very nice man, and I think you'd like his personal aesthetic." Cameron paused, considering. "Masculine without trying too hard, and not the least bit overcompensating with it, either. He had a pink painter's cap on the night we met, and it didn't look like a joke, or like it made him a joke."

"Okay. And I'm always on the lookout for a new necktie."

He smiled. "You look good regardless, but who should be without a variety of neckties?"

"Yeah, uh, thanks, Cam. Anyway. I guess I'll go."

Cameron and I both stood up, and he shook my hand, pulling me in for a clap on the back. "Be safe out there."

"You too."

I guess I'd gotten what I wanted, though I didn't exactly feel lighter leaving than I had when I arrived. It was probably too late to get Green on the phone tonight, so I'd do it tomorrow.

The drive back to Alisha's was quick, and when I got there she was still in research mode, so I made more tea and watched *Sherlock* while she worked.

We didn't even have sex later, just fell into bed, fell into each other, and slept.

CHAPTER 15

Detective Green asked me if I wouldn't mind coming down to the station Monday. I dropped an email to Potter explaining that I had information pertaining to an ongoing investigation and I'd probably be in later.

I'd worried (after all those cop shows) that he'd think I was involved, or that he'd want me to prove I wasn't. I'd almost worried that I'd end up in an interrogation room wondering who I'd call if I needed a lawyer.

Instead, Green got me a cup of coffee that was slightly more shitty than coffee at the paper and sat me next to his desk to talk.

I laid out the newspaper clip of Costello and found the photo on my phone, then explained to him the theme nights at Club Fred's. He nodded along, so it clearly wasn't a revelation that there was a potential connection. I'd passed cops leaving Fred's, so apparently they'd gotten the message.

Had Togg contacted the police? I hadn't questioned their presence, but now I wondered. Of course, it could have been anyone who saw his article, and that included whoever at the *Times-Record* seemed to be reading his blog.

Green, a skinny Filipino guy with glasses and scabbed knuckles, took in everything I said, barely asking a question until I was done. Then he took down Zane's contact information, and Cameron's, and Fredi's. I figured it was probably time for me to leave, except he started talking, peppering his sentences with questions about what I'd already said. It took me a few minutes to catch on that he was verifying my story.

I didn't mind. At least it seemed like he was taking me seriously. Though I was still concerned I'd wind up in a tiny room with a one-way mirror.

"But you never met Steven Costello? Even though his picture's on your phone?"

"Yeah." I paged back and forth so he could see that I'd been taking pictures of everything. "New phone, so I was just messing around. I was trying to get Cameron, but the focus changed without me knowing it."

"And this Cameron Rheingold is your boyfriend?"

"No. He's a friend. Does that matter?"

"To tell you the truth, Mr. Masiello, it's not entirely clear to me what matters in this case. If you're telling me that Costello was gay, that's surprising, since his parents didn't say a word about it. Then again, if he *was* gay, and if he hadn't told anyone, that would go a long way toward explaining why his mom and dad couldn't come up with a single name of a person he'd kept in touch with since leaving La Vista, and how little they knew about his college life. All of that *could* be a normal slightly estranged relationship, but I wondered if there was more to it, so you're not exactly telling me something outrageous right now. Tell me more about this Club Fred's. It's one of those dumps on Steerage?"

I bristled at calling Fred's a *dump*, but he was probably right, objectively speaking.

"Fredi modeled it after Club Med, you know? With a, like, sort of nautical-resort theme. It could use updating, probably."

Green didn't exactly snort, but I got the feeling it was a near thing. "And it's popular? We don't get too many calls out there, and I never worked that beat."

"Yeah, pretty popular. With a certain group of people, I guess." *Fags and dykes and queers and trannies. You should come hang out. We don't bite.*

"Does your phone date-stamp pictures when they're taken?"

"Yeah. Though I have it set not to geo-encode them. Sorry."

He waved a hand. "We can match up pictures with the location easily enough. But I'll need you to send them to me."

"Sure." I pulled my phone back out, accidentally catching a few dollar bills and a matchbook I'd picked up with the vague idea of lighting them in Honey's honor.

"What's that?"

"Uh. Sorry, I have a lot of shit in my pockets."

"No. *That*." His finger landed on the matchbook.

"Oh. It's, uh, a matchbook."

"From where?" He started rustling around on his desk, picking up and discarding files. "I've seen that design before."

Black with a subtle dark-red lifebuoy. No words, though.

"It's, uh, from Fred's. Club Fred's."

"Jesus. It was fucking *right in front of me*," Green growled, thumbing through a folder. "Shit. I can't believe I missed this." He pulled a photograph out and put it flat on the desk.

A Club Fred's matchbook in an evidence bag.

"Where—where is that from?"

"Found it in Costello's pockets. He wasn't a smoker, and none of the matches had been struck. We figured he'd just picked it up somewhere, like you do when something's free, even when you don't need it."

I stared at the picture, then at my own matches. Identical. But anyone who went to Fred's would have known that design without having to check.

Green grunted in frustration. "This puts the kid at your club at some point in the days after he came home from college. With your photo and additional witnesses, we can prove he was there on the night he died. Hell, I gotta get in touch with Baker." He picked up the phone but paused before dialing. "Will you send that photo to the email address on the card I gave you?"

"Sure."

"Great. Thanks for coming down here, Mr. Masiello. I appreciate it."

"Yeah, of course. And I hope you catch this guy. I'd appreciate that."

"We're damn well going to." He punched in a few numbers on his phone, muttering, "Pick up, you bastard."

I took that as my cue to leave.

Trying to focus on work was nearly impossible. I left a fake follow-up message for Steven Costello's parents, pretending I was calling on behalf of the paper and feeling a little crappy about it, but too curious to resist. They probably wouldn't agree to meet me, but between Joe's impression of them and Detective Green's, I really wanted to see for myself.

Then I skipped lunch and left early so I could go visit Abuela and not risk seeing either of my parents.

"Mija, dichosos los ojos que te ven." She kissed both of my cheeks and looked at me closely. "Something is wrong."

"Nothing's wrong, Abuelita. I'm good."

"I can tell when something is wrong, and I'm looking at it right now."

I sighed and set down my bag at my feet. "Nothing's wrong, really. There's some stuff going on, but it really doesn't have anything to do with me, I swear."

"Mm-hmm."

"It doesn't! Also, I, uh, I'm kind of seeing someone."

"Seeing someone!" She sat back, folding her hands over the book in her lap. Spanish romance novels, always Spanish romance novels. "Go on, mija, tell me everything."

After all these years, Abuela doesn't really expect me to date a man, but I still feel like I'm letting her down a little every time I have a girlfriend.

"Her name is Alisha."

"Alicia," she said, pronouncing it as she would in Spanish.

"A*lish*a," I corrected. "English spelling. And she's—she's really great. She wants to go on adventures and travel everywhere. And she's spontaneous and a little bit wild and she's not afraid of anything, Abuelita, you know?"

"Yes, very much. She's a good girl, this Alisha?" This time she said it carefully, tripping a little on the slurred "sh" in the middle.

"She's fantastic. We have so much fun together."

"And she makes you smile, mija, I can tell." She patted my cheek. "Where did you meet?"

"I have no idea. We've always sort of moved in similar circles, but we've never really talked until recently. Then, I don't know, one night we kind of hit it off."

Abuela nodded seriously. "That is sometimes how it happens. Your abuelo had been my neighbor for many years before we married, and we were very lucky. One day, after we had been married, we realized we liked each other very much."

"*After* you'd been married?"

"It wasn't as bad as you make it sound. We 'got along well,' as your mother would say." Whenever Abuela pronounced the English words Mom insisted on, she did it with a little sneer. "But then we found things to like, even love, when we looked at each other. It was very precious, mija."

I can't imagine getting married for family reasons. Abuela always says it isn't as if she and my grandfather's marriage was *arranged*, exactly; both of them knew they'd have to marry someone, so they opted to choose each other before the decision was taken out of their hands. I used to think about that, when I was younger. What it must have been like, fifteen years old, conspiring to marry a friendly neighbor just because you had to marry *someone*.

"Tell me more about this Alisha." Abuela touched my hand. "And get us some of those disgusting cookies tu papá eats."

"Oreos coming right up." I got the package down from the cabinet. "I'll tell you more about Alisha, but you have to catch me up on the ladies."

"Oh, the ladies! You won't believe it. This young man Dotty is seeing? Asked her to marry him!" Abuela threw her head back and laughed. "I wish I had seen her face, chiquita!"

"Me too."

We ate cookies and talked a fair amount of smack about the ladies. I told Abuela more about Alisha's travel plans, and she held my hand as I talked, and told me that she couldn't wait to see the pictures.

I almost clarified that Alisha's plans were for solo trips, not couple trips, but then I figured there wasn't much of a point. It didn't hurt anyone if Abuela imagined me and my girlfriend off traveling the world having adventures, right? And actually, that was a pretty cool thought, if I disregarded things like keeping my job. For a second I let myself picture that, packing my bags, boarding a plane, sitting beside Alisha with her guidebooks out.

Stepping out onto a street in some faraway place with no idea what came next.

Obviously it couldn't really happen, but even thinking about it made me a little bit giddy.

After I kissed her cheek and said good-bye, I picked up burritos and brought them to Alisha's, where she told me all about her next fantasy trip.

CHAPTER 16

As far as I was aware, nothing much was happening with the case. Togg's updates mostly covered the same territory on repeat, and Detective Green hadn't contacted me again, so I had no new information to go off. As expected, the Costellos didn't return my call. I figured I'd head to Club Fred's with Alisha on Friday and I'd ask around, see if anyone else had talked to Steven Costello the night he died.

On Wednesday we were hanging out in my room, about to decamp for her place, when she brought up going to knitting group. I hadn't gone since Honey died, and hadn't planned to go back again, at least until it hurt less.

I blinked. "But do you know how to knit?"

She shrugged. "You could teach me."

"I . . . guess I could." I didn't want to. I didn't want to walk into the yarn shop and not see Honey there. "I don't know. You wouldn't rather stay home?" I waggled my eyebrows at Alisha, hoping she wouldn't realize I was trying to distract her.

Fat chance. Her eyes narrowed on me, and all that focus I loved when we were in bed, or dancing, or even talking, now felt like a weapon.

I looked away.

"Why don't you want to go to knitting? I've seen your yarns"—she gestured toward my stash—"and that bag with your socks, or scarf, or whatever it is."

"Hat."

"You don't want to finish it?"

"It's not that I don't want to finish it. It's like . . . I don't know."

"Babe. Come on." She grabbed my hands and pulled me until I was sitting next to her on the bed. "I miss Honey too. I didn't know her as well as you did, but I still can't believe she's dead."

God, there was no hiding from *she's dead*. I gnawed on my lip for a minute. "She invited me to knitting, you know? She taught me how. And I didn't really care about knitting, but Honey was sort of like... a mentor to me. I'd watch her move, and listen to her voice, and sort of... build myself. I'd think, *Honey crosses her legs like this, maybe I'll try it this other way*. Almost like we were... inverses. Even though that's not true. It was a kind of tool I used, when I was trying to figure out who I was."

Alisha brought my hand to her lips and kissed it. "I can't imagine losing someone like that."

"I feel like I should have appreciated her more. Thanked her. I don't know."

"I'm sure she knew how you felt, Ed."

"I'm sure she didn't. I don't think Honey had anyone like her when she was younger." Which made me even sadder. "It was such a long fucking time ago. And it kind of sucks to be trans now. But back then?" I shuddered. "It was really hard."

She put an arm around me. "I'm glad we're alive now. I know everything's not perfect, but it feels a little less deadly. Most of the time."

"Except when it's not."

"Yeah. But I think not knitting ever again probably isn't the solution. You know? Like, making socks is a good thing. Especially if Honey is the reason you know how to knit. That makes it more powerful."

I tried to imagine it. Holding Alisha's hand. Walking down the street. Walking into the yarn shop. Jaq and Hannah would probably be there. Mildred might be, and if Mildred was, Zane would be next to her.

And an empty spot on the sofa where Honey used to sit. Unless someone took her spot, which would be worse.

"Maybe next week," I said. "I just can't do it right now."

"Yeah, okay, babe." She squeezed my shoulders. "Let's go make guacamole at my place, all right?"

"Sounds perfect."

It was pretty much perfect. Now I had to come up with a reason not to go to knitting next week, but I had some lead time.

I spent the better part of the week fulfilling my assignments at the paper, dodging increasingly frequent *looks* from my editor, and ignoring Caspar (who DGAF about some asshole killing queers, no offense). Just after lunch on Friday I checked Togg's site again and stopped breathing.

Arrest Made in Local Murder Case.

My first thought was *Oh, thank god.* Then I saw who they'd arrested.

Tom Krayak. Longtime bartender at Club Fred's.

I didn't know Tom all that well, but he knew I'd rather drink whatever was on tap than a fancy microbrew. I didn't remember when he'd started working at Fred's, but it must have been years ago. He'd definitely been there for as long as I'd been going consistently. After I graduated from San Francisco State and moved back in with my folks, I'd needed somewhere to escape to, and more often than not, it was Club Fred's.

Tom? Tom was a killer? That couldn't possibly be. I couldn't believe it. Though even as I started to defend him in my head—he was always kind, he was incredibly good-looking, he was the friendly side to Fredi's prickly bartending—I realized that serial killers almost always had people defending them for similar shallow reasons.

But *Tom*?

I scanned Togg's post for hints, but it was brief and unemotional, only stating the facts. Tom Krayak, longtime bartender, had been arrested around 11 a.m., Friday, August nineteenth. Today. A few hours ago.

Damn, Togg was fast. For a second I forgot to feel outraged and freaked out because I was so busy appreciating how quick Togg got information up on his site. I bet the *Times-Record* hadn't even realized an arrest had been made yet. I'd checked in with Rodriguez after talking with Detective Green the other day, and he said as interesting as the theory that the murders were all connected was, it wasn't news until there was some evidence supporting it. Then he'd thumped his hand down on my shoulder and told me, kindly, to get the fuck back to work.

Tom couldn't be the killer. He couldn't.

Except.

He worked at Fred's full-time, was there most nights. He was always there on event nights. Club Fred's locked up at one thirty in the morning, and no one cared if you were still in the middle of your beer. Fredi made it clear that poor time management was not her fault, and everyone knew it.

She locked up alone, I was almost certain. I'd been there, staggering out with the final customers, and I'd seen Tom leave at the same time. Maybe there were certain nights he helped close, and others when he left at one thirty sharp. I hoped for his sake that Fredi kept schedules somewhere accessible.

I wanted them to find the killer. But I really, really didn't want it to be Tom. I wanted it to be someone nobody knew. I wanted it to be someone straight, someone who targeted the community from the outside, someone I could feel free to hate. Intellectually it made more sense that the whole thing was an inside job, that no angry straight white boy was lurking in the shadows outside Club Fred's, successfully luring so many people to their deaths, part of me still grasped for that to be true.

Tom was a fixture. He'd consoled me after breakups. He was the guy who laughed at your jokes, even when they were bad. Handsome, charming, and fuck, he totally fit the profile of a serial killer. How was that possible?

Togg's comment section was filled with people expressing everything from relief to outrage. I couldn't tell from the unemotional reporting what Togg felt, except that the unemotional reporting was an exception, not the rule. He was hiding behind objectivity.

I opened a message. *How convincing is their case against Tom?*

Convincing enough for them to get an arrest warrant.

Tell me something I don't know.

But is there anything actually linking him to the crime scenes, or is it circumstantial? When he didn't write back immediately I added,

As much as I want this guy caught, it's hard to wrap my head around the idea it's Tom.

You and me both. I don't know yet. I'm trying to get more information, but my sources have locked down. Keep an eye on the site. You'll know when I know.

Right. I signed out of everything and sat back, staring at my coffee cup, my part of the table, my phone. The calendar above my head, which was still on July because I hadn't bothered to change it.

Find the destination of your heart. That fucking cruise ship had never looked so good.

CHAPTER

Fredi put up a Closed sign over the door on Friday night, but Alisha and I tentatively showed up on Saturday.

We weren't the only ones.

Tom was still in jail. He couldn't post bail until he saw a judge, and they'd arrested him Friday so they didn't have to put him in front of one until Monday. It was a tactic I understood, but the weekend felt longer now that someone I knew was the one being held.

He was engaged. Carlos wasn't at Club Fred's that night, but a whole lot of people were, and for a group that big, the place was alarmingly subdued.

Zane was the first person we saw, and she gave us both hugs. "You don't believe it, do you? Because I'm telling you there's no fucking way Tom killed anyone."

I hugged her back. "But doesn't he have an alibi? Carlos is always here with him."

"Yeah, but Carlos goes home first. He doesn't stay for the whole shift. He crashes, and Tom comes home when he's off, but because Carlos doesn't even really wake up, he can't say for sure when." She lowered her voice. "I think we convinced him not to lie to the cops, but it was touch and go. This is really fucked up."

Alisha was absolutely convinced of Tom's innocence, which made things easier with Zane. They talked about lack of evidence, and how useless Tom's fingerprints would be since he'd probably served every one of the victims. I stood there, listening, feeling like a horribly disloyal friend. It wasn't that I believed he did it, exactly, but whatever assurance both of them seemed to be running on that he couldn't have done it eluded me.

Why couldn't he have done it? Because he seemed like a nice guy? *They always seem like nice guys.* That's how serial killers were successful.

But I couldn't say that. And I still had too many questions to feel confident that the police had found their man; after a long shift at work, Tom decided to beat four people to death? Why those people? He and Honey had been friends. And why would he pick the event nights? Surely he'd've been smart enough not to kill where he ate.

Most people weren't dancing. A few oblivious couples were on the floor, but everyone else was clustered here and there, talking, casting looks around like they didn't want to be overheard.

"Carlos is inconsolable," Zane was telling us. Her attention was suddenly caught by someone over my shoulder. "Philpott, you son of a gun. Long time no see."

"Hey, hon." The guy smiled and kissed Zane's cheek, then Alisha's. "Heard you found yourself a man."

Alisha laughed. "You're such a gossip. Have you met Ed? Ed, this is Anderson Philpott. He ran the high school newspaper for a few years when we were in school."

I nodded. "Good to meet you."

"We've seen each other around." He shook my hand. He was short, with dark hair and an old scar running from his ear down his neck. "It feels like a wake here tonight. How is Carlos?"

"I was just telling these guys. He's terrible, but wouldn't you be?" Zane shook her head. "This is all so fucked up. Tom's one of the best guys I know. There's no way he hurt anyone."

"I hope it all gets straightened out soon," Anderson replied. "Fredi looks like she hasn't slept since the arrest."

We all glanced over at the bar, where Fredi was mechanically serving drinks and not making much of whatever anyone said to her.

"Fredi can't possibly believe Tom would do this," Zane said.

Anderson shrugged. "Doesn't matter. If he didn't, she's still gotta be wondering if people will want to buy drinks from him after all this. Whether he's guilty isn't the only thing at play. I'm gonna keep walking around, but it was good seeing you guys."

"You too," she replied, still distracted by watching Fredi. "I'm sure she wouldn't fire him over this. I mean, it's Fredi. She's not worried about people buying drinks."

"I can't believe we're even having this conversation," Alisha murmured, shifting closer to me. "Tom's always been such a nice guy. And I can't—I really can't—believe someone's actually killing people we know. That's so wrong."

I put my arm around her. "Everyone who dies is someone that people knew."

She shot me a look. "Yeah, in the abstract. But this is really happening. I wish we could just go away and not think about it."

"That wouldn't change that it was happening though."

Zane shook her head. "You're having two different conversations. Alisha's talking about taking a break from reality, and Ed, you're talking about being unavoidably entrenched in it. When really we're all somewhere in the middle, entrenched and trying not to think too hard about the whole thing."

"It's like that thing your mom says." Alisha poked me. "Don't make me do the Spanish, I'll screw it up."

"De dinero y bondad, siempre la mitad."

"Uh—" Zane frowned. "Always in the middle of money and something else? My Spanish sucks."

"More like strive for the middle of things, you know? Don't go to the extremes."

"Exactly what we should be doing right now. We can't help that Tom's in jail, and ignoring that this horrible thing is going on isn't going to change it. But dwelling on it won't help either." Zane pulled us in for a three-person hug. "This is awful."

"It really is," Alisha said.

I couldn't help feeling like the thing they thought was awful had to do with Tom's arrest, and not the four people who'd already died. I didn't say anything.

"More fucking beer. I'll get the next round. Oh, hey, look who finally decided to come out tonight." Zane greeted Jaq and her girlfriend with hugs.

"So what the fuck do we think of this current bullshit?" Jaq hugged Alisha and me as well.

Zane threw her hands up. "It's ridiculous!"

"No one who knows Tom could imagine he killed anyone." Jaq sniffed at Zane's drink and wrinkled her nose. "Carlos? Carlos could beat someone to death. Tom feels shitty if he kills a spider."

Hannah shrugged. "Not to defend the police, but I can see how Tom is an appealing suspect to those who don't know him."

"Hannah!" Zane looked horrified. "How can you say that?"

"Because I can be more objective than you are. Hon, I'm not saying Tom did it. I'm saying I can see why it looks as if he *could have*."

"I can't. It's too awful to think about."

Jaq nudged her. "This is why we didn't become cops. How's it coming on your side, Ed?"

I shook my head. "It's not my story, but it's not really coming. As far as the *Times-Record* is concerned, Tom was arrested for a string of possibly related murders. Actually, I might have a question for you, Jaq. Did you ever teach Steven Costello?"

"Steven Costello?" She considered it. "The name's familiar."

This time Zane nudged Jaq. "He's the kid I bought a drink for on his birthday, who died. You know. On the night you—" She waved a hand toward Hannah.

"Ohhh. Oh god." Jaq reached for Hannah's hand. "That was a horrible night, and I tried to repress most of it. I don't remember him. Sorry, Ed."

I shrugged. "It was a shot in the dark anyway. He would have graduated three years ago."

"You know, let me ask around. That would have been when my current group of seniors were freshmen, so it's possible one of them knew him."

"Thanks. Anything you can find out would be helpful."

"Sure thing, kid."

Alisha tugged my arm. "Dancing?"

"Hell yes."

Club Fred's was starting to exhaust me and we'd only been there a couple of minutes. We left the three of them and hit the floor.

Whatever control usually held people's behavior in place was slipping. A couple had their hands down each other's pants, another couple was kissing and rubbing against each other in a way that had to be sex. A guy with a cane hanging off his hand was draped over his boyfriend, and the two of them were just swaying in a circle of their own while everyone else moved around them.

The dance floor filled slowly, but by the time Alisha and I got out there, the crush of bodies made it hard to do much more than press against each other. Not that I was complaining.

"You feel so good!" I called into her ear, blushing a little even as I said it.

"Are you coming on to me, mister?"

Oh god. *Mister.* I pressed into her more firmly. "How 'bout you come back to my place, dollface?"

She mimed slapping me. "How dare you insult my virtue!"

"Don't be like that, baby! I only want to talk to you!"

She laughed and grabbed my head. "You better do more than *talk*, you goon!"

"You let me know if you want to do a thirties roleplay sometime!" I said. "I'll call you my dame."

"And I'll call you my man. Take me home, baby."

I took her home.

For a long time I shied away from dildos, as if using a toy was some kind of slight on my cock, like I was betraying it. Once I started T—and after the first wave of depression eased off—I slept with this girl who had, like, seven different dildos. Different sizes and shapes, which she used in different ways. We literally only spent one night together, but she changed my relationship to insertables forever.

Now I had a few basic dildos and one strap-on, with a harness I'd researched for like a month and a half. I didn't know why I'd never shown Alisha any of it before, or why that night, after such a screwed-up week, seemed like the time to do it. But when we got to my house (and ascertained the roommates were either upstairs or out), I flipped open the little box where I kept it all and put it on the bed.

"Oh my *god.*" She stretched out on her stomach, picking each toy up so she could hold it, look at it carefully.

I couldn't keep standing there watching like an idiot, so I started fumbling with stuff, half-assed cleaning, anything to keep from watching Alisha poke through my small collection of sex toys.

The only thing in my collection that I'd used with other people was the strap-on. The dildos I'd kept for myself. I know some guys don't like playing with their pussy, but I don't mind it. I mean, whatever makes you hot, right? Having one of the dildos in while I stroked my cock made me hot, so I did it. Alone. With the door locked.

Alisha touching toy dongs I'd actually had inside my body was a bum rush of embarrassing and arousing. I was getting hard just thinking about the things we could do.

She looked up, holding out the strap-on. "This looks like fun."

"I haven't used it enough to be good at it."

"Really?" She raised an eyebrow. "I've used them a bit. I would have shown you, but I thought it might be insulting. I mean, you know it isn't really like I'm looking at this dick and thinking it's bigger and better than yours, right? This is just a toy."

I grabbed my crotch, a parody of confidence. "This ain't a toy, doll."

"I'm needing a little bit of that right now. Get your ass over here."

She stripped off my jeans and pulled me over her, not bothering with my shirt. I went where she guided, straddling her face, looking down while she licked her lips.

The first touch of her tongue made me shake, and I leaned back a little, trying to stay upright. She played with my cock, teasing it, making it pulse, rubbing her lips across and around it until my toes curled.

I wanted her to suck me, but I held back, trying not to beg.

Alisha licked her lips again. "Do you want me inside you, baby? Do you want me to get you off like that?"

Yes, and no, and I didn't know, because part of me didn't think it was manly to let my girlfriend fuck my pussy, but a larger part of me thought it was stupid to care. If I got off by myself like that, how was this different? Sex acts weren't gendered, damn it. Body parts didn't feel any obligation to conform to cultural expectations. And Alisha wasn't just any woman; she'd known me for years and she never slipped. I never saw that look in her eyes like she was trying to remember that I was a man.

"Yeah." I reached for the dildo I liked best. And the lube. "Sorry, I don't get as wet as I used to."

"I love lube. Give me that."

Her sure fingers lubed the thin black toy, and I had to force myself to breathe waiting for her to use it. This was so far beyond my usual comfort zone I'd never even considered fantasizing about it.

Then her fingers slid down, parting my lips, finding their goal. I braced on the headboard and closed my eyes, lifting up enough so she could press the tip of the dildo against me.

"Oh god, Ed, this is so fucking hot right now." She was breathless. "Baby."

Fingers guiding it into me, the slightly uncomfortable pressure of a strange angle, and then—this. It slipped inside and I arched into it, opening myself for her.

She moaned. "Ohhh fuck. I need another hand. I need to get off while I get you off."

"No—no." I gathered my brain cells, or the ones that weren't preoccupied with the length of that dong and how it grazed across my nerve endings. "No. Don't touch yourself. Get me off. Then I'll fuck you with the strap-on. Deal?"

"Fuck yes. Baby, you're so fucking hard right now. Deeper? Too deep?"

"Deeper. All the way. Oh god."

Some mental sleight of hand overtook me. I shut my eyes again and thrust forward, as if seeking her mouth, and in my head I had the kind of penis other men had. In my mind she fucked my pussy and I fucked her mouth and absolutely everything about that was right.

Then I felt her lips on me, small movements on my small cock, and a circuit connected between my cock and my pussy, lighting up everything in my body.

I moaned, way too loudly, but I couldn't stop and I couldn't care. My hips jolted, and she pressed the dildo deeper, holding it hard against me, its shifting presence inescapable while she licked and sucked and fucked my cock.

The orgasm hit like a freight train going a hundred miles an hour, drilling into my body, rolling over my skin. I thrashed and bucked, but Alisha held me to her mouth, tongue never stopping its teasing little licks until I quit shaking.

"Oh my god," I whispered. "Holy shit." I needed the dildo gone now. Never do dildos annoy me as much as when I've just come. That's when they feel intrusive.

I gently released her fingers and pulled it out, setting it on my nightstand to clean later before flopping beside her. "I think you fucked me senseless."

She laughed and curled against my side, hooking a leg around both of mine. I could feel her heat, her wetness, against my thigh. "Are you humping my leg right now?"

"I have needs, boyfriend."

I pretended to sigh. "You should have thought about that before you did . . . whatever the hell you just did that made me come so hard I couldn't hear for a minute."

"So you meant *literally senseless.*" She giggled. "I'm so powerful. I'm like some kind of sex goddess right now, aren't I?"

"You really are." I captured her lips, sucking in the lower one, nipping lightly with my teeth. "Thank you."

"You're so welcome. That was hot." A few more thrusts against me. "Hint, hint."

"Baby, I'm *tired*," I teased, pretending to go to sleep.

"Hey, if you can't be bothered, I'll get myself off."

I groaned. "That would be fucking incredible. Let's put that on a list or something. But right now—" I reached into the bedside table, where I kept the harness for ease of use. "Let's do this."

"Fuck yes. Will you keep your shirt on? Like you can't even wait to ravish me, you're so hot for it?"

"You say that like it's not true." I ran my hands up her legs, under her skirt. "Keep this on, too. This is a nasty dirty fuck and we're afraid of being caught, right?"

"Yeah." Her lips curled, one hand pulling my neck down. "Yeah. You're some kind of son of a noble family and I'm a serving girl, but we can't deny our feelings for each other."

"I can't deny my feelings for your body."

The usual awkward pause to put on the harness, and seat the strap-on, and make sure everything was secure, didn't happen. I did all those things, but we kept spinning out our story about the nobleman and the serving girl, so it never got awkward. It never felt like waiting, or prep, or anything other than play.

"But what if someone finds us?" Alisha whispered, eyes boring into mine.

I hit the lamp off and climbed on top of her. "They won't. No one will see us. No one will know." One of my hands slid along her thigh, pressing it open. "Relax for me, darling. I don't want to hurt you."

"You never hurt me."

My other hand adjusted the angle of the dick. I used my fingers to guide it past her lips, and she gasped.

"Oh, Horatio! You feel so big!"

I tried to bite back the laugh, but it was too much. "Horatio!"

"Don't call me Horatio, my love! You know I find it strange when you call me by your name when Little Horatio is inside me!"

I choked. "Little Horatio, oh my god."

"Deeper, Horatio! I want to feel your man-meat all the way to my tonsils!"

I collapsed on top of her, burying my laughter in her shoulder. "I'm sorry! I'm sorry, but oh my god, *man-meat*?"

"Your thick, juicy sausage! Your torch! Your baton! Your magic wand!" Her legs wrapped around me. "Oh, fuck me with your wand, Horatio! Fuck me so hard I can feel it all day while I scrub the floors and make the beds and service your father on my knees—"

"Oh my god, Alisha!"

She threw her head back, laughter almost echoing off the walls, heels rhythmically pulling me in deeper.

"You naughty, naughty girl." I let my weight come down more heavily. She moaned. "Naughty girls should be spanked, and forced to do all their chores in only their underthings. Would you like that, my naughty lass? Would you like it if everyone could see how depraved you are?"

"Yes, yes, oh yes, please—" Her pretend moans blurred into real ones as I fucked her, and I was glad I'd come already so I could focus on keeping the angle right, so I could enjoy the way she arched up, breasts standing out beneath her shirt. "Oh please, Horatio—"

Just for that I went in deep and held still.

"Horatio, *please*—"

"Touch yourself. I want to see you impaled on my dick, you wench, thrashing like a hooked fish."

The light was low, but I could see the gleam in her eyes when she pulled her skirt higher and pressed two fingers into her mouth. "Anything for you, my love." She began to rub herself.

I imagined I could feel her muscles contracting around me, that I could feel the heat of her on my cock. I gave her little jolts, never withdrawing far enough to lose control of the strap-on, and she moaned, voice going low.

"Oh god— Fuck— Yes—"

Suddenly I heard the unmistakable sound of footsteps on the stairs. At least two pairs.

Alisha grinned.

"Baby, harder, *harder*! Deeper, fuck me deeper, fuck me so hard I can't walk—"

I leaned all the way over her, almost laughing, caught up in this moment of ridiculous exhibitionism, kissing her like neither of us could breathe unless we stole breath from the other.

Alisha moaned, loudly, into my mouth, and I could feel her fingers frantically frigging her clit, brushing past my cock where we pressed together. She came with a dramatic cry, and I had to laugh again, muffling myself in the smooth skin of her neck.

The footsteps had paused, and after a few beats of silence resumed, with only one audible whisper that we could hear: "Holy *shit*."

We giggled like children, trying to stay quiet, wrapped up in each other. Impenetrable. Everything else disappeared and there was only Alisha and I.

And Little Horatio.

CHAPTER 18

Tom was released on bail late Monday afternoon, which I heard about via text message from Zane.

I was happy for him. Mostly. Only a small voice in the back of my head was worried that he might in fact be a murderer and now he was on the streets again, pissed off and itching to take it out on someone.

It wasn't Tom. I was nearly certain that it wasn't Tom. Too much didn't make sense. Someone would have to be incredibly dumb to hunt for victims where he worked, at the kind of place where people have been going for years, where they have "their" barstool, or "their" corner of the dance floor. But would the cops have arrested him if they had *no* evidence? Seriously? Maybe if he was black and young and poor, but Tom was a big hulking white guy. Statistically that made him less likely to be unjustly imprisoned.

Then again, he was a hulking white *gay* guy, which made him statistically more of a target than he would have been otherwise.

Plus, even if he might have killed those other people, Tom had loved Honey. She'd always pretended she was going to steal him away from Carlos, and he'd always pretended she might have a chance. She wasn't an acquaintance. She was a friend. It made no sense.

Togg posted another totally unemotional fact piece about Tom being released. The commenter tide was beginning to turn. The crew that had rallied around him last week was smaller and quieter now, slowly being drowned out by a larger mob of voices demanding someone pay for these crimes. That Tom might be innocent (that the entire system ostensibly hinged on "innocent until proven guilty") seemed to have slipped their minds.

Convenient justice, even if it was false, seemed like a much better seller than an honest investigation into events. These were people who'd barely noticed when Honey died except to bitch about gender politics; now they were talking about marches and vigils and protests if the court didn't convict the killer.

It made me feel sick.

I took a call a little later from Josh down at the drop-in center, reminding me that their open house was Thursday.

"You'll be there, right? I don't mean to cover it for the paper—unless you want to—but we'd love your support."

"I'll definitely be there. And I'll write it up if I think there's a chance my editor will publish it."

"Thanks, man. Appreciated." He sounded beat.

"You getting any sleep these days?"

"Hell no. I'm running on fumes. But after the open house we'll shut down for final preparations until we open our doors next week, and Keith's made me promise we'll actually go home for at least part of that time, so I'll sleep then."

"Is, uh, sleep what he's talking about?"

Josh laughed. "I think he'll probably enforce some kind of sleep-before-sex rule, I'm not even kidding. I'll see you Thursday, Ed."

"See you then. Thanks for the call."

"Sure thing. Only forty-three left now." He disconnected on his own chuckle, but I had the impression he was serious.

Forty-three phone calls. Plus however many people he'd called before me. I was exhausted just thinking about it.

I checked Togg's site again, but there was no new information and an outbreak of ugly comments had hit since I'd last visited. I shut it down and promised myself I'd knit when I got home, even if it reminded me of Honey and made me cry. It was something to do with my hands, something better than endless web searches and filling more pages in my notebook with disjointed facts and theories.

Alisha wore a red ankle-length dress to the QYP open house, with long sleeves and a high neckline. I staggered when I saw her.

"Dios mio," I said, exaggerating my reaction in the hopes she wouldn't notice how totally bowled over I was.

She twirled. "You like?"

"Should you have a coat or something? An umbrella?"

"Darling, look at this dress. As if I'd screw up the lines of it for anything short of snow. Plus it's not that cold out."

A summer storm had moved in early Thursday morning and even toward dusk showed no sign of letting up. In the space between her building and my car up the street, both of us got alarmingly wet. Rain dripped off my ears and her hair was darkened with water.

"Oh my god, I'm going to be obscene!" she called, laughing, and grabbed me for a kiss before I opened the door. "You look handsome as hell, you know!"

"Thank you, my lady." I bowed.

Then I opened the doors so we could get inside. Fat drops pounded on the roof of the car and my headlights cut indistinct columns into the sheeting rain as we headed downtown toward the waterfront. Alisha held her sleeves up to the heater vents, trying in vain to dry them out before we got to QYP.

"This is so incredible. God, I love weather like this, don't you? It's so exhilarating."

"I guess I never thought about it like that." I reached for one of her hands. "So if we were on an adventure right now, what would we be doing?"

"Walking! We'd be dodging between buildings, ducking under awnings, searching for a little hole in the wall where we could find a cup of coffee, or maybe a bowl of soup. Maybe you'd press me into a doorway and kiss me until both of us were breathless."

"Sounds wonderful. Where would we be?"

"Anywhere. Maybe we'd be in Damascus or Tokyo. Or maybe we'd be in Queensland."

"Is that Australia? I've always wanted to go to Australia."

"We should go! That would be so much fun. Baby, there's no hope for this dress. I hope it doesn't offend you that we're arriving at this do and my dress is plastered to me like I entered a white T-shirt contest and forgot my T-shirt."

"Put a pin in that."

She hit me. Both of us laughed.

The warehouse looked bigger than it had when I last saw it, even though it had furniture now, and a percentage of La Vista was packed in under the rafters. They'd painted the top third of the walls gray, and gone with the vibrant colors I'd seen before for the lower two-thirds, which somehow both made the room feel less cavernous and gave the impression of expanded space, like it didn't end at the ceiling.

Conversational nooks, bookcases, tables, chairs, groupings of clean-lined Ikea furniture everywhere, suggesting possible uses for each area.

"Oh my god, I want this kitchen," Alisha said as we slowly made our way through the crowd. "Ed, look at it."

Right off the showroom floor, an industrial design, including a long island with sturdy-looking stools lined up at it, where people were sitting, nursing glasses of . . . soda? I didn't think anyone would put wine in those glasses.

I glanced around, but no one appeared to be drinking booze at all. "I think this might be a dry event."

"I assume the center will be dry. I think I like the idea they're not even offering it tonight. Plus, there are definitely actual queer youth here right now."

"True." Not exactly droves of them, but some of the folks milling around were teenagers. "Cameron's got a movie tonight, and Zane said she'd be late, but there are a lot of people here I don't recognize."

"You thought it'd be Club Fred's, but with better clothes?"

"I kind of did. Oh, there's Jaq and her girlfriend."

"Hannah."

"Right, Hannah. I always forget her name."

"I know, babe. There's this awkward thing you do when you remember you don't know her name and hesitate while you're talking to her."

"Hey!"

She grinned unrepentantly. "What? I'm helping!"

We went over to talk to Jaq (and Hannah), who were standing with a few kids Jaq introduced as members of the Gay-Straight Alliance.

"I didn't even know that club was still going," Alisha said. "I was one of the founding members."

"You're like the third person who's said that tonight," the white boy (whose name I'd already forgotten) said. "I kind of can't believe so many people are still in La Vista. I can't wait to get out."

"I went to college and came back," I said.

Alisha waved a hand. "I just slacked off and worked a lot of stupid jobs."

The black girl (whose name I'd also forgotten) said, "I'm leaving in the fall. Just to San Francisco, but at least it's a little bit of distance."

"You keep saying 'in the fall' like that's the future," the boy teased, elbowing her. "Isn't orientation like next week?"

"Don't rush LaTasha," Jaq told him. "Oh, that reminds me. Ed, LaTasha remembers Steven Costello."

My pulse sped up.

"Not really." LaTasha turned to me. "You're a journalist?"

"I work at the *Times-Record*." Which technically made me a journalist, even if my beat was blind cats at the senior center.

"Cool. I didn't know Steven Costello. I had PE with him, because he failed it when he was a frosh, so he was stuck in it senior year."

"Do you remember anything about him?"

She shook her head. "Sorry. I'm not a good witness. I know he was always super quiet, and kept his head down. And that Coach Pinedo used to mess with him for being the oldest kid in the class, but always a little meanly."

"Pinedo's a dick," the other kid said.

"I know. It's probably why I remember Steven Costello at all, because Pinedo made it his mission to bully him. Sorry I don't know more."

"No problem. Thanks for talking to me."

"Do you like being a journalist?"

"Uh. It has its ups and downs, I guess."

Jaq sent me a look that said I wasn't fooling her. "Anyway, where's Merin? I want to see this suit."

Hannah smiled. "You just want to scope the competition. I'm sure Merin doesn't look as dashing as you do, Jaq."

"I'd argue that," LaTasha said. "No offense, Ms. C."

"None taken. Oh damn. Carlos and Tom are here."

In the moments after she said it, I noticed the traffic patterns in the room subtly shifting. They made the kind of pair you visually had to stop yourself from staring at, between Carlos's low stature and Tom's height. But tonight it seemed like everyone was determined to pretend the couple was invisible; backs turned and voices hushed as they passed.

"Jesus," Hannah murmured, her voice even lower.

Jaq strode forward, unstoppably, and embraced both of them. Jaq really did look good in a suit. If I had been born a lesbian, I'd want to wear clothes like Jaq did, all pinstripes and straight lines. She led them back to our little group and I felt immediately bad for suspecting Tom for a second; he had dark rings around bloodshot eyes and didn't look anything like a guy who blithely beat people to death.

"How're you guys holding up?" Hannah asked, taking her turn with hugs.

"As you'd expect." Carlos's gaze never stopped moving around the crowd, as if he was searching for attackers from all quarters. "Some people don't know the meaning of the word 'loyalty.'"

"They're afraid," Tom murmured. "You can't blame them."

"Like hell I can't. We're all afraid, and none of them spent the weekend in jail."

Tom's jaw tightened. "Can we not talk about jail? I'd appreciate it."

"Carlos! Tom!" Josh's voice didn't exactly boom, but he clearly intended it to carry. People made room for him to walk. "I'm so glad you could make it tonight." He shook hands with both of them before turning to the rest of us. "I'm glad you're all here as well, and LaTasha, I'm on strict orders not to tell you that Merin is in dry storage rearranging canned vegetables right now."

"I knew it. All that 'Oh no, I'm not nervous, like I care about the open house' was a front. I'm going to—"

"Knock twice, wait, then knock three more times on the main door. That's our signal."

"Got it. Thanks, Josh."

"Anything to coax my assistant out from dry storage. So good to see you guys. Ed, anything you need from us for your article?"

That would be the article I hadn't pitched to Potter. Damn. "No, but I'll let you know if I think of something."

"Great." Josh lifted his head, already moving on. "And Tom, if anyone gives you shit, we'll take care of it."

Tom swallowed, eyes immediately dropping. "Thank you," he mumbled gruffly.

"Keep the faith, brother." Josh squeezed his shoulder. "Keith's working the other side of the room, but either one of us will be around if anyone needs . . . anything."

It was a little hard to imagine Keith, who looked like he was about seventeen, playing bouncer and kicking people out of the open house, but Tom shuffled his feet and thanked Josh again, so I was grateful he'd made the offer.

"Dick-bags, all of them," Jaq muttered.

"Ms. C, it's not nice to call people dick-bags."

"You are so right, Sammy," Hannah said. "These people are all disloyal pricks reeking of fermented smegma."

Sammy choked on his soda. Hannah patted his back amiably and smiled at the rest of us as if nothing were up.

"I love you," Alisha said to her. "Like so, so much right now."

"Back off my girlfriend."

"Sorry, Jaq, but it's true. 'Fermented smegma'!"

"You have a way with words, Hannah. Maybe I can get you a job at the *Times-Record*. How good would you be at writing human-interest pieces about blind cats?"

Hannah pretended to think about it. "How much can I curse?"

"You can't."

"Oh well. Sorry, sugar, guess I'll have to keep up with the lawyering instead."

"Our loss," I said.

"You're damn right it is."

"Thank you," Tom said softly. "This is the least messed up I've felt in days."

Obviously I wasn't an expert, but that didn't seem like a very serial killer thing to say.

Before anyone could respond, Zane was dive-bombing the group, and the music was getting lower, and our attention was being hailed by a young man at the far end of the room.

"The kid looks good," Hannah said.

"Thanks for coming to the open house. Now shut the hell up, Josh wants to say a bunch of inspiring bullshit."

Merin. I'd recognize the voice—and the style—anywhere, even after only one meeting.

And yeah, Merin definitely gave Jaq a run for her money. I didn't know who'd gotten that suit, but it was perfect: tailored in all the right places to emphasize flatter planes and fewer curves.

It was only the beginning of the night, but watching Merin stand up there beside the two young queer men who'd started QYP made me feel a little more hopeful than I'd felt before. And I missed Honey more acutely.

CHAPTER 19

"I want to talk a little bit about the nature of mercy," Josh said. He'd given an elevator pitch about how QYP began, and introduced Keith in entirely ordinary tones that nevertheless made him blush. But now he stepped away, slightly off-center, and everyone in the room shifted to keep him in sight.

"Mercy isn't just about how we feel when we see people who are less fortunate than we are, people with less money, less food, fewer clothes. People who may not have a home as comfortable or safe as our home. You can see those people and feel compassionate without truly feeling merciful. Mercy, in its purest state, is about how we treat people over whom we have power."

Josh paused, eyes sweeping the room.

"Children are the most powerless people on earth. Show me any marginalized group, any intersection of class and ethnicity and gender and ability, and I will point to their children as the least powerful among them. There is a popular portrayal of queer adults as people with money and security who can afford to spend their time lobbying their interest groups and redecorating their urban flats or suburban single-family homes, quite possibly adopting puppies and kittens, driving them around in specially appointed Subarus."

A few people laughed, but Josh didn't even smile.

"Approximately forty percent of homeless youth identify as LGBT. Forty percent. We make up somewhere between one or three or eight percent of the population, and our children make up *almost half* of homeless youth. We are failing them. We are failing the next generation of queer adults when we ignore the children on the street who are meant to become them. The kid couch-surfing because their parents don't like the clothes they wear isn't looking at a Subaru and a nice house in the suburbs. The kid turning tricks because the only person who takes care of them is their pimp isn't going to be shopping for a trendy Scandinavian dining room table five years from now. The kids huddled in their bedrooms, desperately trying to be anything but gay, living in fear one day to the next that their parents will kick them out—we are failing them."

He half turned away and people shuffled their feet uncomfortably. Some cleared their throats. When Josh turned back he looked a little less grim, but no one seemed certain what he'd say next.

"The early feedback on this speech was that it was too much of a downer, that we don't want to set the tone for QYP with such a depressing theme. But the truth is that these stories keep me up at night. And if they don't keep you up at night too, then you're not paying close enough attention. I don't say that to guilt-trip anyone, or to bring the mood down. We'll get back to partying in a minute here. But I can't keep walking through the world thinking giving a couple of bucks to a beggar on the corner is doing my part. Or signing yet another online petition. Or sitting in another well-lit living room, sipping a glass of wine, talking about if only I had the money to help people, or the influence to make a difference. You've all heard that line, 'Be the change you wish to see in the world'?"

People nodded. Someone called, "Gandhi, right?"

"That's what we all think, but Gandhi didn't say that. He said, 'As a man changes his own nature, so does the attitude of the world change toward him.' He also said, 'We need not wait to see what others do,' which is where a lot of us get tripped up. We think to ourselves that if a problem was so big, so bad, someone would be taking care of it. *Someone* would be helping. But there are a whole lot of problems in the world, and a whole lot of good people waiting to see if someone else will address them.

"I want to change my nature. I want to stop waiting for someone else to take action. I want to build a place where taking action, even small action, is the norm. The world is already changing, but we're gonna keep giving it little nudges, right from this room." Now Josh smiled, taking a whole beat to look around. "It takes a hell of a lot of work to change your nature, just like it takes a hell of a lot of work to change the world." He raised his hands, palms open and up. "QYP is a place for hard work and change, and we deeply believe that as we do that work, the world will change as well. Enjoy the open house, feel free to ask questions, give suggestions, and I hope none of you will leave without signing up for our volunteer network. Thank you, everyone, for coming out in the rain tonight."

Applause hit in a wave, and when Josh went over to Keith and kissed him, another wave (including catcalls) crashed through the room. Keith shoved him away, blushing bright, but both of them turned to work the crowd, striking off in different directions.

"I really like those young men." Carlos spun on the stool Tom had brought him so he could see Josh speak.

Zane nodded. "And look at them. You'd think they'd been running this place for years."

Keith made his way over, snagged young Sammy for something, and our group broke up, merging into others. We hung out with Jaq and Hannah awhile longer, until two men I didn't know walked over with an infant.

"There's my baby!" Jaq called. "Come here, James, come see your Aunt Jaq."

"I wish we had one of those little chain of custody sheets for him," one of the guys said.

"Ha. Where's Dred?"

The guy gestured vaguely. "Around. Talking to Philpott, the last time I saw her." He turned to me as Jaq wandered off with the kid. "I'm Obie. I think I remember you from high school."

I doubted it. Unless he was remembering me as a girl, which made me a little insecure. "I'm Ed. Wait, Obie? Do you make ties?"

"Yes! Yes, I do!"

The guy with him groaned. "Another fan, god help me."

"And this is Emerson." Obie leaned forward. "He's secretly a *huge* fan of my work."

"Oh, shut up. Nice to meet you." Emerson shook my hand, then Alisha's.

"Wait, I never introduced you to Alisha before? Sorry. Introductions fail." Obie grinned at Alisha. "Hey, babe. How're those shoes working out for you?"

"They're perfect. They are so, so perfect. Obie painted me a globe on a pair of converse. They're so beautiful I'm afraid to wear them anywhere."

"You gotta wear them! They are meant to be worn, I promise." He turned back to me. "Do you have a tie? Sorry, I don't really remember everyone who orders from me."

"No, no. My friend Cameron was telling me I should, though."

"Oh man, Cam inspires me. I just found this reel-to-reel design, which I'm totally making for him." Rueful smile. "You know, after I'm done with the like two dozen other ties I'm making."

"Your public is very demanding," Emerson said. Was he the boyfriend? I couldn't tell by meeting them. The only real impression I got from Emerson was that he looked like he'd rather be anywhere but at a big party full of people.

"They are! Speaking of which, we should be tweeting right now. Hannah, want to tweet with me?"

"Obie, that's the best offer I've had all night. Let's do it."

They walked off arm in arm, and after a minute Emerson followed them.

"That was a really good speech." Alisha grabbed my hand. "Didn't you think?"

"Yeah. I wish I'd been recording it." The article was writing itself in my head as I stood there; if I didn't have a date, I'd probably be scribbling in a notebook. I squeezed her hand. "Should we mingle?"

"Definitely."

We stayed late and talked to everyone we knew, and met a lot of people we'd either only known of, or didn't know at all. Alisha introduced me to Donald Zhu, who was known to pretty much everyone by his first name as if he were Madonna. He was the closest thing to a La Vista queer celebrity, this old Chinese man you'd never guess was at the forefront of the White Night riots, busting open San Francisco City Hall and tangling with cops at Elephant Walk later that night. I'd seen him at Club Fred's many times—Fredi cleared a table for him—but he was always surrounded by this cadre of stocky admirers who looked like they were still waiting for retaliation for whatever he'd been up to in the seventies and eighties.

Meeting him was a little bit intense. He shook my hand and looked me dead in the eyes from where he sat in his wheelchair.

"I always like being on good terms with the press," he said, and I was pretty sure he was kind of joking with me, but I had no idea if I was supposed to laugh or take him seriously or what.

"What do you think about QYP?" I asked.

"I think it's a long time coming and it's going to save lives. Good to meet you, Ed."

"You too."

And dismissed.

Alisha giggled in my ear as we walked away. "So that was Donald."

"I don't even know what just happened."

"Was he everything you hoped he'd be?"

I thought about the sharpness in his eyes. "Yeah."

We saw Mildred as she was leaving with the baby, Obie, and Emerson, who apparently all lived in a house together. I didn't know if I wanted kids, but raising a kid in a house full of people seemed like a cool idea.

She gave me a tight hug and told me she was making a quilt for Honey, and that she'd sell it and donate the money to QYP when she was done. It was such a great idea I immediately wondered what I could make into a mini fundraiser. I wasn't sure my knitting skills were up for anything super ambitious, but then again, if it was for Honey and QYP, maybe I should figure it out.

Sometime before midnight, people began really clearing out. Alisha and I lingered long enough to say good-bye to Josh and Keith. It had been a damn long night, but Josh hadn't brought the mood down with his speech; he'd elevated expectations. He stood there in front of all those people and basically declared that they were planning to change the world.

Outside, the rain had broken, and here and there between the clouds we could see the dark night sky, strewn with stars. We walked as close to each other as we could, and I gave her my coat.

"I would have loved a place like that when I was a teenager," I said. "Where I could just exist, without Abuela trying to make me Mexican and Dad trying to make me Italian and Mom trying to make me so inoffensive I didn't threaten anyone by being different."

"I, on the other hand, would have loved a place like that to meet girls."

"Well. I wouldn't have ruled that out . . ."

Alisha took a deep breath and exhaled. "God, I love breathing sometimes. You ever think about it? Breathing's such a trip. The whole thing where you inhale oxygen and it gets absorbed into your blood stream? That freaked me out when I was a kid."

"Why?" I asked, trying not to smile.

"Hey, I'm serious! And I think it was because it made me feel so exposed. Like anything could get inside me at any time, you know? I wasn't this closed system, nice and safe, I was all kinds of open and it was scary."

"That's an interesting way to look at it."

"Yeah, and now—now it's the opposite of scary. Now it's this great metaphor for how I want to go through life. I *want* to be open and exposed and take things in. I want to absorb everything if I can. I want to try everything to see if I like it. I want to be brave."

"You are."

"I'm not. But I want to be. I really want to be."

We walked the rest of the way to my car in silence. I wasn't sure about Alisha, but I was taking deep breaths and thinking about how blood traveled an endless path through the body, constantly purifying itself, constantly energizing itself, never stopping.

She was right. The metaphors were pretty much infinite.

CHAPTER 20

No new murders. I checked Togg's site every five minutes Friday morning almost superstitiously, as if any gathering heavy with queers might draw out the killer, but no. The QYP open house hadn't triggered another murder.

I was relieved, obviously, but also a little sick. I expected someone to die. If not last night, then at Apocalypse WOW, Club Fred's next theme night in two weeks. Maybe Fredi would cancel it. I thought I would if I were her.

Not that it mattered. If Club Fred's never held another theme night, whoever this was would keep killing. You don't get over your desire to beat people to death because a local club changes their promotion schedule. In a very real, very fucking grim way, it was probably more convenient for the investigation if everything kept going the way it was. Right now we knew what triggered the murders, and eventually we'd know who was committing them.

I already had my warrior outfit all picked out for Apocalypse WOW. Not that I'm a huge *World of Warcraft* person or anything, but I'd found a warrior cosplay suit that looked awesome and seemed like it might have multiple uses. Sitting at my desk, wondering if Fredi would cancel the theme night, I started imagining some uses for it that Alisha might enjoy.

"Masiello!" Potter's voice boomed from the back. "You working or daydreaming? I sent you an email twenty minutes ago!"

"Sorry!" I called. I may have flushed.

Caspar snickered. "Busted, kid."

"Don't call me 'kid.'"

"Thinking about your boyfriend?"

"Girlfriend, and shut the fuck up."

He did a double take. "Girlfriend?"

I sighed.

Caspar kept on me the rest of the morning, trying to work out if I was joking about having a girlfriend. I ignored him and took quickie notes on the assignments Potter had sent me before dodging out "to interview some people."

Or to sit in my car in a slight drizzle and record a voice message for Alisha about how now that I passed as a dude all the time, everyone thought I was gay, which was weird because when people thought I was a woman, they also thought I was gay, so basically I was gay for all seasons. I figured she'd listen on her break and laugh.

Later, in the middle of a conversation with an administrator at the rec center about the upcoming flag football season, my phone buzzed against my leg. I figured it was Alisha, giggling into my voice mail, but I had to wait until I was back at the car before listening.

It was Alisha. And she *was* giggling.

"I quit my job. Oh my god. Oh my god, Ed, I quit my job. I'm never going back there. I walked out, and I'm done, and I'm never going back there ever again." Giggle. "I'm high right now. Like completely high. I don't even know what to do with myself. I'm just going to wander around town until you get off work. Oh my god, I can't even believe I did that. I'm so *happy* right now. I can't wait for you to get off work. Love you, bye."

I played it again, smiling at her tone, at her laughter. She quit her job. How was she going to pay rent? Or buy food? Did she have a plan? Who'd quit a decent job that paid well enough to live on?

Alisha. That's who.

There was a second message after the first.

"It's just, I've been thinking all day about what Josh said, and this isn't what I want to do with my life, sitting around, talking to jerks on the phone, enabling other people's canned adventures when I want to be having my own. I want to change, and grow, and be a different person a few years from now, you know? I want to look back and see that I've—that I didn't live my life wondering when it would start. It's starting. Today. Oh my god."

All I wanted to do was meet up with her somewhere and celebrate with her, though the idea of quitting my job scared the hell out of me. The clock informed me I had another four hours of work left and I couldn't think of a single responsible way out of it.

They were a very long four hours.

I picked up a vegan pizza and brought it back to her apartment. She buzzed me up and was waiting at the top of the stairs to maul me.

"I am so fucking happy right now, Ed, I can't deal. Oh, pizza, you're amazing, this is *exactly* what I need right now."

Even so, the pizza ended up tossed on the table while Alisha tumbled me onto the sofa.

"You smell like freedom." I kissed her.

"I am freedommm!" Her hands framed my face. "I didn't know it would feel like this. I had no idea."

I wondered if that feeling would change when she had to pay her bills, but figured it wasn't really prudent to point out.

She exhaled, as if she hadn't breathed in months. "I'm so excited for the rest of my life right now, in a way I've never felt before. Like, I have no idea what I'm going to do next week, or next month, but right now I'm so excited."

"Babe, that's great. I'm so happy for you." *And terrified for you, but happy for you too.*

"Come away with me this weekend."

I blinked.

"I'm serious. Just for the weekend. We'll leave early tomorrow and stay the night."

"Um, I—"

"Ed, come on." She hummed a little melody.

"Are you going to serenade me in the style of Norah Jones? Because your answer may influence my decision."

"Please come with me. Overnight, that's all."

I felt like I should sit down and make a list of the things I'd planned to do over the weekend, and how much gas would cost, and what kind of things we'd have to pack. "Where? Where are we going? It's supposed to keep storming through Sunday."

Alisha's smile did this very suspicious twist. "I'm not telling you until you say you'll come with me. I already made the reservation, and I'm going with or without you."

"But—"

She pressed two fingers to my lips. "Come on an adventure with me, Ed. Please."

I mean, a beautiful woman begs you to go on an adventure with her... you'd be a fool to say no, right?

"If it's somewhere posh, I'm not sure we should be spending—"

"I've already taken care of it. We'll just need to stop for food."

That should have been a warning sign, but in the moment I didn't think about it. I kissed her, tugging her in tight against me.

"Let's go on an adventure. Also, remind me to tell you about my warrior costume later."

"You have a warrior costume?"

"Did you ever play *WOW*?"

She collapsed into my shoulder, laughing. "Oh my god, you nerd."

"I'm not a nerd! Nerd would be playing D&D."

Alisha treated me to a raised eyebrow and an unfairly knowing expression. "And you never played D&D?"

"I—I didn't play it enough to be considered a D&D *nerd*!"

"I was more of an *Age of Empires* kid than a *WOW* kid," she said.

"Nerd swoon." I kissed her again. "We should eat pizza. And you should tell me what our adventure is."

"Um. Maybe. You're committed now, right? Even if it's... not exactly what you pictured? Because the reservations are made and we're not backing out."

"I haven't pictured anything! I have literally no clue what you would pick for an overnight adventure to celebrate quitting your job."

"Good. I like being a woman of mystery." She rolled off me, and I groaned. "Pizza, boyfriend."

"Yeah." And she called me that a lot, so much that I thought of myself as her boyfriend, but it still made me shiver. "So," I said casually as I got us paper towels. "If you were planning an adventure in a storm, where would you go?"

"Somewhere tropical. I mean, I don't actually want to be caught in a hurricane, but the intensity of a tropical storm totally intrigues me."

I rolled my eyes. "What if you were going away for only a short period of time? Like overnight?"

"It's on a need-to-know basis."

"But don't I need to know?"

"I haven't decided yet."

Since I knew any further badgering would only make her dig in more, I settled for pouting instead.

"Ha ha ha, your face right now."

"Shut up! I have a good pout!"

"You have a terrible pout."

We argued long enough about whether or not I credibly pouted for me to forget I was wheedling for information. Then she seduced me and I couldn't be held responsible for my inability to focus on anything after that.

CHAPTER 21

"It's raining," I said, for the third time, gesturing to the windshield. "Pouring rain. There's a wind advisory."

"I *know*."

"But—"

"If you don't want to come, you don't have to, but I'm definitely going, so." She stared straight out the windshield without looking over at me.

We'd never fought before. Not really. Maybe a passive-aggressive dig here or there, but never outright, and never an actual disagreement.

Alisha was driving us to my place to pick up my stuff. Which was why she'd finally had to tell me where we were going.

"But camping? In a storm?"

"My tent has a rainfly."

I tried to make my tone sound reasonable. "Well, yeah, but . . . rainfly's not really meant for a storm—"

"Listen, I'm doing this. And it's going to be fun. And if you can't have fun with it, you should stay home."

Ouch.

"I'm not— Alisha, I'm not trying to say it won't be fun. I'm just worried that we'll be miserable the whole time and then—" Okay, maybe I was trying to say it wouldn't be fun. Most of the time we spent together was warm and domestic and comfortable. This sounded like none of those things.

She nodded. "And it's a hike-in site. We'll be totally on our own. Won't even be able to get to the car."

I stared into the massive amounts of water being dumped from the sky and tried to imagine *hiking* in it.

"You don't have to come with me. I'll be fine on my own."

"I don't know how safe that is."

"I'm not asking for your opinion. And considering how safe it is around here lately, I guess it's probably not likely to be less safe in a deserted campground during a storm. I'm sure the murderers will stay home where it's dry."

I winced. "Give me a minute, okay? It sounds completely insane and I can't believe anyone would do it, but on the other hand, that's what makes it interesting. I need a minute to think."

During that minute, as we navigated the last few blocks toward my house, she took my hand. Nothing more. Just her fingers and mine intertwined.

"I'm in," I said. "Oh my god, we're mad. Who does this?"

"We do, babe. We do this. Okay, so here's how I packed."

I studied, but what it came down to was layers and layers and layers. Layers under my clothes, layers of long underwear and socks and an additional sweatshirt, all rolled into plastic bags at the bottom of my backpack. Then food rolled into plastic bags on top of that. Then my sleeping bag also rolled into a plastic bag and affixed to the top with ropes.

As we were getting ready to leave, JP and Troy came down the stairs, both of them with bedhead. They stopped on the landing to blink blearily at us.

"Whoa. Where're you guys going?"

"Camping," Alisha said.

"In the *rain*?"

"Yep." She raised her eyebrows playfully. "Doesn't that sound like a hell of an adventure?"

"Shit. Uh." Troy looked at JP. "Yeah."

"You guys are gonna be soaked. Bring wool. It dries faster than cotton." JP yawned. "Have fun."

"Thanks," I said. "See you."

"Yeah, bye."

When they started banging around in the kitchen, Alisha lowered her voice. "You think that's true? About wool?"

"Yeah. At least, I think I saw it on one of those survival shows. Why?"

She grinned. "Because I almost didn't bring my wool socks since they're so big, but I threw them in at the last minute. Ha."

I kissed her. "We are fucking *nuts* to do this."

"I know! Isn't it great?"

"Yeah. It's great."

It might be uncomfortable, and wet, and somewhat miserable later, but right now, it was pretty damn exciting. "Let's go. Wait, let me get my own wool socks first."

More layers of plastic bags to line the rest of my pack, then I zipped, made sure the sleeping bag was secure, and loaded the car.

I peered into the trunk. "This is the tent? It looks minuscule, even with bags around it."

"It's a two-person tent. I figured we'd cuddle for warmth." The dirty smile said we'd do a lot more than that.

"This is gonna be *great*," I told her. "Really great."

"We might need to be naked, you know, to get the full benefit of our body heat."

"Naughty girl."

She stepped up close against me. "Maybe you're a prince and I'm your servant girl and we're going on a pilgrimage."

"In that case, you're carrying everything and setting up camp, right?"

"Men! Lazy bastards."

We kissed, standing there in the small amount of shelter from the hatch of her car.

"I'm so excited you're coming with me," she murmured against my lips.

"Me too."

The drive wasn't bad. It was stormy, but there weren't a lot of cars on the road once we were past Marin, so that made it feel more like a fantasy adventure.

We played with the backstory for most of the drive, building off each other. I was a prince in a desert land, traveling to meet the princess I was promised to, who reigned in a land that saw rain for most of the year. The mages in charge of royal matches had thought that tying our two lands together would bring balance to the world, but I was in love with my servant, even though I'd never dared touch her, and neither of us had ever been out of the desert. We had been traveling for weeks already and were coming ever closer to the city where my princess awaited me, which meant if we were going to confess our devotion for one another, it would have to be soon...

"I kind of want to read this book now," I said, as we pulled into the visitor center.

"Me too. Like the prince and the serving girl have to end up together, but it can't be fucking *Aladdin*, right?"

"Maybe the princess is a lesbian. It could be like they get married but each of them have a very special serving girl."

"Or maybe you and the princess share me! I could get into that. So much hot, royal sex."

"Insatiable," I teased.

"I totally am."

We picked up our parking permit and map to the campground, which was a mile and a half hike-in. Not bad, right? We could walk a mile and a half, even in the rain. Even with our gear. At least it wasn't really that cold out.

My resolve lasted for probably the first twenty minutes. If that.

I tugged my hands higher into my sleeves. "I'm freezing. Are you freezing?"

"I know! My hands are numb! And it's August."

"It didn't feel this cold when we were standing at the car."

She laughed, the sound of it melting into the pounding rain. "This may go down in history as my worst idea ever!"

I shook out my arms, trying to resettle my backpack more comfortably, and she side-stepped out of the way.

"I'm walking here!"

"I don't think we can be any more wet than we already are!"

Alisha cringed and shook her head. "See, now you're testing the fates, and they get really annoyed."

"Is that your way of saying I jinxed us?"

"It's my way of saying I bet we get more wet than this!"

And we did. A mile and a half is a pretty comfortable hike in sunshine, if it's not too hot or too cold. In torrential rain every step is a slog, your soaking shoes weigh a ton, and your neck and back start aching because you're so desperate to hide under your hood that you're only looking at the trail six inches ahead of your feet.

I found myself mesmerized by the white noise of rain hitting leaves, and thought about Steven Costello again. By all accounts a quiet kid, bullied in high school, a loner in college as far as anyone knew. If he'd been out to his parents, they hadn't accepted him, judging by the fact that they couldn't even say "He was gay" to the people investigating his death. If he hadn't been out to his parents, he'd been living a double life, trying to balance being himself with being who they wanted him to be.

Or maybe I was reading too much into him. Except whenever I saw that picture on my phone, I related to him more. Obviously it wasn't as if he wouldn't have died if I'd been able to talk to him. But maybe he would have felt like there was a place for him in the world, that even if he still died, he'd have known that for a minute.

At least Cameron had tried. If anyone could offer a moment of solace to a quiet, sad boy, it was Cam. What had Steven Costello been thinking at the end? Had he fought back? Or had he taken a beating as his due?

I hoped he'd fought back.

"Wait. Ed, wait."

It took me a minute to get back from my thoughts and stop walking. Damn. I didn't want to be thinking about Costello, or murder, or any of that right now. I wanted to be here, with Alisha, on this plane where everything was an adventure.

"Look around, babe."

We were in a forested area, all redwoods reaching into the sky. I risked the rain and looked straight up.

The view was unreal. Some of the trees topped out inside the clouds, trunks and branches disappearing into white.

"Oh wow."

"I know."

We stood there staring up long enough for the rain to make its way down the front of my shirt, but it was worth it. The storm made for a glorious, wild symphony, wind rustling through the thick trees, drops falling everywhere around us, making slightly different tones when they landed on slightly different surfaces. No thoughts intruded into the moment, and I lost all awareness—even of Alisha, even of myself.

Nothing on earth existed but this: standing still in the center of the storm while branches creaked and water flowed in little rivulets between piles of old needles.

Alisha's hand found mine and we began to walk again, not speaking.

The worst moment of the first day was finally arriving at our campsite, exhausted, drenched, sore, and realizing we now somehow had to set up a tent during a rainstorm without it filling with water before we could get the rainfly over it.

"We need minions for this, princess," I said.

"We really do. Ideally ones who set up an hour ago, left a steaming hot meal, and then disappeared until we call for them again."

"That sounds so perfect."

For a long moment we both surveyed the slightly inclined sheet of mud that was serving as our campsite.

I toed the ground. "So I guess we'll probably set up on the grass, right? Kind of bumpy, but less chance of us falling into quicksand overnight."

She shuddered. "I read a book where that happened once. Sounds like a good idea."

"We should . . . strategize or something."

"Yeah."

Our strategy ended up being me trying to hold the rainfly out over the tarp and tent while she inserted the telescoping pole into the little sleeve and quickly tried to jam posts into the ground. It was so ridiculous—to say nothing of completely hopeless—that both of us were laughing by the time we managed to secure the rainfly.

Then one of the corner posts popped out of the mud and we almost collapsed from some combination of hilarity, hunger, and fatigue triggering a severe case of the stupids.

"Whose dumb idea was this?" Alisha gasped, holding herself up on my shoulder. "Oh my god. The tent's wet."

"Because it's *raining*, dear."

We giggled.

A heavy rock over the troublesome post helped, and the rainfly actually stretched a bit over the outsides of the door flaps so we could at least store our packs where they wouldn't get rained on, or take up space in the tent itself.

She started to mop the puddles on the floor of the tent with a towel. (Bringing a towel would have been a seriously good idea; why hadn't I thought of that?) "You know what would have been smart?"

"What?"

"If I hadn't folded the tarp under so much. Then our stuff would be on tarp instead of muddy grass."

"Live and learn. Next time we go camping in gale-force winds and unrelenting showers, we will totally do that."

"Okay. It's as dry as it's gonna get in here. Let's see if we can get the bags off our sleeping bags and get them into the tent without, you know—"

"Flooding it again?"

She hit my arm. "Be quiet, prince. Or no nookie for you later."

"Damn, you play rough."

"Just wait!"

It took a while to get both sleeping bags in, strip off our most-wet layers, and climb into the tent ourselves. It was a tough choice between trying to maintain the dryness of the tent and trying to maintain at least some of our body heat in damp—if not drenched—clothes. Once we'd carefully unrolled enough dry layers from plastic, neither of us wasted time pulling off the last of the wet clothes and pulling on thermals in the dry safety of our sleeping bags.

"Now we have a lot of wet clothes, a very small area of dry ground, two sleeping bags, and it's—" I checked my phone. "One p.m. What next, loyal servant?" I automatically began to check my email, until I realized I had no signal. "Wow. There is like no reception here. At all."

"Good. We don't need reception. Plus, what're you going to do if you have it? Google search how to stay dry when camping in the rain?"

I pretended to open a browser. "How... to... stay... dry..."

She giggled. "Stop. Meanie."

I slid the phone back into the plastic baggie I'd zipped it into and tucked it in the little mesh storage bag hanging above our heads. "Okay. No phones. No internet. No connection to the outside world."

"I know this is the part where I suggest sex, but seriously, I'm starving. What do we have for food?"

Most of my meals since becoming a vegan were less like "meals" and more like "a collection of snacks." We pooled our food over our sleeping bags. For a spontaneous overnight camping trip, we hadn't done too badly. I was a little worried that our gallon of water and two little bottles wasn't the best prep ever, but then again, we could probably rig a funnel on the rainfly and refill the gallon at any time if we ran out.

"I wish we could light a fire," she said, checking out my double-bagged black beans. "I know these are safe to eat, but wouldn't they be delicious heated up?"

My mouth watered. "Seriously. I mean, maybe if we found a grove under some trees back in the more foresty area we might find some dry wood. Maybe."

We stared at each other, contemplating pulling our wet, heavy clothes back on.

"Nah. This will work. Plus, we're not supposed to light fires outside the barbecue anyway."

"Mmm," I said. "Barbecue."

"Ha. I though you didn't eat things with faces!"

"You can barbecue veg. Though seriously, if someone showed up with burgers right now, I'd eat one."

"Me too. Oh my god. With bacon, and cheese, and—"

I clamped a hand over her mouth. "Stop talking."

She grinned, lips pressing against my palm, sending little sparks of arousal through my body.

"Sex, though. Later. But definitely sex."

That time her tongue traced a line on my skin, and I shuddered and took away my hand.

"You naughty little serving girl."

"Yes, master." She lowered her eyes demurely.

"Oh damn. Okay. We'll get back to that. Right now we're making tacos."

Black beans and corn and portioned-out salsa to make it a little less dry. I took one bite of mine, then scrapped the tortilla for a cabbage leaf, which was better.

"I'm going to choke to death." Alisha eyed my cabbage distrustfully and took another determined bite of her tortilla.

I offered the little bag of cabbage leaves I'd rinsed and rolled before leaving the house.

"No, no. I'm fine. I'm just fine." To prove it she made gagging noises, and we laughed.

"I wish we had avocado," I said.

"But think of the mess."

"True. Though it's not like we don't have enough water to wash our hands. Just unzip, stick them outside, shake them around a minute, and look, clean."

She demonstrated, her flopping hands large in such a small space. "True. I had this crazy idea last night that we'd, uh, dance naked in the rain."

I covered my mouth. "You did not."

"I know! It seemed so romantic and wild when I was lying in my warm bed, with my warm blankets, and running water, and dry clothes—"

"Please tell me we don't have to dance naked in the rain for you to feel good about our adventure."

"No. We really don't. Like, that's the whole point: *not* to make it dependent on some weird idea of what it'd be." She smiled. "I'm so glad you came with me, Ed. Thank you."

"I'm so glad you're completely nuts. I would have never thought to go camping during a storm."

"And it's fun, right? Admit it. You're having a little bit of fun."

"I'm freezing, and wet, and we're now basically stuck in the tent."

"And you're having fun."

I kissed her. "And I'm having so much fun, yeah."

We finished our meals and fooled around, each of us staying half inside our sleeping bags, still trying to get back from numb. It didn't matter that we didn't have sex; cuddling and tucking ourselves into each other until we shared all of our heat was perfect.

Plus, we had the rest of the day. And all night. And tomorrow. Really, that was sounding like a damn long time to be alone in a tent, but I pushed the thought aside and kissed the top of her head as she was lying on my chest.

I should have known we'd be pulling on our clothes and taking a hike. Wet, wet clothes.

"Isn't it beautiful out?" Alisha called from outside the tent.

I gave up on my layers and went with only a T-shirt under my jacket. Less stuff to pull off later, and it wasn't like it'd keep me warm or dry.

It actually was beautiful out. Misty and windswept and ravaged, like the surface had been scraped off the land and what lay underneath was by turns brighter and more raw.

"How far are we going?" I asked.

"Sunset is like seven thirty. We have a few hours."

"Right." Sure. A few hours to get even more wet.

Alisha pulled me in by my coat. "I'll warm you up later, master."

"Damn right you will."

We hiked all the way out to the ocean, which was a choppy field of gray beneath turbulent steel-colored skies.

She held my hand on an outcropping, watching the waves crash below. "I wish we didn't have to leave tomorrow; though I think it'll feel good to get back to the car."

"Can we drive home naked with the heat on full blast? Do you think we'd get arrested?"

"Let's find out."

Making out in a storm on a cliff overlooking the sea was diverting enough for me to forget about the wind and rain.

On the way back to camp I checked for my phone and realized I'd left it in the tent. Without even worrying about it.

"I don't have my phone."

"Me either. It's awesome."

"Is it? I mean, there's a chance we could have gotten a signal out here."

"Yeah, but to do what? Check email? Look online at something? But we're like . . . here. In the world. I think I'd give up my phone if I didn't feel like I needed it for safety reasons. Well. Maybe. Or maybe I'd just delete Facebook and Twitter and email and all those other things and try not to look at it so much."

"I like my phone. I like all that stuff. And my Kindle app."

She put her arm through mine. "I'd rather read on paper, but I think if you're going to be a globe-trotting traveler—and I am—probably reading on the phone is a way more efficient."

"More books in a smaller amount of space," I agreed.

"Do you really like all the apps and everything? I mean, like, it's not just habit or something?"

I thought about it while we walked. My shoes were squishy bricks, and my jacket was so waterlogged I could feel the cold weight of the rain as it made its way steadily from my shoulders south. Still, I was glad we'd taken the walk. And I didn't miss my phone. Though I'd be pretty happy to get back to it when we were safely in civilization. And dry. Being dry was going to be such a luxury.

"Yeah," I said finally. "I do like all that. I like feeling connected, and apps make me feel connected. I think it's possible to balance that feeling with this feeling." I squeezed her arm with mine. "To be connected online and in person at the same time."

"Fair enough. I think I prefer this one, but I can see how both are valuable." She sighed. "I really want us to go away together. Can I plan something? It doesn't have to be super long, just a week or two, but it's important to me."

"A week or two?" Could I even get a whole week off work? I had no idea how I'd ask Potter. In a year and a half I'd never taken a sick day. I wanted to be known for being attentive, reliable. Not taking a week off to go away with my girlfriend.

"Yeah. A week at least."

"I don't know. Maybe. I'd have to think about it."

"What is there to think about? I mean, you might as well ask, right?"

"I'll ask," I promised, even though I couldn't really picture myself doing it. Being a reporter—if you were serious, if you wanted real stories—meant being available. "Tell me where you want us to go."

"Oh, only everywhere. All over the world. I want to visit all the places with you."

"What, around the world in seven days?"

"It would take years, but I'm willing to put the time in. Are you?"

We kissed some more in a grove of fir trees and this time, when we stripped down back at the site, we did a little more than cuddle.

CHAPTER 22

Going away for the weekend made work more miserable than usual. By Wednesday I was killing time, doing way too many crosswords and half-assing my assignments.

I'd just checked my usual slew of news sites (see, that's "work") when Potter shouted for me to come to his office, which annoyed me more than made sense. It was how Potter communicated. He shouted; his staff came to him. But on this particular Wednesday, when I was already feeling put-upon just being there, even that made me want to go off. Who treated people like that? Shouting for them and waiting for them to appear? Damn it, I didn't want to be treated like a fucking servant!

The second he started in, I knew I was going to lose it.

"Look, Masiello, you have some chops, but this whole private-investigator bullshit you're pulling has to stop or be on your time." He tossed a few papers down in front of me. "Your productivity's in the toilet. Everything you've given me this week has been crap masquerading as articles. And I don't want you reading that piece of fucking trash 'truth is invisible' or whatever-the-hell thing on my dime, got that? It ain't research, it's a joke, and you can do it somewhere else."

My hands shook as I reached for the papers.

Tracking. They were tracking everything in neat little columns. Tracking what I did on the computer, hours spent on Togg's site, on the *Times-Record* site, in email. Significantly fewer hours spent in the word processing program where I usually wrote my assignments.

"You're *spying* on me?"

"We're spying on everyone, numb nuts! So we can catch promising young jackasses before they roll all the way off the tracks." He jabbed a finger toward me. "Your ideas aren't always shit, so I give you some leeway, but, kid, you gotta be doing the assignments I give you before you go haring off on these crazy wild-goose chases of yours."

"Wild-goose chases?" I shoved the chair back and stood. "Wild-goose chases like trying to find out who's killing my friends? Is *that* a wild-goose chase? Someone's killing queer people and no one gives a shit! And that's way the hell more important than fucking *bingo*, or what the community garden's harvesting right now!"

Potter took a deep breath and stood up, and shit, right, he was fucking way bigger than me. I didn't step back, but I was distantly grateful for the desk between us.

"You're absolutely right, Masiello. Some stories are more important than others. And when you're no longer a snot-nosed green-behind-the-ears kid, you may even get to write those stories. But at the moment I need someone who's gonna write the shit my grandma reads, and for now, that's *you*. You can do your job or I'll find someone else. Now get the hell out of my office!"

I wanted to fight with him—I opened my mouth to fight with him—but a hand grabbed the back of my shirt and tugged me out of the room.

Joe Rodriguez shoved me roughly to the side. "Boys, boys, let's not forget to be civil."

Potter, face even redder, growled, "Get lost, Rodriguez!"

"Masiello's blood sugar's down. I'll take him for an emergency Snickers run."

"Get him away from me before I fire him."

The words jolted me out of my rage. I couldn't get fired. Shit. I'd yelled at my boss. What the hell was I thinking right now?

"Come on, you."

I couldn't meet Caspar's eyes as I grabbed my bag, and followed Rodriguez out.

Apparently when he said *Snickers run*, he meant *bar*.

"What do you drink?" he asked me.

"Beer. Stella if they have it." I didn't know this place, but it was full of older men. What would they have on tap here? Bud Light?

"I'll be back. You try to resist the urge to yell at anyone else, okay?"

I rolled my eyes.

He brought back a plate of sliders and two beers.

The second I saw the sliders my mouth started watering. I mean, if my mom had made them I'd eat them, so what was the problem with me eating them now? I didn't have to be a vegan all the time. Right? "Oh my god, those look so good."

"I wasn't joking about your blood sugar, Ed. What the hell's going on with you lately? You're moody as fuck." He took one of the burgers for himself and pushed the plate across the table.

I almost hid behind testosterone, which definitely made for moodiness. But that wasn't the problem, and I'd feel like an idiot if I claimed it was. And there was a slight chance he hadn't worked out I was trans, which would mean explaining, and I definitely didn't have the energy for that.

"It's this case. The murders. I can't stop thinking about it." Except when Alisha and I were camping in a storm with no cell service. That had been the first break in weeks, and I felt a little guilty about it.

"Yeah."

That was it? I swallowed my first bite of meat in forever and said, "Wait, was that your pep talk?"

"This"—a hand-wave at the food and beer—"is my pep talk, smartass."

"It just feels like nobody is really trying to find this guy, whoever he is. Like people are going to keep dying and no one even notices because it's just drag kings and trans women and gay people. No one important." I took another huge bite and focused on chewing.

Joe didn't say anything until he'd devoured a slider and half his beer. Then he sat back, surveying me. "Look, kid, I get it. But you're on the outside of this one. I talk to Baker every day. It's a lot of work, putting four crime scenes next to each other, comparing the evidence, judging if the same force was used against each victim. They're trying to find all the inconsistencies and document all the similarities so that when this sonofabitch is found, and arrested, they can lock him up for good."

"So until then, what, we just keep dying?"

"People only move so fast. Let me tell you a story about a bright-eyed young reporter we'll call Roe Jodriguez."

Laughter surprised me, and I almost spit beer all over the table.

"Young Roe was a serious, hard-nosed reporter. This kid never saw a crime he didn't want to write about. He got in with some local cops—other young Turks like himself—and learned a little about how they investigated and how crimes actually got solved, which was a whole lot more talking on the phone and interviewing people who didn't see nothing than it looked like on the TV shows."

I couldn't resist. "They had TV when Roe started out?"

He raised his hand like he was gonna smack the back of my head. "Mind your manners. And hey, it doesn't get better than *Cagney & Lacey*, kid, so shut it."

I laughed.

"As I was saying, Roe wanted to be involved. He wanted to be on the inside of it, where things were happening. He was a journalist, but it wasn't enough to just talk to people after the fact, damn it, he wanted a seat at the table. Or at least he wanted to stand at the outskirts and watch." He took a pull off his beer. "You remember Paloma Santiago Ortiz?"

The name tickled the edges of my memory, but after a second I shook my head. "I know the name, but I don't know the story."

"This was '91. I was working your beat, the shit work, the crap handed down to me by everyone else at the paper. And it wasn't just one guy back then. You may not have noticed this, Masiello, but I'm not a blond, blue-eyed, all-American white boy."

"Me neither."

"And back then, well, it was understood that we token people of color were only there on sufferance, but any excuse would be welcome to get rid of us. So when guys who came in after I did shuffled their shit assignments my way, I wrote them. Maybe not with a smile, but I didn't want to rock the boat because I knew I'd be the first one they tossed overboard."

Shit. I'd yelled at Potter and I was pretty sure he wasn't going to fire me. It hadn't even occurred to me to be quiet because my brown skin might make me a target.

"This ain't a 'you got it so much easier than I did' story." Rodriguez leaned over. "I think all that's bullshit, and you got your own shit to deal with. But I want you to know where I'm coming from so you understand what I risked."

I nodded.

"I was busy enough, between my own work and other people's, so on my off hours I'd hang out with my cop buddies. Guys like Baker and Smith. We'd shoot the shit, they'd tell me about whatever they were working on, I'd bitch about my bosses, you know how it goes. So one day we're sitting around in Baker's garage—he was the only one of us who was married, so we spent a lot of time over there, and Marion, his wife, would give us shit about being lazy bums and keep making sandwiches for us." He cracked a smile. "One day I go into their kitchen and tell her she shouldn't let him treat her like a fuckin' maid, and you know what she said to me? She goes, 'Joe, do you really think I want the lot of you in here? As long as I make sure you got snacks and beer, I don't ever have to hear your horror stories or smell the stink of you.' Then she told me off for tracking dirt in her house and kicked my ass back out to the garage where I belonged. Man. She was a great lady. Died in a car accident, oh, maybe ten years later."

He shook his head and visibly brought himself back to the conversation.

"One day we're in Baker's garage and they're all depressed as hell so I ask what's up. And they tell me about little six-year-old Paloma Santiago Ortiz. They found her body in a trash dump off Horizon and Twenty-third, back when the east side was a hell of a lot more ghetto than it is now. Someone left a sofa that had been lit on fire, and a busted TV, and a little girl's body on the side of the road in front of an elementary school. Since it was just the east side, no one went to clear away the trash for days, which is when they found Paloma. Little tiny kid, beat to shit, broken arms, messed-up face, and the reason they knew it was her was because her mama always put ribbons in her hair and she was from the neighborhood, so when the police taped the whole scene off, but before they'd taken away the body, Paloma's big brother happened to be part of the crowd, only there to see what was going on. He saw the ribbons in her hair as Baker was laying his jacket down over her."

"Jesus," I whispered.

"Poor kid. How do you get over seeing your little sister like that? Anyway, by the time we're sitting there drinking and they're telling me all this, it had been two weeks, and not only did they have no fucking idea who did it, but I hadn't even heard of this little girl. The paper hadn't reported a single word about her." He gave me a rueful look. "Young Roe was a believer in the press, Ed. He believed a free press was almost an arm of government, that's how important it was to democracy. He believed that people had the right, and the obligation, to be informed. But how the fuck could they stay informed if no one was reporting a story like that?

"So I burst into my editor's office the next day and I demanded—*demanded*—to write up Paloma for the paper. I didn't see a downside. She deserved acknowledgment, damn it, and maybe someone had seen something. The cops had come up empty, but surely someone in town knew something, surely this monster, whoever he was, had told someone what he'd done. And if we published it, maybe that person would come forward with information."

"They didn't let you write it?"

"Oh, they did. A very, very sanitized version of it. The girl had been sexually assaulted, which just turns my fucking stomach, and beaten to death, and tied up somewhere. I wasn't allowed to say all that. I was allowed to say a body of a young Hispanic female had been found in east La Vista and anyone with information pertaining to the child's death was invited to share that information with LVPD."

"Hispanic?"

He shrugged. "Those were the times."

"Did anyone come forward?"

"Nah. Well, yeah, but no one credible. Some creepy fuckers who wanted to know more, some little old ladies who thought maybe they'd seen something, but nothing at all helpful. I asked if I could write a follow-up, you know, maybe try to get more energy going around the story, and of course they said no fucking way, we're not wasting column inches on a story that isn't going anywhere. And my cop buddies were getting the same thing from their side. No resources, no time, other crimes that might actually have a chance at being solved. So this little girl was just forgotten, tossed away, and no one knew anything except that she was walking home from school one day and never got there and a few hours later she was dead."

"That's fucking awful." I shuddered.

"Eat more food. You're skinny as shit."

I took another slider, even though the first was sitting like a lump in my gut. "So did they ever find out who killed her?"

"No. At least, the guys had their theories but they never proved any of them. We were obsessed, man. We had a whole bulletin board Marion made us turn toward the wall when we were done for the night. Pictures, notes, a map of her walk home from school and the likely places she might have been snatched. We worked that case every night for months, Ed. I couldn't sleep without dreaming about a little girl I'd never met. It got to the point where sometimes I'd be out in public, in a grocery store, maybe, or walking down the street, and I'd think I saw her out of the corner of my eye." He shook his head again, wiping his lips with a napkin. "It got in the way of my life. I didn't go out, didn't eat, was belligerent at work a few times, until a guy who'd been there a lot longer than me took me aside and told me how it is."

Huh. "So how is it?"

"You can't solve all the mysteries. No one can. If you sacrifice everything in order to focus only on this one case, Ed, you won't have anything left at the end of it. Look, good reporters get obsessed sometimes. It's a hazard of the job. But you gotta know when to pull back. You gotta be able to maintain some perspective or you lose yourself to that obsession, you know what I'm saying? We had Marion. She wasn't my wife, but she damn sure didn't let us get lost down the rabbit hole for too long before flicking the lights at us and either kicking us out or throwing some blankets down on the armchair and the sofa in their living room. You need other people in your life to tell you when you're in over your head, kid. And you're in over your head right now."

I set down the burger, half-eaten. "I hear you."

"Good. Now finish your beer so we can make an appearance at the office before everyone goes home."

"You sure we aren't gonna be fired for leaving in the middle of the day?"

"Hell no. Potter likes you. He's been pushing you for a while now, saying you're better than grunt work." This time he did cuff the back of my head. "If you're ready to really work, kid, long fucking hours, I'll start taking you along. Nights, weekends, forget fucking having a life, because the minute we have a lead, we jump on it."

I looked up. "I'm ready."

"Good. You keep your head down and finish all your assignments and you can get in on the real stories. How does that sound?"

"It sounds good. And thanks, Joe."

"You got it, kid."

We got back to work with just enough time for me to write an apology to Potter.

CHAPTER 23

Despite the fact that Fredi had canceled Apocalypse WOW, a lot of people either hadn't heard, or hadn't cared. The crowd was a mix of people who seemed oblivious and were going about their usual Friday night, and people who were hyperaware of what was going on and couldn't relax.

Tom was back behind the bar, but it was impossible to ignore the cold shoulder he was getting from the people who lined up five deep on Fredi's side to wait for a drink so they wouldn't have to talk to him.

"Fucking bastard *whores*," Carlos kept muttering.

"On the upside," Alisha said, "we're getting really fast service." She grinned at Tom, who returned a weak smile.

"Fredi always gives me her tips anyway. I bet knowing that would really piss all those people off."

Carlos cursed under his breath. "Fucking bastards."

"It's okay. It'll blow over."

Just then a goblin or something came up to order a round of drinks. When the goblin took off, the guy on the next stool over caught my eye.

"You look super familiar to me," he said. Cute, if you're into guys. Real young-looking face.

"Sorry, I don't think we've met." He was too young to have known me before, I thought, though faces like that are sometimes deceptive.

"Huh. Weird." He put out his hand. "Joey."

"Ed Masiello." Alisha was still talking to Carlos, so I skipped introductions.

"Oh shit. Ed Masiello. You work at the paper with my dad."

"Who's your dad?"

"Joe Rodriguez."

"Damn. Yeah, he bought me lunch the other day to keep me from getting fired. Good man, your dad."

"Yeah, he's all right. I knew I knew you from somewhere. I must've seen a picture or something. That's funny." A shadow shifted across his expression, and it definitely wasn't funny. Not that I blamed him; I wouldn't want to drink with my dad's coworkers. He shrugged. "So, uh, how are you liking the theme nights, or whatever?"

I glanced around. "They've been interesting. You?"

"Oh, I guess they're probably not really my thing. I prefer . . . simplicity. You know. Give me a beer and a hot guy and I'm good. But I guess I'm kind of old-fashioned that way."

"I'm not sure 'beer and a hot guy' is ever really going out of style." And if it did, I wasn't about to mourn it, but I'd known younger guys who'd longed for "the old days" before. They seemed to miss the fact that the rest of us had been left out in the cold back then, and that quite a few of them hadn't survived.

"Yeah, true. I guess it's more about who we let in."

I gestured to the costumed crowd. "Too many elves, right?"

He didn't look all that amused, but he offered a weak smile.

"Ed!"

I half turned back to Alisha, who blinked at Joey. "Oh, jeez, sorry. Didn't mean to interrupt."

"It's okay. This is Joey Rodriguez. His dad works at the paper. Joey, this is my girlfriend, Alisha."

"Hey, good to meet you." She reached out.

After a beat of Joey staring at her hand, he shook. "Yeah, you too. Maybe I'll see you guys around." He slid off the stool and melted into the crowd.

Alisha made a face at me. "Oops. Sorry I harshed your conversation."

"Yeah, that was a little weird. We were actually having a kind of interesting discussion about— I'm not sure. Community? Or maybe how it's changing?"

"Ohh. Gay community? Because I'm pretty sure he thinks you're straight now. Or at least bi."

It took a full minute for me to understand what she meant. "You mean— Because you— Huh."

"Yep. Good news: you pass. Bad news: now that dude thinks we're straight people. Just can't win, babe. Anyway, did you know Carlos and Tom were getting married?"

I turned back to the conversation at hand, and the next time a cosplaying *WOW* character approached (an elf?), we moved over to one of the tables where Jaq and Hannah were already sitting.

"I'm only saying there's no point in being here all night freaked out," Hannah was saying. "We might as well go home."

"I'm not worried about *us*. But for fuck's sake, people die after every theme night and where are we right now? A fucking theme night." Jaq smiled apologetically at us. "Sorry, I'm just—concerned."

"Me too," I said. "But I don't know what else Fredi could have done short of keeping the place closed."

"She tried that, but people convinced her not to. They said closing down would be 'letting the bad guys win,' like this is a fucking comic book."

"If we hid in our houses whenever we felt threatened, we'd never see daylight," Hannah mumbled. "Alisha, you want to dance? I can't deal with any more of this talk tonight."

"Yes, definitely." She kissed me. "Come dance in a little bit, right?"

"I will," I promised.

"I think she should have shut it down," Jaq said, voice low. "Just for tonight. It feels too much like taunting this asshole, like dangling all these people right in front of them, daring them to strike again."

I secretly agreed. "Do you think we're sitting here with the person doing this? Like right now?"

"I guess we'll find out tomorrow." She looked up at the guy approaching the table. "Oh good, Philpott, join us. Tell us interesting things about the world."

"The world?" Philpott took Hannah's seat and turned it so he had a line of sight on most of the room.

"Anything to keep me from looking around wondering who's next."

I didn't know Philpott well, but he was funny, and he did seem to have a lot of stories. Josh and Keith pulled up chairs as the night went on, and the conversation inevitably turned back to its original theme.

Josh shook his head, looking exasperated. "Short of implementing a mandatory buddy system, I don't know how we deal with this."

"Triads," Keith amended. "It would have to be triads so that the killer couldn't just overpower their buddy."

"Triads, good point. And we can't implement a mandatory triad system."

"So we sit here and hope for the best," Philpott agreed. "But is that good enough." He didn't say it like it was a question. He said it like all of us knew none of this was good enough.

Jaq shook her head. "Of course it's not, damn it. This is ridiculous."

"But to play devil's advocate, people are allowed to take risks," Keith said. "Every time you get in a car, you accept a risk. Every time you get on an airplane. Right now being at Club Fred's feels like a huge risk, but statistically, taking into account all of La Vista, it's still more dangerous to get in your car."

"I bet that changes if you only take into account attendance at theme nights," Jaq argued. "And car accidents, if you're talking about passive casualties, are random; this person, whomever they are, is specifically targeting *us*. Not straight people, not tourists, but queer people who come to this bar. And that—" She broke off. "It *irritates* me. I know that's weak, but that's how I feel. I'm so annoyed by this person. Aside from the tragedy and the grief, I'm just pissed off that they think they can get away with this."

Nods all around.

"And they can," I said. "At least so far, they *are* getting away with it."

"The cops aren't exactly stirring themselves on our behalf," Josh said.

Philpott held up a hand and tilted it back and forth. "From what I've read, it looks like this person fits the most average profile of a serial killer there is. So do I, and Ed, and Keith's a little young for it, but he'll fit that profile too, in a couple of years. So does Tom, as we've already seen."

I held up my hand. "Hey, keep me out of it. I'm trans *and* Latino. I'm nobody's average *anything*."

He smiled. "Okay, point. But to outside appearances, you could be. A lot of people in here could be. This is a person who doesn't bring a weapon, but finds one where they kill, so there's no connection. That also makes it harder to prove it's the same killer."

"Come on, man, it's gotta be the same person." Josh took a pull on his beer. "It has to be. Please don't tell me we have more than one person running around beating people to death."

"No, I agree. I'm positive it's the same person."

Alisha tapped my shoulder and leaned down to say, "I'll take my dance now, kind sir."

Hell. "Just give me a few more minutes. This is really interesting."

"Really? Okay, I'll be out there dancing all up on Zane, so if you want me to go home with you, you better finish up."

I kissed her. "You're definitely going home with me."

When I tuned back in to the conversation, Jaq and Philpott were talking about serial killer history while Josh made occasional dark interjections about how the two of them were looking more and more like suspects all the time.

I didn't mean to ignore my girlfriend all night. Neglectful boyfriends probably always said that, but it was true. It was just that after weeks of feeling like the only person who cared about Steven Costello, or Honey, or the other victims, I was sitting at a table with people who were paying attention. They'd all read Togg's posts. They'd read Rodriguez's article and follow-up about Honey, and the more recent article about Stephanie Hawkins.

It didn't matter that I didn't know all of them that well, or that we were all coming from different perspectives. In some sense we had a lot in common, and it made me feel less like I was making the whole thing up.

Alisha had tried to get my attention once or twice, but I was in the middle of a conversation, so I'd held her off. I didn't realize she'd gone home until Jaq poked me from across a table crowded with empties.

"Hannah gave Alisha a ride home, by the way. So don't worry when you realize she's not here."

"Alisha went home?"

"Oh damn," Josh murmured. Keith hit him.

I focused on Jaq. "Alisha went home?"

"Um. Yeah. I think she was trying to tell you that the last time she came to the table."

I'd told her to give me five more minutes. She *had* seemed a little put-out. "How . . . long ago was that? Do you know?"

"An hour or so," Jaq said, somewhat apologetically.

"Oh my god. I'm a dick."

"Happens to the best of us," Josh told me. "Though now that I'm looking at the time, we should take off soon too."

Keith patted his arm. "Let's stay a little longer. I'm still getting used to not having the opening shift at the diner on Saturday mornings."

"Ha." Jaq leaned forward. "I forgot you had that job. You done completely?"

"I'm reserve staff now to kind of keep a hand in—"

I gathered my stuff as they talked and excused myself with a wave. I'd been sitting at that table for almost four hours, and I hadn't even noticed time passing. I waved again to Rodriguez's son as I passed him chatting with a guy I didn't know, and got the hell out of there.

CHAPTER 24

Alisha let me in her apartment, but she was clearly not thrilled to see me.

"I'm so sorry. I completely lost track of time."

"I noticed. It's fine."

"Is it fine? It doesn't really sound fine, judging by your voice."

She flopped onto the sofa and stared at me for a long moment. "You said you'd dance with me."

"I know. I meant to. I got caught up talking with people."

"That's the part that's fine. You wanted to talk about serial killers, and I wanted to dance, so that was okay for a while. But if that's really what you wanted to do, I wish you'd told me so I didn't keep waiting for you."

"I didn't mean to. I totally planned to dance, I just— I don't know. I wasn't thinking."

"Because if I'd known it was going to be like that, I would have enjoyed dancing with everyone out there, and when I was done, I would have left. But I thought we were there together, so I kept waiting for you, and when I felt like leaving, I didn't. Still waiting for you."

I sat down next to her and tried to think of something I could say that wouldn't sound like a shoddy defense. "You're right. It just felt like finally people were talking about this stuff that I thought I was the only one even noticing."

She shook her head. "How can you think that? It's all anyone's talking about. People on the dance floor were talking about whether or not the cops are gonna catch this guy, you know? Since Tom got arrested it's practically the only thing anyone's discussing and it's important, yeah, but when it's the only thing we talk about I just feel like we're missing the point."

"What's the point?"

"Are we living our lives? Or are we just trying not to die? Because I don't want to spend my whole life trying not to die. I want to be doing things, going places." She paused, eyeing me. "What do *you* want, Ed?"

Shit. I sat back. "I want to go places too, but I can't turn off the world when it's unsettling. I'm part of it. It's part of me."

"Except, tonight? It was your whole life. There wasn't room for me or anything else. What's gonna happen when they catch this person? Will you get back all those hours and use them for other things, or will you just jump to the next big story you can't stop thinking about? Because once in a while is okay, but if you can't drag yourself away from work to dance with me, that's a problem for us."

"It was one time!" I could feel myself getting defensive and tried to make my voice even. "Jeez, Alisha, I got a little caught up one time and you're acting like it's some huge crime."

"You're constantly checking your phone for updates, and flipping through your notebooks, and talking theory. You do it all the time. Think about how often you have your phone in your hand, okay? Just think about it."

"So when we spend time together I'm supposed to forget that everything else in the world exists? Seriously? Because that sounds a little bit crazy."

"Fine. Then I'm crazy. But tonight we went out to a club and you sat in a chair. For hours. *That* sounds a little bit crazy to me."

That hadn't been how it was, damn it. "I was talking to people. And this isn't— It's not like I'm making this up! People have actually died. People I knew and cared about."

Her face softened. "I know. I know you miss Honey, and I know you're trying to find out who hurt her, but do you really think sitting at a table in Club Fred's all night is getting you closer?"

"Nothing's getting me closer!" I pushed up, pacing to the door and back. "No one's getting anywhere, don't you see that? They arrested Tom, couldn't make a case against him, dropped the charges, and that was it! That was all they did!"

Unbidden, the sight of Honey's body at the waterfront came to mind. She'd been so still, as if frozen in time, except for her veil. Her veil had blown all over the place, tying the moment to the wind, making it real.

I thought of Paloma Santiago Ortiz, a little girl with hair ribbons her brother would have known anywhere.

"These people don't have anyone looking out for them! They don't have a voice, they don't have anyone to protect them, to help them. That's me. It has to be me, if it isn't anyone else, and I can't give that up just because I have a girlfriend. This is my job."

"So is that what you want? Your job, and nothing else?"

"No, no, that isn't—" I shook my head, frustrated and angry. This was so fucking *important*, how could she not see that? "I love you. I love being with you. I love having that, outside everything else, this place where I don't have to think about all the rest of that stuff."

Alisha's eyes narrowed again. "Really."

"What?"

"You like having me—*outside everything else*. Like I'm your vacation. From everything you think is more important."

"What? No. I didn't say that."

"You pretty much did, yeah. There's"—she made a rough shape with both of her hands in the air—"your life, with your job, and all the dead people who have no one to rely on but you to bring their killers to justice, and then there's this"—one hand, a circle made with thumb and forefinger—"our relationship, where you can relax and pretend nothing else exists."

I frowned. "That's not how it is."

"Really? Did you ask your boss if you could get time off to go on a trip?"

"No." Shit, now she looked *really* pissed. "Look, I almost got fired this week, it wasn't a good idea to ask for time off."

She pursed her lips and looked away.

"Jesus, Alisha, what the hell do you want from me? Do you *want* me to get fired? I like my job. I don't want to lose it."

"I don't want you to lose your job."

"So you want to break up with me?"

I expected her to demur, immediately, forcefully, but she just stared for a long moment, until I thought she was going to say yes.

"I need to think about some things. I don't want to be some private little oasis from your life, Ed. That's— For me, that's not what relationships are. If that's what you want, you'll have to do it with someone else."

"That's not fair. You— How many times have you said it was okay I talked about things with other people because you didn't want to talk about them? Now it's my fault I actually did that?"

She leaned over her knees, hands clenching in her skirt. "This isn't you talking about sports with a friend who likes sports more than I do, so don't you dare pretend I'm a shallow bitch for wanting more than the apparently minor role I play in your life. I don't want to be your little bubble of happy, okay?"

"You aren't. How can you say that?"

"Because you just did. Because you stood here, in my house, and told me you want to keep me apart from everything else in your life. Well, fuck that, Ed. I'm not interested."

I hadn't said that. I hadn't meant that. Damn it, how the hell were we having a fight about things we hadn't even said?

"If you didn't want to go on a trip with me, you should have told me, instead of pretending you were going to ask your boss, making me think you were serious. Because I believed you. Like I believed you when you said you'd come dance with me." She shook her head. "You should leave. I can't keep talking to you right now."

"I don't— But— You're kicking me out?"

"I'm telling you to go home, yeah. But here's what you should think about, and it has nothing to do with me, nothing to do with us." Alisha took a deep breath. "This is no way to live. This is no way to honor people. And if Honey were here, she'd sure as hell kick your ass for throwing away your life even if it meant finding out who killed her. Go home, Ed."

I wanted to fight with her more. I wanted to keep arguing until she understood what I was saying, until she could see it from my point of view. I stood there, in her living room, staring down at her, trying to come up with the perfect words, the exact way to phrase what I wanted to tell her so she'd get it.

She wasn't looking at me anymore. Since I couldn't think of a damn thing to say, I left.

It was cold on the street. Last week's rain storm had cleared out the mugginess lingering from summer, and the weather suddenly felt like fall. Or at least like fall was imminent. I'd parked a few blocks away (I would always rather walk a little than parallel park), and my hoodie wasn't quite up to the chill.

I hadn't noticed on the way in, probably because I was looking forward to spending the night with my girlfriend—I thought bitterly—but trudging toward the car was different.

A horn honked at the intersection and I jumped.

Shortly after 1 a.m. In other words: the time Honey was murdered. Was another murder happening as I unlocked my car, started it, turned on the heat full blast? And locked all the doors, just in case.

I drove through a burger place on the way home and treated myself to a bunch of food that would probably make me sick. I didn't care. At least after I ate it my entire body would shut down and I could sleep.

CHAPTER 25

Regret made a hardened lump in my gut when I got out of bed the next morning.

Or maybe that was the burger. And milkshake.

I groaned and made my way to the kitchen in search of coffee. Or possibly a time machine. What I found instead was Troy sleeping with his face in a book.

Coffee-making wasn't the quietest activity. I tried to respect Troy's nap, or whatever it was, but between running water into the carafe and the machine gurgling, he started picking his head up.

"Ummmm. Coffee?"

"Brewing."

"'Kay." He sighed. "Man. I went out last night and ... fuck."

I nodded as if that was a complete thought.

"But like usually I go out with my boys, and last night I went out with these other people. Which I maybe should not have done. Because these people partied *hard*."

"With text books?"

"Huh?"

I gestured to the table. "You partied hard reading?"

"Oh. Oh, no." He shoved the book away. "So, like, I got home, but I was on ... something? And I couldn't sleep, but JP told me I couldn't be in the room because I was bothering him, so I thought I'd come down here, but I got bored."

"So you started reading—" I flipped the book so I could see the cover. "A cookbook?"

"It helped. I mean, I fell asleep, anyway."

Sometimes I wonder what my life would have been like if I'd been born with the body Troy had. We talk a lot about how chromosomes don't matter, how what gender you're assigned by your family doesn't dictate who you are, and I believe all that's true. But it doesn't mean I don't . . . wonder. What being cis is like. What it'd be like to just not think about it all the time.

"You want coffee?" I asked.

"Man, yes. Please. Ugh. So, uh, how was your night?"

"My night." I gave in to the very real need not to sit alone in my room, and leaned back against the counter. "I fucked up with my girlfriend."

"Oh damn. Dude. What'd you do?"

"I hung out with some people at this club we go to instead of dancing with her." That was a good summation, anyway. Sort of.

"Uh. Like I don't mean to be objectifying or anything, but if she was my girlfriend, I would so not turn down dancing with her."

Did he know he talked like Shaggy from *Scooby-Doo*?

"It wasn't really like that. I was in the middle of a conversation."

"Yeah, well, I think that whole 'bros before hos' thing is pretty overrated. Would you really want to be with a guy who picked his friends over dancing with you?"

"I didn't— That's not—"

"Uh-huh. But did you meet up there? Or did you go there together? Because that makes a difference."

I frowned. "We went together."

Troy nodded sagely. "Yep. Douche move, Ed. Harsh but true. Just tellin' it like it is."

Why use one cliché when you can use two?

Another nod. "I bet she forgives you. The first time, at least."

"She was pretty pissed last night."

"Well, yeah. Wouldn't you be?"

"If she wanted to hang out with friends for a little while and I did something else? No. I think that's healthy." Though her last words had worked their way into my brain and wouldn't let go. Honey would be glad I was looking for her killer, wouldn't she? She'd think that was a priority. Except Honey was the queen of impermanence, with her matches and her Robert Frost poems. She might not kick my ass for letting myself become a little obsessed, but she'd definitely give me a stern talking-to.

She'd tell me that this thing with Alisha was good for me. She'd probably also tell me that everyone dies, and losing out on a relationship because I was trying to solve any murder, even hers, wasn't worth it.

"Okay, yeah, I get that." Troy squinted, rubbing his eyes. "But is she saying she doesn't want you to ever hang out with your friends? Or is she saying—"

"Never mind," I snapped. I was not going to take relationship advice from a fucking hipster who'd been so high on "something" last night that his roommate kicked him out of their room.

"Whoa, man, chill. I'm just sayin'. Seriously, I wish I knew what happened last night, but parts of it are shaky. Whew."

Last night. Theme night. Maybe everything was fine today. No one had called my phone, so maybe everyone was all right.

"I gotta go," I said.

"Hey. For real." Troy looked me straight in the eye. "Thank you for the coffee, man. Solid."

"You're welcome."

I filled my coffee to the top and retreated to my room, lifting the lid on my laptop before I'd even sat down. I couldn't remember the last time I'd gone to sleep without looking at my computer, but last night I'd gone straight in and eaten my burger without doing anything else. No podcast or video or website or book.

See? I wasn't addicted to electronics. I'd spent, like, half an hour without using them. *So there*, I told the imaginary Alisha in my head.

Imaginary Alisha pointed out that since I couldn't remember the last time that had happened, I'd actually just proved her point. Whatever, Imaginary Alisha.

I loaded Togg's site and held my breath.

Damn it.

Fifth Body Found at the Waterfront. Killer strikes again.

I clicked through to the article and read it as slowly as I could. I didn't know Felipe Farraway. My immediate relief was quickly overshot by knowing that someone else was staring at this article as stunned and horrified as I'd been when it was Honey.

The comments were a shit show of rising intensity, and I stopped reading them before I'd gotten past the first ten.

Felipe Farraway. I knew of a guy named Felipe, but I didn't know if he was the same one. A big teddy bear of a guy with a smile for everyone. But if I were a killer, would I pick a big guy? Though Honey hadn't been small.

Was this person, whoever they were, escalating? Picking harder targets?

The *Times-Record* site had a hundred words about the murder, but it was almost an exact duplicate of the stub they'd run when Stephanie Hawkins had been killed, with the names and pronouns changed.

I went back to Togg's site. Twenty-three more comments had dropped since I switched tabs. I didn't look at them. After a moment of deliberation I shut down my browser and went back to the kitchen.

JP and David had joined Troy at the table.

"Whoa." Troy squinted at me. "Dude, you look bad. Did she dump you?"

"What? Oh. No. No, someone died."

"How many dead people do you know? Didn't someone else you know die recently?"

JP hit him. "Dude."

"Wait, who broke up with you? Your girlfriend?" David's eyebrows rose like he was interested.

"You're not her type," I said.

"Dude! Not fair. What's wrong with me?"

I briefly imagined David hitting on Alisha and almost laughed. "Alisha's queer," I said, and waited.

David and Troy blinked at me blankly.

JP sighed. "You guys are embarrassing."

"What the hell do you mean, she's queer? You're not a chick."

"I'm not a chick. I'm trans. It works for us. But she only dates queer people." When they just stared at me, I added, "I don't think she's into cis dudes."

"Wait, uh, what'd you call us?"

"'Cis,'" JP said. "It means we aren't transgender." He caught my eye. "I had a friend in college. Uh. Anyway, I apologize for them. No one will be hitting on Alisha."

"She can take care of herself. And we didn't break up, anyway." *I hope.*

"But you know someone else who died? Are you all right?"

"I didn't know this guy. We just sort of hung out in a few of the same places."

"Hold up. This is that gay basher, right?"

"Well, serial killer. But targeting queer people. You know about that?"

JP looked affronted. "Dude, come on. I read the internet. I saw it on Facebook."

"Really?"

"Yeah."

I wasn't that into Facebook. "It's the same person, I think. The killer."

"There's a killer in La Vista, holy shit, you guys." Troy shook his head. "Seriously, like, holy shit."

"Yeah," David said. "That's fucked up."

"Pretty fucked up." I passed them to get another cup of coffee.

JP poked my arm. "Why is Alisha breaking up with you?"

"She's not! At least, I hope she isn't."

Troy assumed a very serious expression. "They went out last night, and Ed totally ignored her the whole time."

"Hey!" I protested.

JP winced.

"I didn't— It's not like she was sitting in a corner bored. She was dancing with friends."

"Uh-huh." JP didn't sound all that swayed to my side.

David frowned. "You turned down dancing with Alisha?"

"I didn't turn it down. We dance. It's like she wants the world to be rosy and cheerful all the time, when bad things actually happen, you know. Like this killer is actually happening and it's like it's not important to her at all."

Troy put his head down on the table. "But, dude. Is she saying it's not important? Or is she saying she wants to dance, you know, anyway?"

"Right," JP agreed. "And are you really saying you wanted to talk about murder instead of dance with her?"

David shook his head. "Yeah, but I see what Ed's saying. You can't just pretend bad stuff doesn't happen."

Great. David was Team Ed. David of the "hot-girl zone" theory was the only guy on my side. That was . . . humbling.

"I think we might be too different," I said to the panel of hipsters in my kitchen.

They looked up attentively.

"She's great. She has all these plans, you know? All these places she wants to go, and she wants me to come with her, but I have responsibilities. I can't just quit my job like she did."

"Why'd she quit her job?"

"Because she didn't like it."

Troy nodded, like this was normal. "Jobs. Yeah."

Because of course they wouldn't understand.

"It's totally ridiculous to quit your job because you don't like it."

"Only if you don't have a plan B," JP said. "Is she still paying her bills?"

"Yeah. I mean, I guess she must be." I thought about her travel money, the money she didn't spend on other things. "I think she has a lot of savings."

JP raised his eyebrows. "I guess I think it's cool she saved her money and quit her job if she hated it that much. Why's it piss you off?"

"It doesn't *piss me off*, it's not— People can't live that way. Normal people can't live that way. It's irresponsible!"

He held up his hands. "Whoa. Okay. But it doesn't actually sound irresponsible to me. Did she ask you for money or something?"

"God. Never mind." Screw it. "Anyway, she didn't dump me, or break up with me, so whatever."

Troy whistled. JP hit him. David opened his mouth to say something, but JP hit him too.

I turned around and left the room.

It took me all day to work up my nerve to go by the house. Saturday evening, so there was at least a chance that my parents would be out and Abuela would be in. But when I got there, my father's car was in the driveway.

I didn't know why I knocked, since it could only end badly. There was always a chance Abuela would be the first to the door . . . Or maybe, after a day of hating everything, I just didn't care.

I knocked, and waited, holding my breath, rehearsing *Hi, Dad. Is Abuela here?* Cool, calm, totally unemotional.

The second he opened the door I lost my words.

"Ana." He looked me up and down once, lip curling into a sneer.

My old name hit me like a blow, and I half stumbled back. I couldn't breathe. I wasn't breathing. My lungs were frozen, refusing to expand.

"You will be welcome here again when you act normal, Ana. None of this—disruption."

This disruption. The disruption of myself, being who I am. This inconvenience of my gender.

He was waiting for me to respond, to get angry. I'd been angry a lot in the last few months I lived there. We'd screamed at each other all the time, two people yelling in the face of a storm neither of us could control.

I backed away from the door and climbed into my car, hands shaking on the steering wheel. I didn't look back. If I went to Alisha, she'd hug me and tell me I was all right, but there would still be all that shit unresolved between us, and I'd know she was putting it aside because I was freaking out. I didn't want pity. And I didn't want to go to Club Fred's tonight, where everyone would be in mourning.

I drove to the Rhein instead.

I told the kid at the door that I was only there to talk to Cameron, so she let me in. Cam, in mid-ticket rush, opened the door to the booth for me and gestured me to the far corner, half-hidden behind the wall.

I slid to the floor, tucked myself under the desk, and began to cry.

Crying's one of those things I tell myself isn't really gendered, but doing it always makes me feel vulnerable, the way being called "miss" used to make me feel vulnerable. I guess because it's externalizing something that can be seen as weak; crying isn't inherently feminine, but it's considered a visible sign that you aren't strong. Even knowing it's bullshit doesn't help.

Of course, usually I liked to cry alone. Not sitting on the floor of the ticket booth at the Rhein during the rush to buy tickets for the evening showing of whatever.

I was distantly aware of everything slowing down, but I kept hiding and Cam let me. I could hear him typing, mumbling to himself occasionally, but until I crawled out from under the desk, he completely ignored me.

Once I did, he passed me a bottle of water and waited.

"Sorry."

"It's okay. That's a pretty good spot, though I don't think I'd fit in it anymore. You want me to ask if you're okay so you can pretend you are?"

I slumped. "No. I'm definitely not okay. Alisha and I had a fight, my hipster roommates took her side, and I just tried to see Abuela and got Dad instead."

Cam's angular, handsome face contorted into a grimace. "I'm sorry. Is that the first time since you moved out?"

"Yeah. He told me to come back when I can act normal."

"Normal," he repeated with distaste. "Can you imagine aspiring to whatever your dad thinks is normal?"

"Yeah. Been there, done that, have the self-loathing to prove it."

"Short of finding someone to *Strangers on a Train* him, I don't know what else to say."

"Too bad I can't harness this douche bag serial killer and point him at Dad."

Both of us froze.

"Oh my god. I can't believe I actually said that."

"It was a bit . . . darker, than you usually aim. No matter, Ed. I'm showing *Jaws* tonight if you're interested."

"No. I think it'd just make me wish a mechanical shark was available to eat me. Fuck, I don't know."

"Sorry. I do not have Bruce available. But." He opened the bottom drawer of a small file cabinet. "I do have these."

Dark chocolate truffles. I took three. "You're a lifesaver."

"I think it's important to be prepared."

I ate the first two and took a break. "So I had a fight with Alisha and decided we aren't meant to be because she wants to be happy and totally in denial that anything bad happens in the world."

"Really?"

I sighed. "It's not just that. She said I try to keep her in a bubble where I don't have to think about other things."

Cam raised an eyebrow.

"Fuck. I think . . . I did that a little. She didn't want to think about anything dark, anything real, so I wrapped that around myself like it could insulate me when we were together. Except I don't think that's actually true. I think being determined to find happiness and adventure despite all the bad shit that happens in the world is maybe the bravest, scariest thing I've ever seen, and that's why I can't deal with it."

"Do you want to do that? Not everyone does, which is okay too. It takes all kinds, you know?"

I wanted happiness and adventure, yeah. I definitely didn't want to be the downer boyfriend bringing up Bad Things to shit on her plans.

"I don't want to live in ignorance. But I don't know if you can think about how truly terrible the world is and also see it the way Alisha does, like it's full of wonder and opportunity." Except that went back to balance again. "And I'm fucking afraid to try, Cam. If I don't try, then I don't have to live with the idea that I fail at happiness."

"Okay. So reframe it. It's not pass/fail. It's ongoing. And you must get better with practice, like anything else, right?"

"Practice at being happy? Come on."

"Not at *being* happy. At taking a chance that you could be. Practice at hope." He shook his head. "I don't know what I would have done in your place, growing up with people telling me how . . . wrong I was all the time. Or knowing they felt that way even if they weren't saying it. School was hard enough, but my parents casually accepted a lot of my strangeness, and I had no idea how lucky I was."

"You're not strange, Cam."

He offered an amused twist of his lips.

"Well. All right. Maybe you're a little strange. But you don't act like it. It fits you."

"I am perfectly strange, thank you very much. I guess I'm just saying I think your battle is a bit more uphill, but that doesn't make it impossible, and it definitely doesn't mean you should give up. People learn from each other in relationships. Maybe being a little more spontaneous is something you'll learn from Alisha. If you want to."

"I think I want to have an adventure."

Now he smiled fully. "Then you should. *That* is something I probably couldn't do easily, at least not with the staff I have. Go on an adventure. Send me postcards and I'll put them up in the window."

For all of La Vista to see. "Maybe I will. Thanks for listening to me cry and ramble and wring my hands."

"I hope for your sake it won't be a habit, but anytime, Ed."

Cameron hugged me tightly before I left. I may have leaned into it for a minute, just to put off the inevitable a little while longer.

This time I drove home determined and ready to take action. And I might have felt the faintest stirrings of hope.

CHAPTER 26

I spent all Sunday planning. I went through all my bills, paid everything that was due in the next few weeks, calculated everything I'd need for next month, and took stock of what was left. I didn't make a lot of money, but my biggest frivolous expense was the occasional round at Club Fred's; everything else just sat in my savings account, waiting for the car to break down or the paper to panic and lay everyone off.

The idea of spending any of that hoarded gold filled me with dread, but each time I thought about it, I remembered what it was like to stand on a cliff in the rain with Alisha, that sensation of endless possibility. Money felt like security, but what was the point of having all that security if it manifested in my day-to-day life as cement shoes, keeping me from doing anything more fun than going out on Friday night?

I also looked up how to expedite a US passport, but it would still take weeks. I didn't plan to wait that long, so I started filling out the forms and located a drugstore that would take decent pictures. We had plenty of time to get our passports and plan big, international trips. There was a lot we could do in the States. Alisha would have ideas.

And anyway, she hadn't agreed to go with me yet.

Trying to figure out what I'd do if she said no was harder. Obviously, the ideal thing would be to go on a trip by myself, to spend the money and stage my own adventure. I didn't know if I actually wanted to do that, though. Part of the fun was definitely imagining the two of us somewhere; thinking about myself alone was nowhere near as intriguing, but it might be worth doing anyway. If I had time off, I didn't plan to spend it in La Vista.

Getting time off was Monday's problem. I was desperately tempted to wait until I knew if she'd come with me before talking to Potter, but that was missing the point. If I was going overboard with this story—and I remembered what Rodriguez had said about needing other people around to remind him not to get too lost—then I had to be willing to reel myself in, with or without Alisha's adventures.

I really hoped it would be *with*, though.

I sent Potter an email the second I got to work, expecting him to basically ignore me and make me beg him for a meeting. Which would be fine, because I still didn't really know what I was going to say. I'd just told Rodriguez that I'd be available whenever he needed me, and now here I was, asking for time off for the first time since I'd started working here. At best, I'd look inconsistent. At worst—I couldn't figure out what was the worst-case scenario. That he'd say no and I'd look like I was picking up lazy from Caspar? Or that he'd say yes and take me less seriously as a reporter?

To my (probably obvious) shock, he actually walked to our table about fifteen minutes later.

"Masiello. You want something?"

Caspar's eyes boggled behind Potter's back.

"Uh, I . . . actually—" Oh shit. No time to think, no time to prepare. "I was wondering if I could have two weeks off?"

"Huh." Potter looked down at me long enough that I started to think he was going to say something like, *Sure thing. Don't bother coming back.*

He didn't, though.

"Yeah, that sounds like a good idea. Don't want you to burn out, kid. Starting when?"

"Next Monday?"

"That works."

"I, uh, Rodriguez said he could use me on— I mean, he told me I should be ready—"

"Rodriguez survived this long without your assistance, he can make it two more weeks." He kicked Caspar's chair. "This means you'll have to get off your ass and do some work around here for once."

"How is that fair? I gotta pick up the slack because boy genius here wants to go on vacation?"

"I think what you actually meant to say there is 'Thanks, boss, for letting me get away with being a waste of space most of the time.' If you do a damn thing while Ed's gone that'll be an improvement on your usual performance around here." He kicked the chair again and waved a hand back at me. "Get your head on straight, Masiello."

"Yes, sir."

"What the fuck?" Caspar shot at me.

I shrugged.

"Two weeks," he muttered. "Jesus. What the fuck. What the hell are *you* gonna do for two stinkin' weeks that's more important than work?"

"Go on a trip with my girlfriend." *I hope. I sincerely hope.*

He shoved back from the table in disgust. "I don't give a fuck, man. Jesus!"

I bit back a laugh as he stomped off to the break room.

CHAPTER 27

I didn't get nervous until I was walking out of the bookstore with a travel guide to Mexico City. We couldn't go next week, but I wanted us to go someday. At least, I wanted her to know I was committed to that. It was a small gesture, but I hoped she'd understand it.

We hadn't talked since Friday night. She'd texted to ask if I heard about Felipe, I'd texted back that I had. That was it.

I called up from the car, crossing my fingers that she was there.

"Hey." At least she sounded happy to talk to me.

"Hey. I'm sort of in front of your apartment. Are you here?"

"I'm so here. But watch out, I've been—busy."

"Busy?"

She laughed. "Come up."

Okay, laughter was a good sign.

It didn't take much to see what she meant: more than half her books were spread around. Some were in stacks beside the bookshelf, the coffee table was full of books splayed open and facedown, and I couldn't see the kitchen table under piles of papers and notebooks and more books.

"Wow," I said.

"Hush. Here." She dumped some stuff off the sofa and used her feet to shuffle it back toward the bookshelf. With an elaborate bow, she said, "Join me."

"Is it okay I just showed up?"

"We're not in the middle of a bitter war. We had a fight. And we have to talk."

"I agree. Totally. But first— I mean, uh, I got this thing." I perched on the edge of her sofa. God, this was so fucking hard all of a sudden.

I passed the bag from the bookstore over to her and waited while she opened it.

"Ohhh, perfect. Are we planning? I will drop everything right now and plan our Mexico City trip, Ed!"

"No. I mean, yes, at some point, but no—"

"What's up? You look really freaked out." She handed me back the book. "Do you not want me to go? Because that's totally fine, like completely, as long as you let me have input on your travel plans, because there are a few places that you, like, *need* to see—"

"No, wait. Stop. That's not what I meant."

She waited expectantly.

"I—" I put the book down over the bag, on the cushion between us. "You're not still mad at me?"

"Well, I think we have unresolved stuff we need to discuss. But I haven't been seething for days over you being a shit boyfriend. I don't want to be your island away from everything that's terrible in the world, Ed, you know? I'm not happy-go-lucky all the time. I don't want to be." She took my hand. "It's like your mom says, you gotta have balance."

"I've been thinking the same thing. I think I maybe . . . made you into my balance. Like no matter what else was happening, as long as we could dance, or laugh, or have sex, that was balance enough."

"When it totally wasn't. It was just completely lopsided at different times."

"Yeah. And I don't want to do that again. But I'm not sure how to . . . approach the world like you approach it. Because I see a lot of the darkness. Maybe more than I see the light."

"And I definitely block stuff out when I don't want to think about it, so maybe we can find a middle ground together. And I get being obsessed, you know? I get obsessed about different stuff than you do, but that part I understand." She gestured to the intense debris on the coffee table. "Sometimes I get totally consumed by a new place. Like I'll go on travel benders where I only watch travel shows about a certain country, or town, and read all the books, and plan these really pie-in-the-sky trips I'll probably never take. And I love that feeling, like I'm immersed in it."

"It's kind of exhilarating," I said. "And addicting."

"Exactly. I don't know where you go in your head, but for me I'll be picturing all these things I could do, all these places, trying to imagine what the light looks like in Hong Kong, or how the air smells in Iceland. But sometimes I forget to eat and sleep when I'm inside that thing, and if you said to me, 'Hey, it's 3 a.m., maybe think about coming to bed,' I wouldn't see that as you trying to tell me what to do. I'd see that as you looking out for me."

I nodded. "Yeah. I get that."

"All right." She hesitated, plaiting some of her braids back as she thought. "So on Friday night you started looking like that to me. Like your shoulders were up around your ears and you were all kinds of tense, and I had this feeling like if I said anything to you, you'd snap."

Ouch.

"Maybe I didn't say it the right way. I was hurt that you kept kind of brushing me off to sit there and talk about death. But you've been inside this thing the entire time we've been going out and when we went camping you relaxed, you know? You took deeper breaths. And I don't know. I think that's related. You didn't have your phone to check, you didn't have your notebooks, it was just you, and me, and some sleeping bags. I think it was good for both of us. But it's your life, babe. I just want you to be happy." She squeezed my hands. "And, like, I think I can make you at least as happy as your phone, at least some of the time."

"At least," I teased.

"But are you serious about Mexico City? Because don't fuck with me, Ed. I take travel *very* seriously."

"I'm serious." I took a breath. Everything seemed fine. We were probably fine. But this still felt like the biggest thing I'd ever done, and I needed a second before I could actually say it. "I asked for two weeks off. From work."

"You what? Wait. You *what*?"

"It's only two weeks—"

"Oh my god!" She launched across the sofa and into my lap, scattering a stack of books at our feet. "Really? You really did? Can you afford it? Are you sure? Oh my god, two weeks!"

I kissed her, relieved as hell to be able to do that again. "I'm serious. I can afford it."

"Oh my *god*. There is like *so much* we can do in two weeks!"

"Well, we can't go to Mexico City because we don't have passports, and even if we expedited them, we wouldn't get them before Monday."

"Monday? Oh, if we're doing this, we're leaving sooner than that. That gives me four days to plan. I'm so excited!"

"We don't have to go for the entire—"

"Don't think about the money. I have some set aside for a hostel and if we split everything and plan out our meals using groceries, we can keep costs pretty low." Her voice rose. "We're going on an adventure, Ed! We're really doing this!"

I still didn't completely believe it. We'd probably kill each other. Or the arrangements wouldn't work out. Or we'd run out of money. Or I'd come back and the paper would have given my job away. (Actually, I didn't think that was legal. Plus, after two weeks of Caspar, Potter would probably welcome me back with, you know, a nod or some other dramatic gesture of support.)

Alisha, though, had no doubts at all. "We're taking my car. I think we'll go down the coast, do a mix of camping with maybe a night in a hotel every now and then. I'll do meal planning so we know we always have supplies. I need an actual ice chest, not a cooler, though I bought this great backpack at Ikea that has spots for those blue freezer things—"

I kissed her until she subsided against my body. "I can't wait," I whispered.

"Me either. Thank you. Thank you for believing in adventure."

I put my hand over my heart. "I believe in adventure. And you."

"And us."

"Yeah. That too."

Eventually we did more planning, and scraped together a meal of snacks eaten at the kitchen counter while dreaming of falling asleep with the sound of the ocean in our ears.

We went to Club Fred's on Thursday night for a spontaneous bon voyage party. Just us, Jaq and Hannah, Zane, and Cameron. It was kind of cool to realize that they were "our" friends in a sense, people both of us had grown a little closer to since we got together (except for Cam).

Zane raised her beer. "A toast to the explorers! May you have good weather, no car trouble, and a reservation in every city!"

"Bite your tongue! No reservations!"

"May your good fortune land you a room in every city, despite pigheadedly not phoning ahead for reservations!"

Alisha smacked Zane. "Jerk!"

"All right, all right," Hannah said. "Seriously, you two, be safe and keep each other warm out there. Hint, hint."

"We will." I grabbed Alisha's hand.

Cameron raised his glass. "Cheers."

"Sláinte!" Jaq added.

"Whatever the hell that means," Zane said.

We clinked all the glasses together.

"Don't think about La Vista at all, the entire time you're gone, okay?" Jaq pointed at me. "Got that, Masiello?"

"Got it. I won't. Much."

"I'll just have to be creative with distractions," Alisha said.

"Call us if you need anything." Zane pulled a bag from under her chair. "Also, Jaq and I made you this."

Alisha took the bag and pulled out . . . a blanket. A knitted blanket, four pieces stitched together in red, blue, green, and purple.

"The colors are a little bizarre," Jaq began, but Zane smacked her.

"They're bold. Just like Ed and Alisha."

"We are bold." I ran my fingers over it. "This is so beautiful. Thanks, you guys."

"We wanted to keep working on stuff, even though it was kind of sad for a while." Jaq shrugged. "Knitting reminds me so much of Honey."

I thought about my half-made project, sitting in a plastic bag under a pile of laundry. "Me too. I've barely touched the socks I was making since she died."

"You should bring them on your adventure," Cam said. "Something to do when Alisha's driving, or when you're hanging out somewhere.

"That's a really good idea."

"You could knit around the campfire at night, babe." Alisha kissed my cheek.

"Yeah."

Zane changed the subject, but I didn't pay attention. I glanced around at Club Fred's, trying to see it with fresh eyes. It was dated and a little dingy, but I doubted we'd find anywhere else that felt as much like home.

"I think I'll miss this place over the next few weeks," I said.

Jaq laughed. "Man, that's how you know you need a vacation. When you're here often enough to miss it."

"Hey!"

We stayed until Jaq said she had to get home because it was a school night, then exchanged kisses and hugs before going our separate ways. I went home with Alisha.

"I love you," she said as we walked to the car.

"I love you too."

CHAPTER 28

The fire crackled in its metal ring, and Alisha's yell of triumph was muffled by the trunk of her car. It slammed, and she gleefully skipped back to the campsite.

"Ha! I knew they were here! Okay, I'm making all sorts of mental notes for next time. Packing's gonna be a whole different thing." She kissed me. "S'mores, boyfriend?"

I held up my knitting. "Last three rows. I can't get sticky yet."

"I'm totally getting a head start on you. I'll be sugar-drunk before you even eat your first marshmallow."

"That's acceptable."

We grinned at each other, faces two-toned—bright, with shifting shadows.

She got to work, assembling graham crackers and vegan chocolate. Now that we were settled in for the night I could see why she'd brought along wire clothes hangers.

"It's not cheating to use those?" I teased. "Shouldn't we be sharpening sticks or something?"

"I like camping, but I'm not a *savage*. Wait, is that racist?"

I rolled my eyes. "Against who?"

"I don't know. Savages of color? People who sharpen sticks? Seriously, 'savage' never means white people, so I hereby take it back. Hey, are you sure you're okay with these marshmallows? Even though they're full of gelatin?"

"Yeah. If I'm a better vegan next time we go camping, we can hit the health food store for super fancy vegan marshmallows."

"Mmm." She pulled her chair (two chairs, two wire coat hangers, vegan chocolate; she'd thought of almost everything) in close to mine.

"I love saying 'next time.' Now, what kind of roaster are you? Do you light on fire and blow out, or do you try for an even shade of brown?"

We debated the relative merits of marshmallow-roasting techniques for a few minutes. Alisha meticulously "experimented" on a few different s'mores for official tasting purposes, but I refused to let them near me.

I could see well enough by firelight to cast off, though it was harder than regular stitches, which I could mostly do by touch.

"I'm done." I dug into my bag for the other sock, and held up the pair of them . . . one slightly larger than the other. "Oops. Oh my god, look."

She giggled, covering her mouth with a chocolate-smeared hand. "Oh no! Your socks!"

"They'll be fine after I . . . block them. Or whatever." They looked like I'd made them for people with different-sized feet. I laughed. "Honey would mock me forever if I showed her these socks. Well, she'd tell me how to fix them, and then she'd mock me forever."

"Are you going to put them on?"

I hadn't even thought about putting them on. "What, here? We're outside."

"So you'd put them on if we were inside?"

"Um." I considered it. But I had a pair of boots, so they wouldn't get too dirty. And they were a decent wool blend. They'd be good for camping. "I think this one will fall off if I put it on right now."

She smirked. "I dare you. Come on. I want to see what they look like."

"You can't see anything! It's practically dark!"

"It's light enough."

"Fine." I pretended to grumble as I pulled them on. If anything, the bigger one fit best; the smaller one was a bit . . . small. "Seriously, how did I make these two different sizes?"

"They're perfect." She leaned forward to kiss me. "Totally perfect. Will you make me a pair?"

"Definitely. I might even go out of my way to make them so they fit." I kissed her again. "You taste good."

"Damn right I do. You ready for a sugar high?"

"I'm ready for anything." I slipped my feet, new socks and all, back into my boots. "I can't believe it's only the first night. I can't believe we have *two weeks* of this."

Alisha offered me a straightened length of wire hanger with a preskewered marshmallow. "I can. It's going to be amazing."

"It really is."

The destination of my heart wasn't a cruise ship, or even a place. It was right here, right now, or wherever I could hear Alisha laugh and feel her skin.

Explore more of the *Queers of La Vista* series:
riptidepublishing.com/titles/universe/queers-la-vista

Dear Reader,

Thank you for reading Kris Ripper's *The Queer and the Restless*!

We know your time is precious and you have many, many entertainment options, so it means a lot that you've chosen to spend your time reading. We really hope you enjoyed it.

We'd be honored if you'd consider posting a review—good or bad—on sites like **Amazon, Barnes & Noble, Kobo, Goodreads, Twitter, Facebook, Tumblr**, and your blog or website. We'd also be honored if you told your friends and family about this book. Word of mouth is a book's lifeblood!

For more information on upcoming releases, author interviews, blog tours, contests, giveaways, and more, please sign up for our weekly, spam-free newsletter and visit us around the web:

Newsletter: tinyurl.com/RiptideSignup
Twitter: twitter.com/RiptideBooks
Facebook: facebook.com/RiptidePublishing
Goodreads: tinyurl.com/RiptideOnGoodreads
Tumblr: riptidepublishing.tumblr.com

Thank you so much for Reading the Rainbow!

RiptidePublishing.com

ACKNOWLEDGMENTS

My grateful thanks to General Wendy, as ever, for keeping track of all the details, murder victims, and various things Ed might or might not have been knitting at any given moment.

I am indebted to May Peterson's thoughtful comments regarding identity, controversy, and, uh, grammar, though I don't really understand what she's talking about with the grammar stuff.

Lucky writers have friends who volunteer to read and give feedback. Alexis Hall took a spin through this book at a crucial moment and pointed out a matter of empathy, and also a matter of wedding dresses. JR Gray dropped everything to read this and offer a few significant clarifications (and a note on the variety of vegan cheese). This business would not be nearly as fun without my fellow scribblers. My thanks. Let me know when I can return the favor, lads.

Anyone who wants to read the book Alisha references while camping, in which the main character goes to sleep in his tent and wakes up in his tent . . . in quicksand, look no further than *The Vor Game* by Lois McMaster Bujold.

Far more seriously, Paloma Santiago Ortiz, the young girl whose murder haunted Joe Rodriguez and his contemporaries, is a fictional character. The idea of her, of a young girl whose murder was brushed off, was inspired by two real-life cases of young girls who galvanized the public and consumed the local media.

Real-life young white girls.

Amber Swartz Garcia disappeared while jumping rope in front of her house in Pinole, California, in 1988. Polly Klaas was kidnapped from her home in Petaluma, California, in 1993. Both cases inspired obsessive searches, constant television attention, and even now the Google hits are eager to tell me all about them. I wanted Joe's personal obsession, like Ed's, to be about someone whose story wouldn't be told otherwise. Someone whose death had been a footnote, whose life could not be fruitfully googled twenty-five years later.

Some of us were born to tell those stories, to honor the people whom others forget.

ALSO BY
KRIS RIPPER

Queers of La Vista
Gays of Our Lives
The Butch and the Beautiful
One Life to Lose
As La Vista Turns

Scientific Method Universe
Catalysts
Unexpected Gifts
Take Three Breaths
Breaking Down
Roller Coasters
The Boyfriends Tie the Knot
The Honeymoon
Extremes
The New Born Year
Threshold of the Year
Surrender the Past
The Library, Volume 1

New Halliday
Fairy Tales
The Spinner, the Shepherd, and the Leading Man
The Real Life Build
Take the Leap

The Home Series
Going Home
Home Free
Close to Home
Home for the Holidays

Little Red and the Big Bad
Serial One
Serial Two

The Erotic Gym:
Training Mac
The Ghost in the Penthouse

For a complete book list, visit: krisripper.com

ABOUT THE AUTHOR

Kris Ripper lives in the great state of California and hails from the San Francisco Bay Area. Kris shares a converted garage with a toddler, can do two pull-ups in a row, and can write backwards. (No, really.) Kris is genderqueer and prefers the z-based pronouns because they're freaking sweet. Ze has been writing fiction since ze learned how to write, and boring zir stuffed animals with stories long before that.

Website: krisripper.com
Newsletter: krisripper.com/about/subscribe-what
Facebook: facebook.com/kris.ripper
Twitter: twitter.com/SmutTasticKris
YouTube: youtube.com/user/KrisRipper

Enjoy more stories like
The Queer and the Restless
at RiptidePublishing.com!

The Burnt Toast B&B
ISBN: 978-1-62649-217-2

Roller Girl
ISBN: 978-1-62649-418-3

Earn Bonus Bucks!
Earn 1 Bonus Buck for each dollar you spend. Find out how at RiptidePublishing.com/news/bonus-bucks.

Win Free Ebooks for a Year!
Pre-order coming soon titles directly through our site and you'll receive one entry into a drawing for a chance to win free books for a year! Get the details at RiptidePublishing.com/contests.

CPSIA information can be obtained
at www.ICGtesting.com
Printed in the USA
LVOW03s1930200417
531554LV00003B/551/P

9 781626 494381